A trained medic and crisis counsellor, C.J. has assisted with many difficult cases involving abuse, rape and homicide. Winner of the Golden Gateway, Readers' Choice and Daphne du Maurier awards, her short story 'Scutwork' was selected to appear in *First Thrills*, an anthology edited by Lee Child, featuring the best of today's thriller bestsellers and the future stars of tomorrow. Her first novel, *Blind Faith*, was a self-published ebook phenomenon in the US, debuting at Number 2 on the *New York Times* print and ebook bestseller list and garnering her legions of fans. *Blind Faith* was also shortlisted for the International Thriller Writers Awards 2013 for best original ebook novel.

ALSO BY C.J. LYONS

Blind Faith

Black Sheep

HOLLOW BONES

C.J. LYONS

sphere

SPHERE

First published in the USA in 2013 by St. Martin's Press
First published in Great Britain in 2014 by Sphere
This paperback edition published in 2014 by Sphere

Copyright © 2013 by C.J. Lyons

The moral right of the author has been asserted.

*All characters and events in this publication, other than those
clearly in the public domain, are fictitious and any resemblance
to real persons, living or dead, is purely coincidental.*

A CIP catalogue record for this book
is available from the British Library.

ISBN 978-0-7515-5767-1

Printed and bound in Great Britain by
Clays Ltd, St Ives plc

Papers used by Sphere are from well-managed forests
and other responsible sources.

MIX
Paper from
responsible sources
FSC® C104740

www.fsc.org

Sphere
An imprint of
Little, Brown Book Group
100 Victoria Embankment
London EC4Y 0DY

An Hachette UK Company
www.hachette.co.uk

www.littlebrown.co.uk

CHAPTER ONE

FBI Supervisory Special Agent Caitlyn Tierney was glad she'd skipped her morning coffee. The adrenaline she mainlined when the Escalade's driver pulled a .45 was quite enough to jump-start her heart. Wide awake now, thank you very much, have a nice day.

"Lower your weapon, Commissioner Schultz!" Sheriff Mona Holdeman shouted from where she stood behind her cruiser stopped on the other side of the Escalade from Caitlyn's position.

The early-morning March wind cut down the lonely country road, bringing with it the promise of snow. A stray memory flitted through Caitlyn's mind even as she sighted along the barrel of her Glock 22, aiming at the driver. Waking up on mornings like this as a child, rushing to the window, ignoring the sting of the cold floor on her naked feet, and looking outside, searching for snow, only to be disappointed. Not by the weather, but by the fact that by the time she reached the window, she'd be awake enough to remember her father was gone. Dead. Buried back in North Carolina at the home they'd left behind.

Caitlyn shook free of the childhood memory and focused on their subject, a corrupt county commissioner with a penchant for weaponry. Holdeman's cruiser and two state trooper vehicles blocked Schultz's path forward, creating a barricade. Not that there was anywhere to run. They'd chosen their spot carefully, here in the middle of Pennsylvania Dutch Country, where the only civilians to worry about were a trio of horses grazing in the field across the road.

Caitlyn was here as backup—something the newly elected sheriff was in dire need of after discovering two-thirds of her force were on the county commissioner's payroll and that Schultz had ordered a hit on her.

When your county's population numbered twice as many cows as people, and most of the people didn't get involved in elections or vote, it made for interesting politics. Which was exactly how Schultz had been able to control this quiet patch of Pennsylvania countryside for the past decade, growing rich as he decimated tax-payers' coffers. Public corruption was one of the FBI's top priorities, so when Holdeman and the Pennsylvania State Police needed assistance building a case against Schultz, Caitlyn was happy to help.

She hadn't intended on being on the front line. But after two months in her new position as the FBI's Local Law Enforcement Liaison, juggling cases via phone, Skype, e-mail, and paperwork, it felt good confronting a bad guy in person. From what Caitlyn and the other investigators had dug up on Schultz, he was a very bad guy, into everything from taking bribes, extortion, and now, contracted murder.

Knowing that the commissioner always traveled armed and had a stockpile of weapons at both his house and office, they'd chosen the location for their take-down carefully: an empty road surrounded by farmland on one side and rolling hills covered in forest on the other. Schultz drove the road every day on his way into work.

"Place the weapon on the ground and back away," Holdeman's voice came over the loudspeaker of her patrol car blocking Schultz's vehicle from the front. "Keep your hands above your head."

Schultz hesitated. Turning his weapon on Holdeman would only invite certain death from Caitlyn positioned at the rear of his vehicle or the two state troopers behind Holdeman who both held long guns aimed at Schultz. Exactly how they'd planned it: Give the subject no reason to resist, and things would go quietly. Their plan called for a quick takedown and arrest, back at the sheriff's station in time for coffee and homemade doughnuts drizzled in maple syrup.

Slowly, with exaggerated movements, Schultz bent forward and placed his weapon on the pavement, keeping one hand in the air. He raised the second hand and turned to back away from the pistol on the ground.

That's when everything went wrong.

Caitlyn was in charge of covering the rear and passenger side of the Escalade. Easy duty since Schultz was supposed to be alone. At least that's what their intel said. No one was visible through the Escalade's tinted windows. Schultz stood at the driver's side of the vehicle, all guns and eyes trained on him except Caitlyn's.

She was too busy trying to figure out what to do with the little girl who had jumped out of the passenger door, aiming a rather large semiautomatic pistol at Caitlyn's heart.

Caitlyn's training had her sighting her own Glock at the girl, but she stopped herself from pulling the trigger. The girl was a skinny thing, looked to be around eleven, with twin blond braids and freckles on her nose.

She wore a purple jacket with puffy sleeves decorated with a grinning kitty cat with impossibly long whiskers embroidered on the front. The cat's whiskers crisscrossed right over the girl's heart, making for a perfect target.

"Put the gun down," Caitlyn called to her.

"Let my daddy go!" The girl jerked her weapon at Caitlyn.

All eyes turned to the girl. Except her father's. Schultz used his daughter's diversion to attempt to escape by running into the woods beside the road. Immediately the sheriff and one of the staties followed, yelling at him to stop.

Caitlyn didn't move. Didn't even blink. Her entire universe was filled with the girl and the gun.

The girl had a good stance, looked like she knew how to use the semiautomatic. Even more reason why Caitlyn should shoot her—lethal weapon, not responding to commands, everything in her training told her to take care of the threat. Now.

She was just a kid. If she'd been endangering someone else's life, Caitlyn would have shot her. But it was only her and the girl on this side of the vehicle. Caitlyn knew it was stupid, risking her own life to save the girl, but she had to try.

"This isn't helping your father," Caitlyn told her. It felt like they were the only two people in the universe. Even the springtime serenade provided by birds pecking through the field alongside the horses had vanished, leaving just her and the girl. "What's your name?"

The girl frowned. For a moment Caitlyn thought she was going to start crying, lay the weapon down. But then Holdeman and the statie dragged Schultz back, now in handcuffs.

The girl straightened, eyes narrowed. With Caitlyn dead center in her aim.

"I said," her voice tight with anger, "let my daddy go. Now!"

"We can't do anything until you put the gun down." Caitlyn's vision eclipsed to a black-edged tunnel, but she forced herself to break through it and scan the periphery. The other statie had moved to cover the girl from behind. One wrong move and he'd take the girl down for Caitlyn.

It wasn't going to come to that, she vowed. Releasing one hand from her weapon, she stretched it out to the girl. Twenty feet separated them, but she wanted her to feel like she was closer.

"Your dad is going to be fine, sweetheart." Damn, she'd forgotten the girl's name from the briefing. "He wouldn't want you to get hurt, now, would he?" Or hurt anyone else, she hoped. "Just put the gun down and come here. Then you can go with your dad."

On the other side of the SUV, the sheriff moved to put Schultz in one of the squads. The girl whirled, stepping back at an angle so she had both Caitlyn and her father in sight. "Leave him alone! Back away, now!"

Time to play hardball. Caitlyn shifted both hands back onto her Glock and leaned forward. "Look at me," she commanded. The girl obeyed, squinting over the barrel of her pistol. "Feel your fingers going numb? How heavy your gun feels? That's adrenaline. Look at how your hand is shaking."

It was working. The girl glanced at her hands knuckled white around her pistol. The gun wavered and she hunched her shoulders to steady it, but it kept trembling.

Caitlyn continued, "Shaking like that, you'll never hit me. Pull that trigger and the gentleman behind you is going to shoot you dead. Worse, that will make your dad run to help you, and I'll have to shoot him dead, too. That what you want? Want your dad dead?"

What she wanted the girl to hear was: *dead, dead, dead*. It must have worked. The girl began crying, shoulders shuddering. She shook her head. But she didn't lower her weapon.

C'mon, kid. Don't take all day. Caitlyn wasn't sure how patient the staties would be.

She kept her voice firm and level. "If you want to stay with your dad, you need to put down the gun and come with me. Now."

The girl hesitated; blinking hard and fast, glanced at her dad, looked back at Caitlyn, then finally nodded and carefully set her weapon on the ground.

Caitlyn kept her in her sights as one of the staties moved around the front of the SUV and took the kid into custody.

Even after the danger was over, it took Caitlyn a few breaths before her hand was steady enough to holster her own weapon. She sent a quick prayer up into the clear blue Pennsylvania sky. Thankful she didn't have to kill anyone today. Especially not a little girl who only wanted to save her father.

CHAPTER TWO

Maria Alvarado's feet touched the concrete below the cruise ship's gangplank. Her first step—ever!—on the land where she was born. Tourists, mostly fellow college kids from the spring break "booze cruise" swarmed around her, jostling her as they rushed to grab tour guides or cheap souvenirs from native vendors hawking their wares. She inhaled deeply. Scents of cocoa and coffee and exotic spices tantalized her nostrils. Even the air here in Guatemala felt different: It tasted of freedom.

And danger. Because once her father found out what she'd done, how she'd disobeyed him . . . It was worth risking his wrath, coming here to follow her dream. It had to be.

Besides, she was an Alvarado, and as her father was constantly telling her, Alvarados never retreated. No matter how fierce the enemy, no matter how great their fear.

Maria blinked against the bright morning sun. She might have half her father's DNA coursing through her veins, but she wasn't at all confident that she'd inherited any of his courage. Uncertainty flickered through her—she could still change her mind, go with her friends, cancel her plans to join Professor Zigler at the site.

A bird's raucous call cut through the air. Exotic, unlike anything Maria had heard before. Exactly the reason she was here. To decide her own fate, make her father proud. Always forward, no retreat.

"So, Maria, where's your hunky grad assistant?" Linda, one of Maria's friends, asked. Tracey and Vicky joined them, pocketing their passports.

"He'll be here," Maria said, trying hard to take in all the various elements. The port wasn't what she expected. She'd imagined something out of a movie, thatch huts and colorful bungalows, maybe a steel drum band to welcome the *Caribbean Dream*.

Instead, Santo Tomás was a working cargo port. Stacks of shipping containers towered past the horizon to the south, and the only building in sight was a thoroughly modern concrete warehouse with a utilitarian steel roof. It would have been right at home on the streets of Miami if not for the sign overhead that read: WELCOME TO GUATEMALA.

"You sure about this?" Vicky, always the worry-wart, asked. "You could come with us, forget about this crazy treasure hunt."

"Miss my chance to meet Professor Zigler and work on the discovery of a lifetime? No way." Maria still couldn't believe how lucky she'd been, meeting the professor's grad assistant in an online archeology forum, helping Prescott decipher clues that might lead the professor's team to a Maya treasure trove that hadn't seen the light of day for two thousand years. It was her chance to redeem herself after being turned down to join her own university's dig. Not to mention proving to her father that at nineteen, she really could take care of herself.

He was going to be so angry when he discovered her deception—he thought she was here only to enjoy spring break with her friends. Served him right; she was certain he was behind the rejection of her application to join the UCF dig in Belize. Neither of her parents wanted her to continue pursuing a degree in archeology, much less her chosen area of interest: Preclassic Maya culture.

She'd been only a few months old when her parents fled Guatemala and made new lives for themselves in America. They never spoke of their homeland; never even spoke Spanish if they knew Maria was around. They insisted their family be true Americans. If they'd had their way, she'd be spending spring break just as she had last year: at home in Coral Gables, lounging by the pool or playing tennis at the club. That was her parents' idea of fun.

They were so boring. Maria wanted more. She wanted adventure, excitement, a chance to meet new people, see new places. A chance to explore the world, maybe even help people understand it better. She took a deep breath—so deep, it tingled the whole way down to her toes. Freedom.

"When my father asks where I am," she reminded her friends as they navigated through the crowd of tourists and natives, heading past the tour buses lined up on the concrete in front of the cruise ship, "tell him I'll call when I'm ready to come home."

"And he can send the company jet to pick you up," Linda said, rolling her eyes. "We got it, we got it."

Vicky wasn't so sure. Her eyes were wide as she took in the vista of jungle-covered mountains beyond the bustle of the town with its crowded, brightly colored buildings, none taller than two stories high. "I still don't think this is a good idea."

"Professor Zigler is from Cambridge. He's highly regarded," Maria argued. "He even came out of retirement for this dig. It might be my last chance to work with someone of his stature. Besides, I was the one who thought to combine Irfan View with the NASA imaging programs to isolate the exact location of the temple. I deserve to be here, a part of the archeological find of the century." Her travel pack slipped off her shoulder as she sped up to a jog in her excitement. She couldn't help herself; there were so many feelings spinning around inside her she might just explode.

Yes, fear was part of it. After all, she'd be heading off into the jungle with strangers—except they really weren't. She and Prescott had Skyped for hours. And she felt like she knew the professor, had read all his papers although he hadn't published in years and his methodology was hopelessly outdated—exactly why he needed someone more tech-savvy like her on his team. She glanced around, the foreign sights and sounds and smells leaving her light-headed. A little fear was good for the soul.

Even if her father would probably lock her up in a convent after she got home. She pushed the thought away, feeling guilty about disobeying him for the first time in her life.

A handsome man in his late twenties pulled up in an open-topped Jeep and honked the horn. He hopped out without opening the door, one hand balancing lightly on the roll bar, springing to the ground, graceful as a cheetah. Or jaguar, Maria thought. There were jaguars here in Guatemala. Fear tickled her senses once more but was quickly overruled by excitement.

"Maria?" he called as he weaved through the other vehicles, his blond Hollywood features a strong counterpoint to the darker-skinned Spanish and Maya surrounding the tourists. Without waiting for an answer he hugged her, lifting her off her feet. "It's so good to meet you! Sorry I'm late; the professor had me running errands. We don't get into town very often."

Maria struggled to regain her composure. He was even more handsome in person than he'd appeared in their Skype chats. She turned to her friends, proudly introducing him. "Prescott, this is Linda, Vicky, and Tracey."

"Pleased to meet you, ladies." He reached for Maria's bag. She'd filled it with all the necessities for living in the primitive conditions of an archeological dig: sleeping bag, ripstop shorts and pants, mosquito netting, mess kit. Unlike her friends, who wore casual, bright-colored tourist clothing, Maria wore khaki shorts, hiking boots, a tank top, and an ExOfficio long-sleeved shirt wrapped around her waist above her fanny pack. Despite her dark skin, she even had a hat—a wide-brimmed squishable khaki-colored sun hat that she wore at what she hoped was a jaunty angle.

"Now, don't you ladies worry about your friend here," Prescott said as if reading their minds. "We have a satellite phone at base camp—as long as the weather cooperates, she can call her boyfriend, tuck him in for the night anytime she wants." He laughed and turned to Maria, one hand pressed flat against his chest, mimicking a posture of lovesick despair. "But please, please tell me you don't actually have a boyfriend; it will break my heart if you do!"

Maria blushed. "No, no boyfriend. Yet," she added with bravado foreign to her usual introversion. She hugged her friends as Prescott carried her bag to the Jeep. "Remember, not a word to anyone," she admonished as she gave Linda her cruise ship passenger ID. "And tell my parents not to worry."

They smiled, enjoying the intrigue, and waved her off. "Have fun!" called Linda.

"Bring us back some treasure," Tracey said.

"Be safe!" yelled Vicky.

Maria felt like a movie star as she drove away in the Jeep with Prescott at the wheel, weaving through narrow streets lined with brightly painted adobe brick and cinder block buildings. It was as if her life was finally starting. And what an exciting start it was, working with a world-famous professor on a dig that could change the way they viewed Mayan culture. Not to mention the treasure—if she was right, they could be talking about the location of the Dresden Codex's lost gold, millions of dollars' worth of treasure that had been missing for centuries. More than money, though, the treasure represented a glimpse into the ancient Maya, perhaps even solving the mystery of their demise.

"The professor is looking forward to meeting you," Prescott said as he steered them around slower-moving trucks and brightly painted "chicken buses" filled with locals. He kept one hand on the wheel, the other draped casually behind her, resting on the back of her seat. "He was quite impressed with your theory connecting our site to the location mentioned in the Dresden Codex."

Maria felt her cheeks warm as Prescott beamed at her. "Thanks. Anyone would have put the two together if you discounted the common belief that the codex is talking about Lake Izabel. And of course, I had modern satellite imaging to help me."

She was actually quite proud of that not-so-small feat. By combining a unique series of image translation algorithms, she'd been able to confirm her theory about the river shifting its course after the earthquake two years ago, revealing evidence of a vast quantity of metals at a location just a few miles away from Lake Invierno. With further enhancement and using historical images to reveal how the terrain had changed over time, she realized she'd uncovered the location of a Maya temple, devoured by the jungle, hidden from human sight. Until now.

She only wished she could have found a way to join the professor's expedition sooner. His team had spent the last month exploring her discovery, working to unearth the temple. Prescott had Skyped her almost daily progress reports, which had mainly consisted of getting the road built, supplies transported in, and the start of the surveying work. Still, how thrilling it would have been to be there from the beginning.

She'd been surprised by how quickly the professor had been able to get funding and permission from the Guatemalan authorities to start the project—the perks of being a world-famous archeologist. Maybe someday she'd be able to command such influence. As it was, she was lucky to be here now, even if it was only for two weeks as a volunteer.

There had been reams of paperwork: applications, followed by insurance waivers, health history forms, nondisclosure forms, forms to acknowledge that she wasn't receiving any compensation or university credit, travel checklists, and liability waivers. No wonder the professor left all the details to his grad assistant—she was surprised anyone ever got any work done, mired down in academic bureaucracy. If the professor was pleased with her work, Prescott had promised her an actual for-credit internship for the summer—although it would mean plowing through even more paperwork.

After she returned home. For now it was two weeks of adventure, soaking up as much knowledge and experience as she could from one of the leaders of her field.

"The greatest minds in the world have been working on that codex since it was found during World War Two," Prescott said. "But you're the first who came up with the idea that the codex pointed to Lake Invierno. Much less found a temple that was previously undiscovered. If your theory is right, this find is going to be bigger than even the Brown University El Diablo discovery last year." El Diablo was the archeologists' name for a previously unknown temple of the Mayan sun god, painted bright red to catch the sun's rays and create an incandescent display. Before the jungle swallowed the temple whole a thousand years ago.

Prescott paused, slowing the Jeep, checking all the mirrors. She twisted in her seat and looked behind them. The road was empty.

He caught her look of concern and said, "You can never be too careful." For the first time she saw a hint of uncertainty cross his face. "Do you really think the gold is there?"

"Oh yes." Maria forced herself to curb her enthusiasm and sound professional. "I think there's a good chance. Wouldn't it be thrilling if it was?"

They turned off the main highway, heading into the jungle and climbing the hills leading up to the mountains. The road was wide enough for only one vehicle, dirt and gravel, but not too rough. Then they came to a fork where the road narrowed and turned into two muddy trails, each barely wide enough for the Jeep. Prescott stopped the Jeep, looking down both paths.

"Are you lost?" she asked, suddenly aware that she hadn't seen any other cars for the past hour. Without the breeze generated by the Jeep's movement, the humidity closed in on her like a smothering blanket. They were alone in a wilderness filled with every shade of green imaginable, the only other color the occasional swath of blue sky overhead. But the farther they went into the mountains, the more crowded the treetops and fewer glimpses of sky.

"Is something wrong?" She reached for her phone. An urban instinct—there would be no reception this far from civilization.

Prescott turned away, scowling down the left-hand turn, then yanked the wheel to the right. "Nothing wrong. I just want to make sure we get there before dark."

Made sense, she wouldn't want to be caught on this road in the dark—even though it was just past noon, the jungle's gloom was so thick that he'd already turned on the headlights. This far into the mountains, night fell earlier than down in the lowlands. Prescott no longer looked at her or smiled. Instead he drove hunched over, swearing every time he had to slow down to avoid a fallen tree limb or navigate through a patch of mud as the road quickly devolved into something barely resembling a path.

Thank goodness for Prescott. She never would have made it here on her own. They rounded a sharp curve. A mud-splattered pickup blocked the trail before them. Men with machine guns flanked the truck, motioning to them to stop.

"Prescott!" Maria shouted as he wrestled with the wheel, steering them into a U-turn. The Jeep lurched and wobbled. Its wheels spun in the mud and they drove over some small bushes, but somehow he kept it upright. They sped back the way they came.

"Who are they?" She grabbed the door handle and ducked her head in case the men began shooting. Her heart pounded so hard, she felt it in her throat, but Prescott kept driving, cool and capable. "What do they want?"

"You." He hunched over the steering wheel and looked both afraid and angry. They rounded the curve, leaving the men with guns behind.

"Me? Why me?" Panic surged through her as she remembered every urban legend involving rape and kidnapping female tourists. Then she realized. The treasure. They thought she knew where the treasure was. No, that couldn't be it. How could they know?

The Jeep fishtailed into a skid as Prescott slammed on the brakes. Maria looked up over the dash. A large yellow Land Rover blocked their escape. A man stood in front of it, arms crossed, leaning against the bumper casually, as if waiting for a date. He was Spanish, his handsome chiseled features marred by a pale scar slashing across his right cheek.

The Jeep stopped, twisted diagonally across the road, the driver's side closest to the man. Prescott blew his breath out and narrowed his eyes at Maria. "Wait here. Don't move. Do exactly what I say."

How could he be so calm? Crouched down in the wheel well, she nodded. None of this felt real. It couldn't be happening, not to her. Nothing ever happened to her. Her life was even more boring than her parents'.

Prescott climbed out of the Jeep and warily approached the man.

"I think you made a wrong turn," the man said. His voice sounded almost cheerful, but when Maria edged her gaze above the dash, his scowl appeared deadly.

Despite Prescott's admonition to stay put, she inched her door open. Whatever happened, she wanted to be ready. Her side of the Jeep was on the edge of the road, surrounded by bushes and ferns; if she ran, she'd be swallowed by the wilderness in a few steps. Of course, she'd also be hopelessly lost.

Hoping it wouldn't come to that, she slid out of her

seat and planted her feet on the soft ground, hiding behind the door. Prescott knew what he was doing; he'd get them out of this. Soon, they'd be sitting around a cheery campfire with the professor and his students and workers, laughing at their adventure in the jungle.

"You had one job," the man said in the tone of a father scolding his wayward child. "Bring her safely to *el doctor*. But you got greedy."

"I'm sorry," Prescott said, arms stretched wide in surrender. He sounded scared—which escalated Maria's own panic. And what did that man mean, "greedy?" Maybe Prescott wouldn't be able to talk them out of this after all. All those questions about the treasure— could Prescott want it for himself?

Following her instincts for survival, she pushed her confusion aside and sidled toward the edge of the door, ducking low as she slid between large leaves of some kind of ferny type of bush. Moving very slowly, creeping an inch at a time so the leaves wouldn't rustle and betray her, she crouched behind a palm tree, angled so she could see the men standing on the road.

The man with the scar nodded at Prescott's apology. He even smiled, showing his teeth, as if all were forgiven. Prescott's posture relaxed.

Then the man drew his gun and shot Prescott in the head.

Everything moved in slow motion. Prescott's body jerked, then sagged, finally dropping to the ground.

Maria screamed but it was mainly in her head because her throat had spasmed shut with terror, swallowing the sound. She couldn't stop looking over her shoulder at Prescott even as her feet moved her away from the horror.

The man walked past Prescott toward the Jeep. Like a thunderclap, time began to move forward again. Maria turned away from Prescott—he was obviously dead, there was nothing she could do for him—and she ran.

Head ducked low against the possibility of bullets flying, arms held in front of her, branches and leaves and vines slapping against her body, she ran as she'd never run before. Wished her father were here to save her, to protect her.

Why had she ever left home?

CHAPTER THREE

During the eight-mile drive to the sheriff's station, Caitlyn counted seven barns and three houses. The only people she spotted were an Amish farmer and his sons plowing a field in the distance. Their horse-drawn plows kicked up a cloud of dust that made the March sunshine shimmer gold. Hard to believe they lived in the same reality as Caitlyn.

She wondered if the Amish ever accepted converts. Specifically semi-atheist FBI agents with blood staining their souls. Probably not.

She rounded a curve, and the farmers with their horses and tranquility vanished from sight. The sheriff's station was in a town named Blue Ball. A village of less than a thousand souls, it was created when an intrepid trader built a hostel at the intersection of two Indian trails two hundred years ago.

She pulled into the station, a utilitarian cement block building, behind Sheriff Holdeman and parked her car beside a familiar Harley. Her lips quirked into a smile that she fought to suppress and failed. What the hell was Carver doing here?

She followed the sheriff into the station, her feet practically dancing a jig as she scoured the reception area. No sign of Carver.

The staties and Holdeman's deputies began processing Schultz and his daughter. Sheriff Holdeman paused in the open bullpen, watching as the door to the holding area closed behind Schultz. She eyed her few remaining deputies, all men.

They didn't applaud or do anything overtly demonstrative, but each man sat up straighter and met the sheriff's gaze, most with a small nod of satisfaction and acknowledgment.

The sheriff nodded back. Mission accomplished. Then she opened her office door.

At least Carver had had the good grace not to take the sheriff's chair, Caitlyn saw as she followed Holdeman inside. Instead he lounged in one of the spare chairs, legs stretched out, ankles crossed, a self-satisfied smirk creasing his face.

"Carver, what are you doing here?" Caitlyn asked. She hated the way the words came out in a rush, as if she cared.

"When you said you were working a public corruption case in Blue Balls—" He drawled the colorful town name with a grin.

"It's Blue Ball," Sheriff Holdeman corrected automatically. "Singular."

"No, I'm pretty sure both my—"

"Don't encourage him," Caitlyn cut him off, but she didn't bother hiding her smile.

Carver's gaze roamed over both women, spending more time on Caitlyn. She and Holdeman were dressed alike in tactical gear, were both redheads, about the same height, five-six, although Caitlyn definitely had more curves.

"I think you ladies might be the cure for my unfortunate condition," Carver continued, his voice practically twinkling with restrained laughter. "I've always had this fantasy about twins—"

"Unless that fantasy includes handcuffs—," Holdeman warned, fighting back her own laughter. Caitlyn had noticed that about the sheriff. She took her work seriously, the people she was there to protect and serve always foremost in her mind, but she had a wicked sense of humor. Probably how she'd lasted so long in a job where testosterone ruled.

Carver nodded eagerly. "Handcuffs are good."

Caitlyn had work to do, and now that Carver was here, she had even more reason to get it done quickly. "Cut the crap. Sheriff Mona Holdeman, this is Special Agent Jake Carver, who—despite his adolescent demeanor—is one of the FBI's top forensic accountants."

"They stole me away from the IRS." Carver flexed his biceps as he bent his arms behind his head. Until two months ago he'd been deep undercover with an outlaw motorcycle gang, precisely for the reason that he looked like anything but an accountant. Now, wearing his leathers for the ride up from Virginia to Pennsylvania, he was reprising his role of sexy outlaw hunk.

"Seriously, Carver, why are you here?" Caitlyn asked again.

He was supposed to be crashing at her place in Manassas, safely out of sight from grudge-holding bikers, while the Assistant U.S. Attorney debriefed him on his year and a half of undercover activities. The preliminary hearings for the first of the biker defendants were scheduled to start soon and the AUSA wanted to make sure his star witness was ready to go.

Carver stared at her, a tiny sigh escaping his lips,

quickly covered by another smirk, but she saw the truth: He'd missed her.

Even more surprising, she felt the same way about him. It wasn't the reaction she expected—or wanted—so she quickly masked it. Hopefully before he noticed. Otherwise, she'd never hear the end of it.

"I finished early with the AUSA, figured most public corruption cases are won by following the money, so thought I might be able to help. Tell me about your case, Sheriff." He glanced at Caitlyn. "And call me Jake."

As Holdeman laid out her case against Schultz, Caitlyn moved to take the seat on the other side of the office. She never called him Jake. She wasn't sure why—after all, they'd been sleeping together for the past two months and he was practically living at her place.

Except somehow it didn't feel like living together. Not with her constantly on the road, working cases in her new position as the Bureau's Local Law Enforcement Liaison—a fancy title for a job that basically meant helping communities unravel crimes they didn't have the resources to handle but that also didn't strictly fall under federal jurisdiction.

Besides, both she and Carver were self-proclaimed loners. Her last relationship had ended disastrously, something she wanted to avoid repeating at all costs, while he had sworn off commitment after his first marriage crashed and burned. His fault, he admitted readily. And that was as far as any talk of taking their own not-a-relationship-or-a-commitment to the next level went.

So she called him Carver. Better than using his undercover biker name, Goose. Yet lately, sometimes, only in her mind, Caitlyn found herself slipping and thinking of him as Jake. Wanting to ask his opinion on a case or share an interesting tidbit from her day, she'd call him up while she was on the road. He was so easy to talk to, always had great ideas, and she'd hang up, lie alone in bed in some motel far from her home, and fantasize about what her world would be like if she had him in her life every day.

Wasn't going to happen. As soon as he was done testifying, he'd be shuffled to a remote field office far from any vengeful bikers, probably stuck behind a desk the rest of his career. Hell, given the way the Bureau and AUSA threw a fit when he'd first outwitted his security detail and came to Caitlyn's place after refusing to be placed into protective custody, he'd probably end up in Guam. If he was lucky. If not, then Fairbanks, Alaska.

Carver was just a visitor to her world; that much was clear. Taking things further would only hurt them both in the long run. So Carver he would remain. At least outside her fantasies.

Sheriff Holdeman was finishing her summation. "Schultz has been giving county projects to the crooked contractors for years, taking kickbacks, and then giving them new contracts to fix the shoddy work they do in the first place. Our schools are falling down, the hospital has a roof that leaks like a sieve—actually had to evacuate after a blizzard when the snow began to melt, short-circuiting their electrical systems—and there are bridges just waiting for a strong gust of wind to blow them down.

"It's a miracle no one has been killed—and it's my job to make sure that this all stops before it gets that far." No one could claim the sheriff wasn't passionate about her job. It was one of the reasons why Caitlyn had taken this case, come up here in person to help.

"Wow," Carver said. "Now I know how you got elected, Sheriff. What can I do to help nail this bastard?"

* * *

Maria pressed her face into her palms, inhaling her own sweat and fear. She'd quickly realized that running wasn't her best option—not with all the noise and rustling branches pointing the way for her pursuers—so while the man with the scar called for reinforcements, she'd found a place to hide.

Hiding was what she did best. Emotionally, hiding the pain of a lonely childhood, constantly trying to prove herself worthy of her father's love, escaping into a world of books and imagination. She had a gift for physical concealment as well. Her father said her vision was better than 3-D glasses, the way she could look at something and translate it into multiple dimensions—it was that gift that had helped her locate the temple from the professor's satellite images. Instead of studying archeology, her father wanted her to use her talents to figure out puzzles like protein structures and enzymes—stuff that would help his biotech company. Boring stuff.

Even as a kid, she could spot the best hidey-holes, places that to the casual observer appeared too small or not the right shape for a person to fit inside. Like this rotten tree stump. The ground around it appeared empty, but Maria spied a depression beneath one large root, partially covered by low-hanging branches of another tree with wide, flat leaves. She had no idea what kind of tree it was—palm, banana, manna from heaven—but the shadows it cast onto the hollow carved out by the roots of the dead tree made for perfect concealment.

Curled up in a ball, ignoring the scurry of insects as she burrowed deeper into the soft soil left by the decomposing stump, she hid and waited, barely breathing.

Her heart pounded so hard and fast, she was sure it would knock over the dead stump above her or make the leaves of the other trees rustle and quake. But unless her pursuers took the time to poke and prod every dead tree and raise the lower branches to look beneath every live one, they'd never find her.

At least not quickly. Not unless there was an army of them. But she'd counted only five, including the man with the scar, the one who'd shot Prescott.

The man's words still puzzled her. Had Prescott led them here, lured by the prospect of finding the treasure? But the man said Prescott was supposed to take her to *el doctor*—that had to be Professor Zigler. And the professor—what would the men be doing to him and his team? He was old, in his seventies—surely they wouldn't hurt him. . . . The image of Prescott's bloody face destroyed that small hope.

As she crouched, arms and legs going to pins and needles, she created a mental map of the area. The temple was less than two miles to the northeast in a direct route, a little longer via the twisting road—but she would need to avoid the road. The nearest town was over thirty-five kilometers—about twenty-two miles—away, so forget that. But if she could make it to the river, she could follow it downstream to a hospital she remembered seeing on the map. Following the river would take longer, with its twists and turns, but safer than trying to follow the more direct route the road provided. All she had to do was make it to the river.

"Maria," a man's voice called, setting off a wave of raucous echoes from the birds. He spoke English with a slight Spanish accent. "We're not going to hurt you. We're here to help. Come out now."

Yeah, right. Did they think she was stupid? Even if Prescott had been after the treasure, these men were still killers.

The men were between her and the road, but that

was a good thing. She wasn't going back to the road. They wouldn't expect that.

"We need her alive," the man told his partners. "Fan out and cover back to the road. She couldn't have gotten past here, we'll drive her into the open."

No, you won't, she thought stubbornly. Her legs cried out for release, and the urge to shift her weight was overwhelming. She bit the inside of her mouth, using one pain to distract from the other.

Men stomped through the jungle, rustling the undergrowth around them. She imagined them wielding machetes and machine guns. They moved all around her, one actually raising the leaves on the other side of the tree covering her.

Maria closed her eyes, waiting for a bullet to hit her. Her pulse pounded through her temples and her chest tightened.

Then he was gone. She had the sudden need to pee, but forced it aside by thinking of something— anything—else. Her father with his military posture and stern scowls, daring anyone to disobey him, yet beneath it all he was so unhappy that Maria treasured every smile he gave her. Her mother, regal in her beauty, so poised and confident, everything Maria wasn't.

She wished she'd never left home. She should have listened to them. They were right. She didn't belong here. She belonged safe at home, curled up with one of her books.

"Maria, please, let us help," the man called. "Your father sent us. We're old friends of his from the army. He's very worried about you."

Maria listened hard, hoping against hope to hear a familiar voice. Had her father discovered her deception? Was he coming to rescue her?

"It will be night soon," the man continued. "You

can't survive out here alone in the jungle. Not at night. That's when the jaguars feed."

Still she said nothing. If these men knew her father, wanted to save her, then why had they killed Prescott?

Lies. Everything the man said was lies. Her father wasn't coming. She was on her own. Her tears mingled with her sweat as she struggled to stop crying, to keep still and quiet.

"Maria, have you ever seen a jaguar? Their claws are so sharp, they can eviscerate a man with one swipe."

Now she had something else to fill her mind as she huddled in the darkness, smothered by the stench of decay. The jungle fell still, its silence oppressive.

One of the men shouted and fired his gun. Suddenly a howling noise, someone screaming in pain, broke through the air, making every muscle of her body clench.

"Don't shoot!" the man yelled. "We need her alive."

The screams got louder and multiplied as if a horde of tortured souls stampeded through the jungle.

"Damn howler monkeys," one of the men said as he passed Maria's tree stump, jogging toward the man who'd fired the shot.

There was a mix of Spanish and English, ending with laughter. From what Maria could make out—her Spanish was limited to hello, good-bye, and ordering beer—it sounded like the man had tripped and fired accidentally. Good thing he wasn't aiming anywhere near where Maria was.

"She couldn't have gotten this far, let's head back to the road." Their footsteps retreated as they moved past her.

She didn't risk raising her head to look, but she felt the trees sway around her as the troop of howler monkeys passed, their screeches deafening. After they were gone, the jungle returned to normal. No sounds of the men. Just parrots squawking, frogs belching, and small animals rustling through the undergrowth.

Still she waited. Wasn't sure if she could move even if she wanted to—her legs had gone numb. Her mouth was dry; she longed for a sip of water but couldn't risk reaching for the bottle at her waist. Her fanny pack was now all she had left to help her survive: a bottle of water, protein bar, bandanna, notepad and pencil, compass, and her cell phone.

Plus her mind. Her will, her determination. She was an Alvarado, and Alvarados never surrendered.

The sound of a truck engine came from the distance. Traveling west, down the road. Her cue to move farther into the jungle, find the river.

They wouldn't stop looking for her, not if they thought she was the key to finding the treasure. And men like that—they wouldn't stop at killing Prescott, she was sure. The professor and his entire team were in danger.

Slowly, she unfolded her body from its contorted position and brushed the bugs and detritus from her hair and clothing. Somewhere along the way, she'd lost her hat. She took a drink of water—only half a bottle left—and stretched her legs, taking her bearings. Her compass had cost her only a few dollars at a camping store, but now it was her most valuable possession. It confirmed her natural sense of direction, pointing her north, in the direction of the river. Her only hope.

CHAPTER FOUR

There really wasn't much left to do except for the paperwork, but the sheriff was happy to have Jake's second opinion on Schultz's finances while she and Caitlyn interviewed Schultz and made arrangements for his daughter. It was dark by the time they finished their after-action reports and had everything tied up for the state prosecutor.

"So why did you really come here, Carver?" Caitlyn asked as she led him into her room at the Blue Ball Inn, a single-story 1950s-era wood frame motel. "Worried about me?"

"Not about you being on the job." He threw his knapsack onto the second bed and looked around the dingy room done in various shades of scratchy brown tweed. "Hey, Magic Fingers. Got a quarter?"

"Then why?" she persisted, standing against the closed door, arms crossed. She didn't like surprises—not even pleasant ones. They had a way of turning sour, spinning out of control. Caitlyn thrived on control. Yet another reason why she lived and worked alone.

"I was going crazy cooped up in that apartment of yours. I needed a little action."

His "action," leaving the safety of her apartment, was likely to give the U.S. Attorney apoplexy, but that was none of Caitlyn's business. She also didn't point out the fact that there probably would never be a next time for Carver to get in on any more field action. Not after he testified against the Reapers.

She knew how it felt to be sidelined from a job you loved—she'd had emergency brain surgery after an encounter with a killer last year, and it almost ended her own career. Now she had one last chance to prove herself with her new assignment as Local Law Enforcement Liaison.

Then he added, "I couldn't help but notice how close this place is to Chambersburg and your grandparents. Figured it was the first time you'd seen them since you learned the truth about how your dad died, so . . ."

He shrugged, obviously uncomfortable. So was she. Sometimes she forgot he knew things about her and her family that no one else did. So much easier to hide behind the jokes and sex and the idea that he'd soon be wandering out of her life as easily as he'd strayed into it.

Since he and Caitlyn met two months ago at the end of his undercover operation, Carver had been shuffled around by the FBI and U.S. Attorney to debriefings, depositions, and the dreaded post-operation psych evals. One rainy night he'd shown up on her doorstep, looking a lot like a stray cat with his wet hair straggling down to his shoulders and his duffel carrying everything he owned in the world. "Figured the Reapers would never come looking for me here," he'd said—his way of inviting himself into her apartment and her life.

Every night when Caitlyn came home from Quantico,

she expected to find him gone. That was the kind of relationship they had—no strings attached, nothing to curtail their independence or freedom.

It was the kind of relationship they both wanted. Needed even, as he eased his way back into a normal life after being undercover for so long and Caitlyn dealt with the challenges of her new job. At least that's what Caitlyn told herself. When it came to relationships, her track record was worse than dismal. There was a stray cat she'd tried to befriend. When the weather turned cold, it abandoned her to move in with her landlady, sacrificing freedom for regular meals and a warm lap to sleep on. Then came the neuroradiologist who'd wanted to marry Caitlyn. She'd abandoned him for irregular meals; a cold, empty bed; and her career.

Yet lately, every night as she reached for the keys to her apartment door, she had this strange feeling of anticipation, anxiety, uncertainty, and . . . hope. All because of Carver.

"Saw my dad's folks on the way up." Talk about uncomfortable. Her grandparents had dragged her to Meeting. People sitting around, solemn, quiet and still, waiting, when all she wanted to do was scream and curse at God for taking her dad the way he had. For the lies and betrayals she now had to face.

It was their way, the Quaker way. Definitely not Caitlyn's. Probably why she'd been so aggressive with her approach to Sheriff Holdeman's case. But it all worked out in the end.

And Jake—Carver, she corrected herself firmly—had worried about her enough to come hold her hand. He need not have bothered. She could take care of herself, thank you very much. She'd been doing it since she was nine and her dad died.

He plopped down on the bed, patted the gold paisley bedspread. Arched one eyebrow in a suggestive leer. "They're fingers *and* they're magic."

She glanced at his body stretched out across the bed. His T-shirt had bunched up, revealing the well-defined lines of his abs. And the way those jeans hugged his hips . . . She didn't need hand-holding, but there were definitely other needs he could satisfy.

Digging a quarter out of her pocket, Caitlyn tossed it to him. "I'm in the mood for a little magic."

"Your wish is my command," he said, tugging her onto the bed with him.

Later, after they'd run out of quarters, she lay back, eyes closed, and for the first time since she'd left her home four days ago, relaxed.

"You know why I like you, Carver," she mumbled, only half-aware she was even speaking out loud. He lay behind her, his hand lazily stroking her breast, avoiding the scars that crisscrossed her chest. "When I'm with you, I don't have to think, don't have to work. I can just . . . be."

His hand fell away. Shit. Had she really just said that? It was the truth, but it wasn't exactly the nicest thing to say to a guy. He'd think she was just using him for sex. And she was, of course she was—wasn't she?

She opened her eyes and twisted to face him, expecting to have to work hard to soothe his bruised ego. But he was smiling at her, a smile that brought out the wrinkles around his eyes as if he was holding back laughter.

"You know," he drawled, the Kansas farm boy he'd long ago left behind reappearing in his voice, "that's the nicest thing anyone's ever said to me."

He leaned forward to kiss her, a kiss that felt like it meant something more than a prelude to sex. Caitlyn sank back against the pillows and let his embrace ease the confusion of emotions tangling her mind. Thinking too much. That was always her problem.

A few moments later, it wasn't a problem anymore.

If Maria had any tears left, she'd be crying. Her stomach twisted in an empty ache. It had given up on growling. She'd already eaten her only food, a protein bar, to keep her spirits up. Had to swallow it dry; she'd run out of water hours ago.

The sun climbed high, turning the jungle into a sauna. Then, too quickly, it moved to brush the tops of the mountains to the northwest, stranding her in darkness. The jungle was a strange mixture of small trees fighting for any sunlight and towering trees that soared into the sky before spreading their branches. Both conspired to trap her inside a bubble of humidity and shadows.

As soon as she knew the men had gone, the sounds of their vehicles banished by the constant chatter of jungle noise, she'd pushed her way through ferns and palms and scraggly pine trees with long needles that stung when she brushed against them, hoisted herself over dead logs using a walking stick and clinging to the vines that twisted around tree trunks as if intent on strangling their hosts, using her phone as a light to guide her through the jungle's gloom—it wasn't good for anything else, as there was no cell signal—until it died at about the same time the sun had.

She'd dreamed of being an explorer all her life. But this was the first time she'd ever found herself actually in the wild. Unless you count camping out on the deck surrounding their pool when she was a kid. Her whole life had been spent pretending—all this reality hit with a shock.

Like the image of Prescott's bloody face that kept inserting itself into her vision.

Alone in pitch black more immense than anything she'd experienced in her life, she'd wanted to cry, to scream, even run to the man with the scar if he'd save her from the darkness and the dangers hiding in it. Yet she continued on, moving forward toward the river.

Something scurried across her foot and she jumped, shaking her leg into the air, flinging it away. A snake? No, too small. But there were snakes here—deadly ones. The next step she took could be fatal.

Or she could stand here cowering and let the jaguars find her. As it was, she was being eaten alive by mosquitoes.

Frozen with fear, she closed her eyes and concentrated on the map in her head. She couldn't be far from the river. Its headwaters were on the mountain, near the temple she'd discovered. From there it flowed to Lake Invierno, where, according the map, there was some kind of hospital or clinic. Only a few miles as the crow flew, but the way the river meandered, it would be six or seven miles across country.

But a hospital meant help, a phone, maybe even a security team who could rescue the professor and his people. So that's where she was headed.

That was the plan. All she had to do was find the river. Then she could save herself and the professor's team. Even if she was too late to help Prescott.

Keep calm and carry on, she imagined the professor's voice—really Sean Connery's voice, as she'd never actually spoken to the professor—in her mind. All her life she'd dreamed of having adventures, becoming a real-life Indiana Jones. Surely she could survive one night in the wild?

She opened her eyes. Stared into the night. Shapes

of tree limbs and vines and leaves slowly took form, gathered from the black-on-black shadows. Better yet, beneath the chirps and squawks and rustling noises of the jungle, was the low-pitched rush of water. The river was close.

Using her walking stick like a blind person—a twist of the ankle and she could be stranded here in the jungle, left to rot and die—she stumbled across the treacherous terrain.

The sound of the water grew louder. Almost there, almost there.

CHAPTER FIVE

A piano riff jangled through the night. Both Caitlyn and Carver jerked awake, backs to each other as they sat up in bed. She held her Glock on the front door and window while he covered the shadows that crowded the rest of the room, including the connecting door to the room beside them.

The jazz notes sounded again. "Phone." She exchanged her Glock for the cell.

He remained at full alert, tension vibrating through his muscles, arm held straight, his weapon an extension of his body. She ignored the phone even though the number on the screen belonged to her boss, and took a moment to press her body against his, stroke her hand down his taut muscles, coming to rest on his gun hand. Carver allowed her to take his semiautomatic from his now trembling grip.

His gaze darted from one shadow to the next. Then he met her eyes. He hauled in a breath, swallowed twice, hard, jerked his chin in a nod to let her know he was back, safe again in the here and now. She gave him a quiet smile: been there, done that, had the scars to prove it.

Her phone rang again. This time she answered it. "Tierney."

"It's Yates." The Assistant Director had set up her new position as Local Law Enforcement Liaison and she now reported directly to him. "I need you to head out to Miami. Have you booked on an eight A.M. flight from BWI."

She sat up straight. The AD never played travel agent. Certainly not in the middle of the night. "What's up?"

"Cruise ship crime. I'll e-mail you the details."

Crimes involving U.S. citizens on cruise ships fell under FBI jurisdiction, but no one liked them. By the time the FBI had a chance to begin its investigation, there were always delays in reporting, crime scenes contaminated, witnesses scattered. She'd read about one case where a girl had gone missing and the cruise line never notified anyone, simply gave her luggage and belongings to Goodwill when they docked and forgot all about her. Poor parents finally found out weeks later when she didn't come home from her dream vacation. Never did learn what happened to her.

"Wouldn't a cruise ship fall under the Miami office's purview?" Her deal with Yates was that she got to choose her own cases—no way in hell would she ever pick a cruise ship crime.

"Parents happen to be close personal acquaintances of the Director. Not to mention the Attorney General, Vice President, and several prominent party leaders." His tone made it clear that he didn't like this any more than she did. "Given your repeated forays into the public spotlight—"

"I never asked for—"

"Doesn't matter. You're the FBI's bright and shining star and now you have to pay the price and make us look good. Damn good." A hint of warning undercut his last words.

No sense arguing. She hung up and threw the phone back onto the nightstand.

"What time's your flight?" Carver asked, glancing past her to the bedside clock.

"We have time," she assured him. She ran her fingers down his breastbone, slowly, teasing. But her mind jumped back to ten minutes ago when the phone rang and they'd both jerked awake.

Even coming out of a deep sleep, body charged by adrenaline and the hypervigilant reflexes that had kept him alive every day while undercover, Jake hadn't looked to the front of the room, the most likely direction to invite danger.

He'd trusted Caitlyn with his life. As a partner, someone whose skills he respected, he relied on her to protect them both.

Caitlyn's cheeks suddenly felt cold and she couldn't meet his eyes. She covered by nuzzling his neck, avoiding the Reaper tattoo that ran up beneath his hairline. She was used to holding strangers' lives in her hands— not someone she cared about.

He cupped her chin in his palm and raised her face. His lips found hers. She forced herself to stop thinking. Always thinking too damn much.

They stopped for breakfast at a diner off the interstate. From here Caitlyn would head south to the airport and Carver would continue to her apartment in Manassas. A fact he didn't seem too happy about.

"Weather's supposed to be great all week," he said, shuffling and reshuffling his pancakes as he smothered them with apple butter instead of syrup. "Be a nice ride down to Miami."

"Yeah, and all of it through Reaper territory," she reminded him. "Not to mention the U.S. Attorney would probably slap you behind bars as a material witness just to protect your sweet ass."

"Protect his case is more like it." He shook his head sorrowfully. "It's such a game with those guys. I can't stand sitting there listening to them argue and dissect every decision I made, talking about whether or not it will play well in front of a jury. Like this is a sitcom and me risking my life just isn't funny enough to grab the ratings."

She wished there were something she could do to help. But big cases like this one meant a long time before justice was served. The whole thing could drag out for years. With his life and career left in limbo. "How about I call LaSovage? You could help him out with tactical training, still be close enough to D.C. to run up if the AUSA needs you."

He brightened at that. LaSovage was a member of the Hostage Rescue Team stationed at the FBI Academy at Quantico. He was always looking for people with street smarts to work with the new agents in training. "Thanks, that'd be great."

They dug in to their food, both in no rush to leave despite the clock ticking away the minutes until Caitlyn's flight.

"That guy yesterday," he said.

"Schultz?"

"Yeah. I saw the video of the takedown. Saw how he left his kid there, hung out to dry. What would you have done if she hadn't listened to you? Would you have shot her?"

Every rule of law enforcement said yes. Noncompliant subject with lethal intent and a weapon, officer safety came first. If it were anyone else, that's exactly what she would have said, would have quoted procedure verbatim. But this was Carver and she wanted to always tell him the truth.

"No."

He nodded as if expecting as much. "You saw yourself in her. Defending a parent."

"Being betrayed by one's more like it. You know what Schultz told us when the sheriff asked him about why he ran and left her? Said it was her own damn fault for not shooting us like he'd taught her to. If she had, he would have had time to get away clean. Can you believe that? Didn't care if we shot her or if she shot us."

"What did you expect? The guy's obviously a sociopath."

"Why are you so obsessed with Schultz?" Then it hit her. "This isn't about him. It's about my mother." Another sociopath—a fact she herself didn't recognize until two months ago. Talk about blind spots.

He reached into his jacket and pulled out an envelope. "I've been debating whether or not to give this to you. It came while you were gone."

The address was a prestigious criminal law firm in Asheville, North Carolina. She was tempted to throw it away unopened, just as she had her mother's numerous letters written to her from jail. Funny, her mother had never written her a letter in her entire life—not until she was locked up behind bars for murder. Now she seemed to have all the time in the world to reach out to her daughter.

Caitlyn opened the letter, conscious of Carver watching her. She unfolded the stationery with the fancy letterhead designed to impress and intimidate. The words that followed were chosen for the same impact. As she read them, she heard her mother's voice instead of some anonymous lawyer's.

"They're informing me that they'll be subpoenaing all of my medical records for the preliminary hearing." Threatening her was more like it.

Carver got it right away—sometimes it freaked her, the way he could tune in on her thoughts and feelings. "That guy you dumped, the doctor, they want him."

"Why? Paul was a radiologist, never involved in my case after he made the diagnosis." And saved her life by finding the brain aneurysm that was close to rupturing. The one good thing to come from her encounter with a psychopath who had almost killed her.

"No, but he was involved with you." Carver frowned at the remnants of his breakfast. "He told me he didn't think you should be working, carrying a weapon. Said you'd somehow fooled the FBI doctors into letting you back on the job after your brain surgery."

Her job was the thorn in her relationship with Paul and one of the reasons why she'd left him. Then she realized what her mother was after. "They want to discredit me as a witness—"

"As the prosecution's *only* witness." His frown deepened and he surprised her by reaching across the table to place his hand over hers. "If they destroy your credibility, implying your brain surgery made you unstable—"

"She could get away with murder." A cold-blooded, premeditated murder. The idea sparked through her veins with fury. Mother or not, she wasn't going to let someone commit murder right before her eyes and walk away. She couldn't—it was what made her different from her mother. Caitlyn believed in justice. If she lost that, she would lose everything.

Then Carver took the scenario to its logical conclusion. "I don't care about your mother. Caitlyn, you could lose your career. You'd never be able to work again with something like that on your record."

CHAPTER SIX

Jake regretted his words as soon as he spoke. Caitlyn was headed out on a case; she didn't need her focus divided between the job and this shit her mother was dumping on her.

They made a hasty good-bye in the diner's parking lot and sped off in opposite directions. He fought the urge to turn the bike around and go after her. But she'd hate that, hate him for assuming she needed him, needed anyone.

Never should have brought her the letter, he thought as he steered the Harley through the predawn gloom. Should have just left it at home for her to deal with when she got back. Or better yet, he could have opened it and found a way to deal with the scumbag lawyers and Caitlyn's bitch of a mother himself, saved Caitlyn the worry. But he'd wanted to remind Caitlyn there were no secrets between them—and that he wanted it to stay that way.

They both had issues with trust. He understood that. Hell, she was the first person he'd told his real name to in a year and a half. He was the only one who knew everything that had happened in January when she went home to visit her family. They were both vulnerable and skittish about how much they shared with the rest of the world.

He wanted her to know that her life, her secrets, they were safe with him. Didn't matter if this thing between them, sweet as it was, didn't last—

The thought brought with it a burning that reached up from his gut through his chest like bad Chinese food cooked by Mexicans and served in a Jewish deli. Heartburn.

The damn Employee Assistance shrink the FBI had ordered him to see was right. She'd said that after long-term undercover operations, agents responded in one of two ways: They either holed up, digging into a psychological bunker, shutting out the rest of the world. Or they found someone they could form an attachment to, use as a lifeline to guide them back to their life.

When he was a kid on the farm, he'd seen a chick do that. Thought the beagle was its damn mother. It was funny then, watching that fuzzy little bird follow the beagle all over the yard. Not so much now. He was no innocent chick and Caitlyn was definitely no damn beagle.

She was everything he wasn't right now, everything he needed: brave and bold and fierce and passionate and smart and kind and fearless. . . . At first he'd been worried about putting her in danger by staying close to her. But she'd pointed out that the Reapers had as much reason to want her dead as they did him. So then he'd told himself he was protecting her by being with her.

But he knew in his heart, it was the other way around. He felt like he could breathe when he was with her. The rest of the time he just went through the motions: repeating his story for the record over and over and over again, jousting with lawyers and the brass who picked apart each of his actions and decisions, all the while knowing that a case like this could drag on two, three years and when it was all done, he'd be done. No more undercover work, no more career, no more . . . anything.

Caitlyn kept him from looking into the dark clouds of his future. Kept him anchored in the here and now.

She'd left twenty-three minutes ago and he already missed her.

Caitlyn used her time waiting at the terminal and then on the flight getting caught up with her other cases and gathering background on her new one. When her boss created this position, he'd warned her that a lot of her job would be triage: learning to say no to cases she didn't have the resources to help close. Especially as the entire Local Law Enforcement Liaison Office consisted of her and a shared administrative assistant who handled her paperwork and phone calls. No budget other than what Yates approved on a case-by-case basis—not until she proved her worth.

Still, she insisted on reviewing every case before saying no. Wrote up a letter to the originating agency providing suggestions of new investigative avenues they could pursue. Ended each with an offer to stay in touch.

After two months on the job, she was juggling seventeen active cases—mostly cases she was working long-distance, thanks to the wonders of modern technology. She'd already helped close nine: three with boots on the ground and the others via phone and Skype—and had three dozen to finish reviewing with more arriving in her in-box every day as word spread.

Time spent on a plane was time spent incommunicado, away from her cell phone, giving her the chance to catch up. Yates, her boss, was pleased with her progress and so was she. She loved the work. Yet when she left the office every night and realized there would be even more pleas for help waiting for her when she returned in the morning, it was exhausting.

Carver helped. He reviewed cases with her—his accountant's eye for detail was a huge asset, finding things she overlooked at first glance. He seemed to enjoy it as well. She knew he was bored to tears, shuttling between the AUSA's office and the FBI's Washington Field Office for debriefings and spending the rest of his time trapped in her one-bedroom apartment. A man like him, forced to hide out like that—it was worse than a prison sentence.

She was mostly to blame for the danger he was in. Usually undercover operatives weren't present for the takedown and arrest. If things went right, they were far away from the final action, their real identities protected.

Things hadn't gone right in North Carolina. There'd been no time to call anyone else, so Carver had been the one to arrest the Reapers' leaders. Before they could kill Caitlyn. Or she them. She really hadn't been in the mood to kill anyone that morning, so she owed Carver for that. Big-time.

More than owed him. She liked having him around. What she'd said back at the motel was the truth: He was easy to be with. Unlike work, where she had to guard against getting overinvolved in cases she'd have to later decline. Plus, she had to present herself as always in control: to the locals who came to her for help, she was the face of the FBI. It had never felt like that before when she was in the field working cases, and she still wasn't quite sure how to handle it.

Carver was the one piece of solid ground she had to

stand on. He knew about her family, the lies, the betrayals, and he didn't care. She could tell him anything and he would never use it as a weapon against her.

He was the one person she trusted. Which was scary as hell. Not because she was afraid of him ever hurting her: she'd been betrayed in the worst ways imaginable and had survived.

Carver frightened her because the people Caitlyn trusted tended to end up dead.

CHAPTER SEVEN

To Caitlyn's surprise, she was met at the gate in Miami by a man in a pilot's uniform holding a sign with her name on it.

"Special Agent Tierney, I'm Captain Nouri, the Alvarados' pilot. Do you have anything at baggage claim?"

"No." She'd learned to travel light and had assembled a collection of clothing that would work for anything from a press conference to a tactical raid. In fact, the only things that she missed bringing on these trips were her ballistic vest and long guns. She could pass through TSA with her service weapon and backup Glock, but had to leave the rest behind.

She followed Nouri through the terminal. He didn't offer to take her rolling travel pack or smaller messenger bag, but she didn't ask. "Where are we going?"

"Maria's friends and the ship she is supposed to be on are docking at Cozumel this afternoon. We're flying out to meet them." He glanced over his shoulder at her. "You do have your passport?"

"Of course. But I'd hoped to speak with Maria's family, learn more—" She'd used the jet's Wi-Fi to research as much as she could via the Internet, but that was no substitute for meeting witnesses up close and in person.

"Mr. and Mrs. Alvarado will be traveling with us. You can talk while we are en route." He led her into a private corridor that he accessed with a special pass. A few minutes later they were on the tarmac in the back of an SUV being driven past the commercial jets and out to a private section of the bustling airport. It was too noisy in the SUV to talk, so Caitlyn got caught up on e-mails. She'd done a quick Google search on the Alvarados during the flight down and found they owned a privately held company called BioRegen that specialized in human tissue procurement for research and medical use.

Not very glamorous; in fact, the company's Web site had been filled with so much technical data, aimed at physicians and scientists, that her eyes had glazed over. But as they drew up to a sleek Gulfstream, she realized medical research must be more lucrative than she imagined.

Nouri bounded up the steps and into the cockpit without looking to see if she followed or needed help with her luggage. Obviously playing errand boy sent to fetch a lowly FBI agent was beneath him. She wished Carver were here to annoy the haughty pilot with his biker persona. The thought made her smile.

She entered the plane, and a young man in a business suit immediately relieved her of her bags and ushered her to a seat at a table. He presented her with a glossy folder stamped with BioRegen's logo, then after offering her a drink, he showed her her seat belt and the call button. "We'll be taking off in a few minutes."

The engines started and the steward closed the cabin door. Caitlyn leafed through the folder. In it were photos of Maria, a copy of her passport and driver's license, contact info for her and each of her parents, class schedule, cruise itinerary. Very thorough. She wondered who had put it together—the distraught parents or an anonymous employee?

Just as they began to taxi, a door in the rear of the plane opened and a man and woman emerged. Maria's parents were older than Caitlyn expected: Sandra Alvarado in her late fifties and Hector Alvarado his early sixties. But they moved with grace and strength, in sync with each other, the plane's movement not bothering them at all.

They were both tall, with dark hair and dark eyes, Latino coloring. Hector was dressed in a conservative suit, tie tight, not a wrinkle in sight. Sandra wore four-inch heels and a silk dress that reminded Caitlyn of the designers her mother favored. Even though the swivel chairs were bolted to the floor, Hector still held hers for his wife, his hand brushing her neck before he sat down. Possessive and more than a little controlling.

A united front was the impression Caitlyn had. A true power couple. Two against the world. Where would their daughter fit into that dynamic?

"Thank you for coming on such short notice, Special Agent Tierney," Sandra said. She made it clear her words were simply a formality, but inclined her chin as if waiting to be thanked for the gesture.

"Actually it's Supervisory Special Agent," Caitlyn couldn't resist correcting her. Then immediately chided herself. It wasn't her place to judge how parents grieving their child's disappearance should behave. "But please, call me Caitlyn."

"Caitlyn," Hector said in a smooth, businesslike tone, as if Caitlyn were a dawdling toddler, "I'm sure you understand there's no time to waste."

Definitely no need for handholding with these two.

"How did you learn Maria was missing?" Caitlyn asked, opening a notebook. People were always reassured when you took notes by hand, even if a recording would be more accurate and easier. Her own notes tended to serve as mnemonics rather than a verbatim record. Especially during conversations like this, where the subjects couldn't possibly be involved in the crime. "Did the cruise line call you? Do they know when she was last on board?"

"We can't get any straight answers from the cruise people," Hector said with disdain. "They still refuse to confirm that she's not on board. That's why we need you." His tone implied that it was the only reason they'd allowed an outsider to intrude into their private affairs. "If they listened to reason, this entire trip would be unnecessary."

"What makes you think she isn't still on board?" Caitlyn didn't care what kind of political clout the Alvarados had. If they'd brought her all the way down here on a wild goose chase . . .

"She calls me every night. Ten o'clock," Sandra said. "She didn't call last night."

"And she's not answering her phone. She must have also disabled the GPS tracking on it. We called the cruise line and had a steward page her but she didn't answer any of those messages."

Caitlyn kept her head down so they wouldn't see her eye roll. This was sounding a lot like overprotective parents and less like a federal case. Didn't these two remember what it was like, being a nineteen-year-old college kid, giddy with your first taste of freedom? "She's on the cruise with friends, right? What do they say?"

They glanced at each other and shifted in their seats. "They're her friends from college."

"I kept asking her to bring them home. We wanted to meet them before they went off together. . . ." Sandra's voice trailed off, and finally the two made eye contact with Caitlyn once more.

Hector took over. "Her so-called friends insist that everything is fine and we shouldn't worry. They won't say anything more."

Caitlyn focused on her scribbling as she thought about that. These two were obviously biased, but . . . even college kids would understand the importance of a friend missing from a ship at sea. "Perhaps she met someone? A romantic involvement?"

Both parents bristled, as if her suggestion were outlandish. "Maria would never date a boy without our approval," her father said in a tone that didn't allow for compromise. Sandra nodded in agreement. "And she has far too good sense to be involved in any kind of shipboard dalliance."

Right. Clearly these two didn't remember their own college days. The Alvarados were a generation older than Caitlyn. To someone Maria's age, it must have seemed like her parents belonged to an entirely different world.

"Tell me more about Maria," she suggested. "What was she studying? Any interests outside of school? Did she have a job?"

"She's an excellent student when she applies her mind. We encouraged her to study something that would provide her with lasting skills. Biochemistry or engineering. Even architecture. But . . ." Hector's shrug threatened to wrinkle his Italian suit.

"Always with her head in a book, even when she was a child. I guess we should have done something about that, not indulged her so much."

Caitlyn looked at the parents, waiting. Finally the

mother confessed, "She's studying archeology, of all things. Thinks she's going to get a job exploring ancient ruins and digging for treasure. It's quite impractical, of course, but the more we argued with her, the more she dug her heels in."

"She gets that from you," Hector said. "Stubborn."

"At least I'm also practical." She sighed. "But I assure you, she is very practical in other matters, Special Agent Tierney. Very responsible. She'd never not contact us, not unless something happened to her."

"And she's never missed a day calling before this?" Caitlyn asked.

"Never," they said in unison. The father picked up the narrative. "Ten o'clock at night before she goes to bed. Without fail. It was one of our requirements for her to go to school so far away from home."

Like Orlando was so far from Miami? Talk about strangling on apron strings.

"So, if you're correct, she went missing yesterday or sometime after ten o'clock the night before?" That was a long time when you had a few thousand people tramping all over the potential crime scene. If there was even a crime.

Caitlyn began to wonder if maybe Maria had run away. That would explain the friends' reluctance to talk with the parents. Only problem was, a naïve nineteen-year-old trying to escape smothering parents would make for easy prey for streetwise predators.

It was the worst-case scenario, but worst-case scenarios were Caitlyn's expertise. She glanced at her notebook where she'd jotted down the ship's itinerary. Key West, Belize, Guatemala, followed by Cozumel. Was Maria still on board? Could she have slipped past the ship's crew and gotten off at one of the ports?

Was she still alive?

CHAPTER EIGHT

Apparently money talked even louder in Mexico than it did in Miami, because Caitlyn and the Alvarados were whisked through customs with lightning speed. After a short taxi ride, they soon found themselves ushered into the office of the *Caribbean Dream*'s chief of security, Ian Broadman, and were asked to wait for him.

Hector and Sandra groused that they weren't being given access to the ship's captain. The *Caribbean Dream* was nine stories high, and from the activity on the dock and on the various decks they crossed through, Caitlyn figured the good captain had plenty on his hands to worry about. It must be like running a small country, only in addition to the administrative headache of feeding, housing, and entertaining thousands of passengers and crew, he'd have to also worry about external concerns like the engines and storms and navigating the ocean.

Not a job she'd want, that's for sure. After keeping them waiting for several minutes, a tall man with military bearing wearing a suit and tie rather than a uniform strode into the office. "Mr. and Mrs. Alvarado," he said without shaking hands as he slid behind the desk to take his seat. "I'm Chief Security Officer Ian Broadman. It's good to meet you, but really, I'm not sure how I can help."

Hector bristled at that. "What do you mean, you're not sure how you can help? You can either bring my daughter to me now, as you insist she's still on board, or you can allow Supervisory FBI Special Agent Tierney here full access to your data so she can begin a proper investigation."

"As I told you on the phone, your daughter is an adult, and I can't violate her privacy. However, I understand your concerns and I can verify that to the best of our knowledge, she is still on board."

"You've seen her?" Sandra leaned forward, one palm pressed against Broadman's desk. "Is she okay?"

He frowned at the impression her hand left behind on the polished hardwood, and Caitlyn knew he wanted to wipe it clean again. A by-the-book kind of guy. "I don't need to see her to know that she's on board. We have a state-of-the-art security system and—"

"What led you to that conclusion, Mr. Broadman?" Caitlyn asked before either of Maria's parents could leap over the desk to throttle the security officer. Both had edged almost off their seats—the most emotion she'd seen from either. "That Maria is still on board?"

Broadman didn't back down. "Each passenger has an ID card that must be carried with them at all times. It has a RFID device implanted, so they can use it to purchase onboard amenities, and we can track usage of our facilities, which meals are most popular, et cetera."

"And Maria's ID is still on board?"

"Yes. Last used at breakfast on the Lido deck this morning."

"Can you tell us where she is now?"

He frowned. "I'm afraid that would be a violation of her privacy."

"How do you know she's the one using it?" Hector demanded. "Why hasn't she called us or answered her phone? She could be anywhere and all you'd know is where a damned card is."

Caitlyn tried to smooth the waters. "He has a point, Mr. Broadman."

"In my experience," Broadman said, "cruises such as this one that appeal to our younger clientele often lead to shipboard romances. Perhaps your daughter has simply been otherwise occupied."

Both parents jumped to their feet. Caitlyn pushed out of her own chair and stood between them and Broadman. "Nevertheless, I am a federal agent who would like to speak to Ms. Alvarado and verify her well-being. Mr. and Mrs. Alvarado will wait here while you take me to where Ms. Alvarado is now."

He frowned at that but was smart enough to realize it was the only thing that would get the Alvarados off his back. "Very well. If you need anything, Mr. and Mrs. Alvarado, my assistant will be right outside. Agent Tierney, if you'll come with me."

No one was very happy with the arrangement, and for a moment Caitlyn thought Hector was going to barge after them, but to her surprise he and his wife merely sank back into their seats while Broadman escorted her from his office.

As large as the ship had appeared from down on the dock, it seemed even larger as they journeyed through it. They ended up at the rear of the ship where there was a climbing wall, a large water feature that simulated surfing, two pools, and an outdoor bar. Despite the beach being just a short distance away, the deck was crowded with laughing young men and women.

Caitlyn couldn't remember her last vacation—unless you counted her trip home two months ago. The trip that had ended with her mother under arrest for murder. She decided it didn't count. Maybe she and Carver . . .

"Her ID card indicates she's at the bar." Broadman interrupted her fantasy. The man was inhuman, not even sweating despite the fact that it was eighty degrees and he was overdressed—especially compared to the co-eds who wore bikinis that used less material than the rags Caitlyn cleaned her guns with. Which also made her think of Carver, stuck back in Virginia. He would have loved this.

A trio of giggling girls purposely brushed their oiled bodies against Broadman as they passed. Maybe it was a good thing Carver wasn't here. He would have enjoyed this too much. Yeah, cross cruise off the list. Besides, if she was going to be trapped on a boat, she preferred to be the one in control. Maybe a rafting trip?

They navigated through the crowd of sunbathers and reached the bar. No Maria.

During the flight from Miami, Caitlyn had done some basic background checks on Maria and her friends—finding the most useful data, including photos, on their Facebook pages. Standing at the bar were two of the girls. Linda Cervino and Tracey Morton.

"I don't understand," Broadman said, his haughty demeanor slipping for the first time. "She should be here. Perhaps she's in the pool or showers, took her ID off."

Caitlyn saw the two girls eyeing them. "Why don't you go look? I'll wait here." She waved her hand and wiped her forehead. "In the shade."

He gave her a look of disdain for her weakness and left her at the bar. Linda, who had obviously overheard them, grabbed her purse and tried to sidle past, but Caitlyn grabbed her arm. "Want to tell me where Maria really is?"

The girl had acting chops. She shook off Caitlyn and glared at her. "I think you have the wrong person. Whoever you are."

A third girl joined them. Vicky Smith, if Caitlyn remembered correctly from her perusal of Maria's social media. "Why are you asking about Maria?" she said in a worried tone. "Has something happened? Who are you?"

Linda rolled her eyes. "Shut up, Vicky."

"That might not be the wisest decision, Linda." The girl flinched at her name, glared at Caitlyn. "And to answer your question, Vicky, I'm FBI Supervisory Special Agent Caitlyn Tierney." She flipped her credentials open, showed them to the girls. "Before any of you say anything, you should know it's a federal offense to lie to a federal agent. Tracey, you're pre-law, you already knew that, right?"

Tracey bit her lip and nodded.

"Tell you what, girls. Let's go back to your cabin where we'll have some privacy and you can tell me everything. Linda, you lead the way."

Broadman was going to be furious that she was wandering the ship unescorted, much less that she'd stuck him with Maria's parents, but better him than her. And no way would these girls answer their questions. But she could get them to talk.

She only hoped their story would have a happy ending—a prank gone on too long, Maria holed up in a romantic liaison with another passenger. Typical college spring break adventures.

From the worried look on Vicky's face, she had a feeling that wouldn't be the case.

CHAPTER NINE

The girls shared a small stateroom with a bunk bed, foldout sofa bed, and window. Clothing and souvenirs were scattered all around and there was no place to sit except for the sofa, which Vicky hastily folded up, shoving the dirty linens under the cushions.

"Where is Maria?" Caitlyn asked once the girls were seated on the couch. She remained standing, the better to intimidate. They seemed to respond to authority, even Linda, who was obviously their leader.

"Having the time of her life digging through some ancient ruins in Guatemala," Tracey answered. Her tone was wistful, as if she wished she'd had the courage to go on an adventure instead of being stuck on a cruise filled with the same kind of drunk college kids they could have hung out with back home.

"Ancient ruins?" Maria's parents had said her passion was archeology—a passion they disapproved of. Hence, the deception. "Start from the beginning."

"Well," Linda said, "it all started with a cute guy."

"Prescott," Tracey put in. "He's a grad student at Cambridge."

"So he's English?" Caitlyn asked.

"No. American. Studying abroad. He and Maria met in a chat room devoted to pre—" Linda paused, frowning.

Vicky supplied the details. "Preclassic Mayan Civilization of Mesoamerica."

Whatever that was. The girls began to fill in the blanks without Caitlyn's prompting, so she stayed quiet and listened.

"You see," Linda said, "Prescott works with this Professor Zigler. He's been looking for this Dresden Codex something place his whole career. Maria volunteered to help and go over his data using modern technology."

"And she found it!" Tracey interrupted.

Linda shot her a look and continued, "So the professor came out of retirement and organized a dig at this lost temple. Apparently folks have been searching for it for like a century but they were looking in the wrong place."

"Of course they had to keep it a secret. Not just because of the treasure and looters it might attract, but also the natives—"

"Indigenous people," Vicky corrected.

"The Mayans have this big political deal, their land, their heritage, something like that."

"They're just trying to stop the exploitation of their culture and history."

"Yeah, but that leaves all those temples and buildings just rotting in the jungle when people like Prescott and Maria could be studying them, learning tons of stuff—"

"And finding tons of treasure." Vicky's voice held a hint of disapproval. "There's no way in hell the government will let the Mayans keep all that gold for themselves. They'll confiscate it, sell it to the highest bidder."

Caitlyn intervened. "Tell me more about this Prescott guy. And the professor, Zigler. Are they with Maria now?"

"Of course," Linda said. "Maria's not stupid. Professor Zigler is famous—if you're an archeologist. He's been retired, so out of the spotlight for the past few years, but she couldn't pass up the chance to work with him."

"He met her in Guatemala?"

"No. A man that important wouldn't leave his work just to pick up an undergrad volunteer. He sent Prescott."

"Does Prescott have a last name?"

"Prescott Wilson," Vicky supplied. She got off the sofa and rummaged through one of the bags scattered around the room, then handed Caitlyn a sheet of paper. "Maria took this screen shot of him during one of their Skype calls."

It was a color printout of a man in his late twenties. Blond, handsome, aristocratic. "So Prescott picked Maria up—"

"At the port. Santo Tomás. We all met him."

"Maria definitely lucked out there. Compared to the drunken frat boys we've met here, at least," Tracey said.

"And where's this dig, this lost temple?"

They looked at each other. "We don't know."

"They had to keep the location a secret," Linda explained. "Maria said everyone thought the temple was at the bottom of a lake—"

"Lake Izabel," Vicky supplied.

"Right, Lake Izabel, but they were wrong. It was really like thirty-some miles away, in the jungle, near another lake, where it'd been forgotten for centuries. All that time looking, and Maria's the one who finally found it."

"How'd she do that?" Caitlyn asked, not liking the creepy tingling crawling up her spine as she listened to their story. It was too involved and convoluted to be a routine con—and there was no money exchanging hands. If they'd just wanted to kidnap a college girl, there were easier ways. And there'd been no ransom demand . . . at least not yet. But this whole thing felt so very wrong. "Maria is only a sophomore. How could she help this famous professor?"

"She's very gifted," Linda defended her friend. "Especially with maps and satellite images and shit like that."

"Prescott showed her the professor's data," Vicky explained. "They had tons of it. Geological surveys, thermal and infrared scans, satellite imagery going back twenty years, even aerial photos they'd found in some archive. Problem was, they had too much data. And no way to interpret it."

"Until Maria," Caitlyn said. Talk about reeling in your mark. But why? What did they want with Maria?

"Right," Tracey said with pride. "She worked for weeks on it, used all her spare time. Used tons of crazy special computer programs and stuff to analyze it. Even one she got from NASA. But then she put everything together and figured out where the temple and treasure were. So of course the professor invited her to join them. She had to jump through tons of hoops, fill out all sorts of forms, plus there's no credit, but she's hoping the professor will let her join for real come summer."

Linda nodded. "But her parents would never approve. So she decided to prove to them that she can take care of herself and we came up with a plan."

"Right." Caitlyn fought the urge to roll her eyes. "The plan. How did you guys pull that off?"

"We left the boat together at Santo Tomás. Prescott picked up Maria and we went sightseeing with this hunky guide, Jorge."

They all smiled simultaneously, remembering Jorge.

"But the ship's records show that Maria got back on board."

"Before she left, she gave us her passport and passenger ID. When we got back on board, Linda dropped her bags, distracting the security guy, while I scanned her passport under the bar code reader."

"Then we just carried her ID with us, taking turns to use it to buy stuff so the computer would think she was still here."

"And that's all there was to it," Linda finished with a smirk. They all sat back, crossing their arms, daring Caitlyn to find fault with their plan.

It took everything she had not to lash out at them. Had she been that foolish and naïve and plain old stupid when she was their age? She took a breath and calmed down. Yes. She had. And so had all her friends. Made you wonder if Darwin was right after all.

Caitlyn didn't waste time reprimanding them—it wouldn't help her find Maria. "How was Maria going to get back into the country without her passport?"

"She was born in Guatemala. Her parents moved to Florida when she was only a few months old. But she has two passports. She was going to use her Guatemalan one."

"And if that didn't work or if she had any trouble, she'd go to the U.S. consulate in Guatemala City."

"We made sure she had their phone number programmed in her cell."

"Worst case, she'd call her parents. They'd bail her out—and then probably make her quit school and join a convent or something."

"They're so strict."

"And old. They just don't understand what it means to have a dream."

"Not a clue. Just because their lives turned out boring doesn't mean ours have to." They nodded in unison, condemning parents everywhere.

"Do you have the professor's contact info?"

Linda and Tracey looked away. Vicky answered, "Prescott said they have a satellite phone. That way she could call if she needed anything."

"But she hasn't called?"

They all shook their heads. "See, she's fine," Linda rationalized. "If she was in any trouble, she would have called."

Right. If Prescott was legit, if the sat phone was working, if the trouble happened after she arrived at the dig, too many ifs to count. "And none of you know exactly where this site is?"

"It's a temple hidden in the jungle. It belongs to the Mayan rain god, Chaac," Vicky supplied with a gush, trying to make up for their lack of helpful information. Teacher's pet, Caitlyn guessed.

"Do you know where in the jungle?"

She drooped with disappointment. "Maria showed me the satellite photos, but I didn't see a map or anything. All you could see was green everywhere, it was on the side of a mountain and there was a huge waterfall beside it. You couldn't even tell there was a building there hidden in the trees. Not in the regular photos. It just looked like another hill. Part of the mountain."

Not much help. Caitlyn thought again about the elaborate ruse that lured Maria to Guatemala. It was clear Maria had been targeted. Far too risky not to have someone watching Maria, making sure she didn't alert the authorities or change her mind. "How about before you left Orlando? Have any of you noticed anyone watching Maria? Maybe someone out of place?"

Linda and Tracey exchanged glances. "You mean like the pervs?"

"What pervs?"

"A few old guys, always following us around," Tracey answered.

Linda rolled her eyes. "They even showed up when we went out dancing the night before we left."

"I thought I saw one of them here on the ship," Vicky interjected as if she didn't want to be left out. "Well, maybe. I haven't seen him for a few days."

"Not since Maria got off?" Caitlyn asked. The girl nodded.

After grilling the girls and receiving only vague descriptions of three men, Caitlyn took Maria's U.S. passport from them and handed them her card with her contact info. "If you girls think of anything more, if you see one of the men, if you hear from Maria—or Prescott or the professor—I want you to call me. Right away. Day or night. Do you understand?"

Another group nod. This one the slightest bit sheepish—but not sheepish enough. Finally Vicky asked, "She's going to be okay, isn't she? I mean, she's not in any danger. Not there with the professor and all those archeology people."

Caitlyn couldn't resist. "She's alone in the jungle a thousand miles from home with strangers who may or may not be legit. And she hasn't made contact with anyone in over thirty-six hours. What do you think?"

Suddenly they got it. Eyes went wide, hands clutched for each other's comfort, a few tears appeared. Caitlyn reached for the door.

"Tell Mr. and Mrs. Alvarado we're sorry," came a quiet plea from the couch. She didn't bother to turn back to see which girl had uttered it. "We thought we were helping."

Caitlyn left to find her way back to the security office. Friends like that . . .

CHAPTER TEN

Maria had spent the night at the river. At first she worried about animals coming to the water to drink, but she felt safer there than trapped in the claustrophobic confines of the thick jungle undergrowth. At least at the water there were no snakes. She'd rather take her chances with jaguars than snakes. Well, maybe not, but it was harder to imagine jaguars with every rustle below the ground cover.

She'd found a relatively dry patch along the riverbank and used a rock to carve a niche into the mud, then lined it with ferns to make it waterproof and add insulation. She used more ferns and palm fronds to defend against the chilly mist that gathered over the river.

Of course she hadn't counted on the torrential storm that flew down the gorge, thunder ricocheting from one rock face to the next, leaving her teeth aching. No amount of padding with plants could protect her from the rain and water splashing up to her feet. But moving up into the jungle seemed even more dangerous as the ground grew muddy and unstable while lightning flashed between the trees, each strike closer than the last.

Finally she just huddled, letting the rain lash her, trying to imagine she was somewhere else. Her teeth chattered as she curled up in the mud, knees to her chest, hugging herself for warmth, rigid with fear, alternating between crying for her parents, weeping over Prescott, and sobbing in terror with each new sound and motion the darkness brought.

As for any possibility of sleep, fear took care of that.

At first light she drank her fill of the river water, filtering it through her folded-up bandanna into her bottle. After bathing in the water, she turned to the thought of food. She'd had heart of palm salads back home, but had no idea what part of the palm tree they came from. The root? Stems? Inside the trunk? Didn't really matter, since she had nothing to cut into the plants with. She settled for peeling back some of the palm fronds, slicing her hands with their sharp edges, until she reached the stringy white fibers at the center of the stalk.

Bitter and they did little to take the edge off her hunger, but it made her feel like she wasn't totally inept. After all, she'd survived a night alone in the jungle, in a storm that rivaled the tropical squalls back home. Not many kids her age could say that.

She hiked downstream, feeling more confident that she could actually make it to the hospital that day. Until she stopped to rest and exhaustion and hunger and the heat of the day combined to knock her off her feet for several hours. Hours when anything could be happening to the professor and his people. She woke with her mouth dry and her heart heavy with fear and guilt. Never should have stopped, even if she had practically fallen to the ground, she was so damn tired.

Despite her nap, she was dizzy when she pushed to her feet. Her arms and legs moved slowly, as if the air were thicker than mud. Welts left by lashing branches during her race through the trees and insect bites from her night spent huddled in the mud covered her body. She scratched absently as she checked her watch. Almost four. From the topography around her, she guessed she still had at least a mile to go before reaching the lake—maybe two. And the light was fading fast.

The river burbled cheerfully beside her, oblivious of her panic. It was a fast-moving river carved out of the foothills, but the largest waterfall she'd had to climb down as she followed it was maybe ten feet high. And it had gotten flatter, smoother, the farther west she came. Could she risk it?

Her father would say yes. But what decided her was the thought of spending another night in the wild, of what might be happening to the professor and his people, the blood on Prescott's face, and yes, the deep, primal need for human contact, for civilization.

She stepped into the water, icy cold from its trek down the mountains, walked until it came up to her knees, then sank into it, feet facing downstream, and let the current take her.

Staying afloat in the river with its rocks and turns and churning water wasn't as easy as it looked in the movies. Maria had once gone tubing down the Ichetucknee when she'd visited friends in Gainesville—that river was nothing like this one.

After being sucked under for the third time, Maria realized she had to get out, risk going by land, even if it did take longer. She tried to swim for shore but the current held her tight. Then she heard the noise she'd been dreading: the roar of a waterfall.

The sun was barely a scarlet memory in the sky, leaving shadows that filled the river gorge. The current smashed her into a boulder, trying to spin her under it where she'd be trapped, but she managed to keep her head and arms above water, hugging the rock face as she inched along it, aiming for the shallower eddies that ran toward the riverbank. The current forced her to the south bank of the river where the gorge wall was a steep cliff and large boulders had tumbled into the river.

It took the last of her energy and she got pretty banged up along the way, but finally she collapsed faceup in the mud. Shivering uncontrollably, she watched as stars began to appear overhead. She wouldn't last another night out here, not as cold and wet as she was. And the professor and his people needed her to get them help.

Coughing out the water she'd inhaled, she pushed herself to her feet and struggled on. The roar of the waterfall got louder, the rocks and boulders she had to navigate over or around got larger, until she climbed onto one final rock ledge only to realize that she'd come to the end.

The river vanished into churning white water plunging over the side of the mountain. On her side of the water a sharp rock face reached toward the sky, a few scraggly trees breaking its knifelike silhouette. She couldn't climb up. Couldn't swim over to the less rugged terrain on the other side of the river where trees sloped down the mountain to the lake below. She crept out to the edge of the limestone cliff and looked down. It was about twenty-five feet or so to the bottom of the falls. They emptied out into a lake and on the far side of it she saw lights. Not stars, but man-made, real lights.

The clinic. She'd made it. Almost.

No way to tell in the dark what lay at the bottom of the cliff. The water was probably deep enough, but what if there were boulders and rocks waiting below?

Or alligators—did they have alligators in Guatemala? She couldn't remember reading about any.

She peered into the darkness. The water roared like a freight train. The rock face beside it was polished smooth. Even in daylight, she wasn't sure she'd be able to climb down it.

She stood, inching her toes out over the edge of the cliff. Back home, as a kid, she'd never been afraid of heights, had loved racing up the high dive and shouting to her father to watch as she hurled her body through the air as far as she could push gravity. This was just like that.

That's what she told herself as she backed up to get a running start. Her best bet was to land as far out into the lake, away from the rocks and rapids as she could. Given the height she had to work with, she thought she had a good chance.

If the lake was deep enough, if there were no hidden rocks or submerged trees or alligators waiting for her.

She heaved in one breath after another, filling her lungs to capacity. Prescott's bloody face, the sound of the gun roared through her mind, eclipsing the sound of the waterfall. Then she pushed off, running, until she ran out of ground and found herself soaring through the air.

The last thing she thought of before hitting the water was she wished her father could see how brave she was. She hoped he'd finally be proud of his little girl.

CHAPTER ELEVEN

The only good thing about the intel she'd gotten from the girls was the look on Broadman's face when Caitlyn told him how easily they'd outwitted his state-of-the-art security system.

Hector and Sandra, aghast at the idea of their daughter left behind, wanted to fly to Guatemala immediately, but the pilot quashed that idea, saying that he couldn't get clearance until morning. They settled into a hotel for the night, the Alvarados in an executive suite, Caitlyn in a regular room, hoping they didn't fly off without her.

Because, as she told Carver later that night, trying to make a joke of the weird vibe Maria's parents left her with, wouldn't that be terrible, getting stuck in Cozumel?

"Have a margarita on me." His chuckle sounded wistful. She wished he were here as well. But of course she didn't admit that. Not to Carver and not to herself. "Yates is authorizing you to go with them to Guatemala?"

"Wants me to find the girl, keep the parents out of

trouble, and save his career. Not necessarily in that order." She stretched out on her bed and stared at the tasteful black-and-white photos of seashells that adorned the wall.

The Alvarados had chosen an expensive, upscale hotel, so everything was in black-and-white with a hint of silver thrown in. Forget that right outside the window was a stunning palette of blues and greens and gold. The message the art deco style furnishings sent was that they were too classy to indulge in such commonplace beach decor.

"All this fuss for some college kid run off on an adventure?"

"I hope that's all it is, but I don't think so. Too much just doesn't feel right. This Prescott kid—I can find his name and a superficial Web presence but nothing that goes back past a few months ago. It's too late now with the time zones, but first thing in the morning I'm calling Cambridge to see if I can talk to Professor Zigler. He's definitely real enough, tons of publications and appearances."

"E-mail?"

"It seems the good professor lives off the grid. I can't find any contact info for him other than a mailing address in care of the university."

"The plot thickens." He paused. "There's more, isn't there?"

She squirmed, trying to get comfortable. Apparently rich, art deco furnishings also meant uncomfortable; it was the hardest damn bed she'd ever been in. "The parents. I've dealt with tons of grieving parents, parents of missing kids, but these two. Cold, aloof, clinical one moment, then suddenly distant, like they're hiding something."

"They're forty years older than Maria. They just

don't get it, why their kid could run off, need a little space, find herself. . . ."

"Maybe." Doubt filtered into Caitlyn's voice. "But everything changed after I told them Maria left the ship in Guatemala. Especially with Hector, the dad. He totally clammed up, wouldn't answer any questions about his past, said it was none of my concern."

"That got your Spidey senses tingling?" Carver believed in the magical properties of Caitlyn's intuition even more than she did herself. Maybe because it had saved their lives a few months ago. "Want me to check into them?"

"Sounds like you're bored."

"You don't know the half of it. Cleaned my guns— and yours—so many times, I'm getting high on the fumes. Hey"—his tone brightened—"want me to come down? A little Caribbean sun might be just what I need."

She blinked. Imagined her and Carver on a beach. Couldn't help but smile at the thought. But aloud she said, "Don't you dare. The AUSA will have you locked away as a material witness."

His sigh rattled through the airwaves. "Okay, okay. I won't come down. You said the parents were from Guatemala. Maybe something in their past?"

"If so, I haven't been able to find it. Looks like everything is on the up and up. They left Guatemala when Maria was two months old, started their biotech company in Miami, got rich, became U.S. citizens. Nothing pops on their background checks."

"Maybe you're just not looking in the right place." She heard the grin in his voice. Carver loved a challenge. "A forensic accountant might be just the person you need on this case."

"Maybe. But it will have to be off the books. These

guys are too well connected. Any hint of trouble, and they could fry all our asses—including Assistant Director Yates." Like it or not, Yates was her key to job security. No Yates meant no Local Law Enforcement Liaison.

"No problem. I'll be like the wind. Invisible."

She gave up on the bed and rolled to her feet. It was too dark to see the ocean from the sliding glass doors leading onto her balcony, but still, she pressed her hand against it, looking out. To the side she could see the lights of a cruise ship dancing over the water—she wasn't sure if it was the *Caribbean Dream* or not.

"I can't stop hoping that we'll get there and find her having the time of her life. Digging in the dirt, finding lost treasure, whatever. Just enjoying her freedom." She sighed. "God, it makes me feel so old. I barely remember being that young."

"You're only thirty-five. Wasn't that long ago."

"Feels like forever."

"What kind of crazy things did a kid like you, growing up with your Quaker grandparents, do when you got to college?" He didn't mention her mother, Caitlyn noticed.

She thought back. A smile warmed her face despite her fatigue. "Guess I was a lot like Maria. Did a ton of stupid shit."

"Like what?"

"Like meeting a guy at a party and we both realized we'd never seen New York City, so we took off right then and there in his car. No one knew where I was or who I was with; I didn't know anything about the guy, but it just felt right. Some kind of grand adventure. Like I was in charge of my own life."

"Obviously he wasn't a serial killer or anything."

"Nope, just a kid from Hagerstown. We ended up

hitting the city around two in the morning, drove all around because we didn't have enough money to park the car or stay in a hotel. Saw Times Square—tons of people even in the middle of the night—and Broadway, that pretty triangular building that's in all the pictures—"

"The Flatiron."

"Right. We passed a lot of parks, but I don't think any of them were Central Park. Ended up watching the sunrise parked at a loading dock near the river until some angry truckers made us leave. Realized we barely had enough money for gas, so we turned around and drove back home. No one even knew we'd gone."

A sigh as she remembered the freedom. No rules or regulations, no boss to answer to, no lawyers trying to discredit her. She felt a little envious of Maria for having the courage to take a risk and choose her own path as she had. Given the girl's overbearing parents, it couldn't have been easy.

"How about you?" she asked Carver. "An accounting major at Kansas State, I'll bet your idea of a good time was tipping cows."

"Very funny. We did tons of crazy shit. Once I even moved a decimal place for the heck of it."

"Hah. CPA humor. You never messed with a decimal point in your life."

"Okay, you got me. Well, our RA was really strict about no girls overnight, since our floor was guys only. Guess it got the religious types riled up or something. We used to penny the doors to other guys' dorm rooms. Lock them in with the girls they'd smuggled in the night before."

"Penny?"

"Yeah. There's a gap when you shut the door. Fill it with pennies and you can't open it from the inside—do it right and you can't open it from the outside, either, not without a screwdriver or chisel to get the pennies out."

"Locking guys inside their rooms with their dates, that was your idea of a good time?"

"Does kind of sound lame now that I think of it. Probably helped that we were drunk."

"And obviously without dates yourself."

"Go ahead, rub it in. What can I say, I was a late bloomer."

A yawn overtook her. "I still have work to do before I hit the sack."

"Get some rest," he said. "Call me if you need anything."

"Thanks, Carver. Good night." She hung up the phone. Suddenly the room seemed so empty. Hell, her entire life did. She'd fought so long and hard to get where she was with the FBI, but what did it really matter if her life was simply traveling from an empty apartment to empty hotel rooms and back again?

She pushed the thought aside and opened her laptop. Her life was just fine, thank you very much. She had plenty to fill it. Didn't need anything else jumbling things up.

Especially not Carver. At least that's what she told herself. But it didn't stop her from wishing he was holding her when she finally crawled into bed an hour later.

Jake hung up from Caitlyn feeling more energized than he had in weeks. He grabbed his laptop and began digging into the Alvarados' and BioRegen's finances. Even as a privately held company, there were still a lot of public filings, not to mention all the info relating to its biomedical products.

Turned out BioRegen specialized in tissue procurement. It had started almost twenty years ago as one of the few places where scientists could legally obtain stem cells for research. It also hosted a stem cell bank for private individuals wanting to protect their children's futures. It had grown to now provide tissue to medical facilities and laboratories all over the world, expanding from research into the burgeoning plastic surgery and orthopedic markets.

Given the company's rapid expansion and skyrocketing net worth, apparently human tissue was a hot commodity. BioRegen leased a fleet of jets and planes to transport the fragile, time-sensitive tissues like stem cells and bone marrow, and had also established local procurement centers partnering with funeral homes, allowing the deceased to donate their tissues and still be allowed an open-casket viewing.

How noble. Except that all those families thinking their loved ones' bodies were going to aid medical research probably didn't realize that most of the donated tissues ended up being used as filler for breast augmentation and other plastic surgeries. Given that it was illegal to sell body parts in the United States and that all the tissue donations were made voluntarily, that meant BioRegen operated with little up-front costs, leading to a very tidy profit from each body entrusted to its team of "tissue procurement specialists."

Good business, but he didn't like the ethical shadow land BioRegen occupied. During his time undercover with the Reapers, Jake had forgotten how cutthroat corporate America could be. At least with the outlaw motorcycle gang they'd had a sense of honor, commitment to each other.

The more he read about BioRegen's business and filled in the blanks behind the public documents, the more he sensed another type of gang: greedy bastards out to fleece grieving families and honor the bottom line.

He closed down his computer and thought about it. When he was with the IRS, he'd never gotten emotional about a case. Yet here he was, ready to accuse the parents of a missing girl of fraud and questionable ethics.

He blamed it on Caitlyn's influence. Her sense of justice didn't tolerate shades of gray—not even when it came to her own mother.

BioRegen hadn't broken any laws, the best he could tell. In fact, if it was a public company, it'd be praised for enhancing its stockholders' profit margins. Yet, no matter how he tried to look at the company's business plan from an objective point of view, he couldn't get over his distaste and distrust. There was something shady going on behind the healthy profits; he was sure of it.

He was sure of it because his gut told him so. He chuckled out loud, glad Caitlyn wasn't there to see it. Not exactly sound investigative procedure, especially for a forensic accountant.

Jake grabbed his phone. Lynn never went to bed before midnight. And he needed a second opinion. A cold, detached, completely unemotional second opinion.

Who better to ask than his cold, detached, completely unemotional ex-wife?

CHAPTER TWELVE

Caitlyn woke at six, grabbed a quick shower, and packed. After several disastrous trips when she first started this new job, she'd developed a routine that had led to the rebirth of an obsession with camping gear, large zipper-locked freezer bags, as well as clothing that was versatile and easy to wash in a hotel sink, quick to dry. Just like her summers in college spent as a river guide, always in search of clean, dry, comfortable clothing.

Since they might be following Maria into the jungle, or at least off the beaten track, she exchanged the lightweight dress boots she'd worn yesterday for her tactical boots. Decided on khaki cargo pants, a navy Under Armor T-shirt, and her favorite travel jacket: a windproof, waterproof, breathable parka with tons of secure pockets inside and out. Thank you, REI.

She went downstairs to the lobby, where she checked out and worked on her computer while eating breakfast. The worst thing about travel was no time to exercise, and after five days on the road, her muscles were crying for a good long run. But Alvarado's pilot had said he hoped to be cleared to leave by eight o'clock and that he'd pick up Caitlyn and Maria's parents by seven thirty, so she'd have to skip another day.

While she was clearing the most pressing items from her in-box, Caitlyn's phone chirped with a text message. Vicky, Maria's friend, the one who had been the sole voice of disapproval about Maria's adventure.

Caitlyn waved to the waitress for her check as she dialed the girl. "Caitlyn Tierney here."

"Oh, I didn't realize you'd call back so soon," Vicky stuttered.

"I have to leave in a few minutes. Did you hear from Maria?"

"No. But I think I know where the professor's research site is. The temple Maria found. I thought that might help."

"Absolutely. Can you e-mail me the info? How did you find it if Maria didn't contact you?"

"I'm the only one of us who brought a laptop, and she was using it before she left. The history was all there, so I followed her tracks and found a Google Earth search with GPS coordinates for an area not far from Santo Tomás."

"Good work."

"It's even more remote than I thought. I checked and there's no towns or anything for miles around it. Just a clinic of some kind. She could be lost for days in the jungle and no one would ever know." Fear strained her voice. Vicky struck Caitlyn as the kind of high-strung person who always found something to fear in every situation, but this time she might be right.

"Also, she didn't log out of her Gmail account. There are a few emails from Prescott—I hope it's okay that I looked."

Damn it, why hadn't the girl thought of the computer

yesterday? "They might be very helpful. Do you know how to expand the header to show the original info?"

"Wait. Okay, yes, I see."

"Do that, then copy that info into a text file and forward it along with the originals so I can examine them."

"I hope they help."

So did Caitlyn. "Thanks, Vicky. I'll let you know as soon as we find Maria." She hung up and glanced at her watch. Still a few minutes before the pilot would be here to take them to the plane. No sign of the Alvarados yet. She did the math; early afternoon in Cambridge. She dialed the number she'd found for the archeology department. "Professor Zigler, please."

"I'm sorry, the professor is unavailable," the clipped British accent of a secretary replied.

"I understand he's not there at the moment. I'm a FBI agent calling from America," Caitlyn explained. "It's important that I speak with the professor regarding his current research project in Guatemala. Could you please give me his contact details?"

"I'm sorry, ma'am. I'm afraid the information you have been given is incorrect. The professor isn't in Guatemala. In fact, he retired several years ago."

"I was told that he returned for a final project. Perhaps it isn't sponsored by the university?"

"You don't understand." The woman paused. "Professor Zigler had a massive stroke three years ago. He's been in a nursing facility in a vegetative state ever since."

Caitlyn froze. Damn it, her gut instincts had told her there was something more going on. "I see. Could you tell me if you have a student there by the name of Prescott Wilson? I believe he's American."

"Oh yes, Prescott. Delightful boy. Do you want to speak with him? His office is just down the hall."

"He's there? Hasn't left?" So, definitely not the guy who met Maria two days ago.

"Of course he's here. He has responsibilities. I'd know if he missed a class or practicum. But he'll be leaving to teach class in about five minutes, so if you want to speak with him—"

"No. Thank you very much. I've gotten everything I need." Caitlyn hung up. There was no reason why Maria would actually call the department—in fact, an undergrad like her, not even an official participant of the research project, only a volunteer, she'd probably avoid talking to administration for fear of being kicked off the team.

The first of Prescott's e-mails to Maria arrived in her in-box. They appeared to come from the university's IP address, but that was easily spoofed. She'd have the techs back at Quantico work their magic on the original code and see if they could trace where they actually came from.

Whoever was behind this had created the perfect trap for a girl like Maria. Caitlyn headed for the small business center in the lobby. She printed out the maps Vicky had forwarded to her. They traced a route from the port at Santo Tomás north into a remote mountain area. A river twisted east to west, originating near the coordinates marking the temple. The only other landmark was someplace called Clínica Invierno on a lake with the same name in the foothills. According to the map's legend, the clinic was only a few miles from the archeological site if you could cut across the mountains and hills in a straight line, but was at least three times as far if you traveled the faint lines that indicated single-lane roads.

Switching to satellite view, all she saw was trees, hills, mountains, and clouds. The occasional glint of silver from the river where the gorge widened enough that it was visible amid the tree cover. The only sign of humans was a cluster of buildings along the north side of the lake: the Clínica Invierno. Talk about back of beyond.

Why would someone pretending to be Prescott lure Maria to such a remote area? Definitely not to go digging for a lost Mayan temple, that was for sure. It had to have something to do with the parents' past—maybe the area meant something to them? She glanced around the lobby. Still no sign of the Alvarados or their pilot, and it was twenty to eight.

"Could you ring the Alvarados' suite?" she asked the desk clerk.

"I'm afraid they checked out, ma'am."

"They did? Could you tell me when?"

"Six o'clock this morning. Are you Ms. Tierney? They left a message for you." He handed her an envelope with the hotel's insignia on it.

Caitlyn bit back her curse and moved to a quiet corner of the lobby to open the letter. Written in a delicate, feminine hand, Sandra Alvarado apologized for wasting the FBI's time and resources, stating that Caitlin's services would no longer be needed as they'd received word that Maria was in fact visiting distant relatives back in their homeland, Guatemala.

Great. Just great. Ditched in Cozumel—wasn't that what she'd joked about with Carver? Damn, she hated it when she was right.

Not just about the parents. About the fact that Maria was in a hell of a lot more trouble than anyone realized.

She called Yates. Despite the early hour, the Assistant Director was in his office, answering his own phone. She explained the situation.

"Do you think they're involved?" he asked, obviously

peeved at the Alvarados' yanking their chain. As if the FBI were at their beck and call.

"No. If they were, why call us and make such a fuss in the first place? I don't know what their game is, but clearly there's something going on in Guatemala that they don't want us investigating. Maybe there was a ransom demand? Instructions to not get any police involved?"

"They are originally from Guatemala. Maybe it's some kind of family feud. Ancient history."

"With their daughter as bait to get them to return?" If so, that meant this was about more than just money. Which meant the danger to Maria could be worse than she'd suspected.

"What do you want to do?" he asked.

"I want to find Maria. If her parents don't have her best interests at heart, someone has to be there to protect her."

"I thought you hated this assignment. They really pissed you off, didn't they?"

"They wasted your time, my time, taxpayer and Bureau resources, and there's a girl's life at stake. Damn right I'm pissed." She held her breath, waiting for Yates's decision. If he told her to get on the next plane home, she'd be screwed, because no way was she abandoning Maria now. But it would be a whole lot easier with Yates and the Bureau supporting her as she traveled into a foreign country with no backup.

"Here's how we're going to play it," he finally said. "We now have three missing U.S. citizens whose welfare we are concerned for. And since you're there and already have knowledge of the case, I'll call State and make sure they know you're coming, prepare the locals. Let me check with the FAA and see if there's a way to see where they'll be landing—"

"Actually, I already checked," she said, pulling up the screen on her laptop. "There's only one place their jet could land: Guatemala City. If they're going to Santo Tomás, the last place Maria was seen, it looks like at least four or five hours by car. But I can get a flight to Punta Gorda, which is closer to Santo Tomás. It's only a ninety-minute flight, and Punta Gorda is a hour behind Cozumel. If I can find a way from Belize to Santo Tomás, maybe I can beat them there."

"You head to the airport, I'll have someone get started on local intel. And digging into the Alvarados' personal backgrounds."

"Jake Carver would be excellent at that, sir. And he's currently unassigned. Good use of resources."

"I'll call Carver, get him on it. And Tierney? No international incidents. No bad press on this one. The FBI better come off looking like fucking heroes saving the lives of U.S. citizens with the help of whatever locals you need to involve. We need to be bulletproof. Understand?"

He meant that if the Alvarados began throwing their political weight around, he and the Bureau had to be protected. Which translated as: it was her ass on the line.

"Understood." She hung up and swung her travel pack onto her shoulder. The weight settled into place, she headed out to navigate through three foreign countries without knowing the language, the land, or who the hell she could trust.

And people wondered why she had control issues.

Everything hurt and everything was fuzzy. Like she was floating. Was she still in the water? No, it was dark but quiet; she was on a bed, inside a building. Maria blinked but nothing came into focus. People moved around the room, just out of sight. One of them came close, touched her arm; then everything went dark again.

She fought to open her eyes, to speak. She had to tell them about Prescott, about the men with guns, about the professor. She had to save them.

The more she struggled, the more exhaustion overwhelmed her. The last thing she sensed before she surrendered to sleep was a man's voice.

"Everything depends on her."

Was he talking about her? Couldn't be. Maria had never done anything important in her life—not like her parents, whose business was saving lives. That's why she'd been so determined to come to Guatemala, make a big discovery. All on her own. Not because of her parents' money or influence, but because she was smart and talented all on her own.

On her own . . . All alone . . . Did someone call her parents? They'd be so mad, so very mad.

She tried to stir again, ask the man, but her limbs were too heavy to move.

Then his voice came again. "Guard her with your life."

CHAPTER THIRTEEN

Jake could have worn one of the new suits he'd bought for his meetings with the lawyers and court appearances. Lynn would have approved. Which was probably why he'd skipped the suit and gone with jeans, a T-shirt, and his leather jacket. Hey, at least he'd shaved.

Lynn would have hated the scraggly beard he'd worn when he was with the Reapers. His hair still brushed his collar, camouflaging the Reaper tattoo on his neck and skull, but no way was he going to trim it until he finished getting the tatt lasered off. He wanted the damn thing gone as soon as possible, but turned out it would take months. The idiot AUSA even talked about using photos of each painful laser session as an "in" with future juries. Damn lawyers. Wished he could laser them out of his life.

He got to the diner right on time, but still had to wait a few minutes for Lynn to make her appearance. Typical corporate mind games. The person who had to wait was always at a disadvantage. He leaned back in the booth, arms stretched out over the top of his seat, and smiled at her as she crossed the diner. He wasn't playing her games, making him the ultimate winner.

She looked good. Slim build, suit a shade of pale green that brought out her eyes and highlighted her blond hair. Made her look feminine, soft—everything she wasn't. Camouflage.

He grinned at her, and her step faltered a microscopic beat. Not enough for anyone who didn't know her intimately to notice, but her loss of control spoke volumes to him. He still had what it took. Funny. He no longer cared.

He wasn't expecting that. Game over. He lowered his arms and waited for her to slide in across from him. "Thanks for seeing me, Lynn."

She settled her ostrich-skin attaché case onto the seat beside her and lined up her utensils and napkin in a precise formation before meeting his gaze. "What's the game, Jake? Calling me in the middle of the night, asking for help with an off-the-book investigation into a couple with political clout and their extremely well connected company?"

"Actually I just heard from the Washington Field Office. The investigation is official now. Background checks on persons of interest."

She shrugged that away. "There's more going on here, and you know it. You're setting me up, trying to steal another case from me, hog all the glory."

"If I recall, that was your play, not mine." Lynn's passion for the job had been what initially attracted him to her—until he realized it was a passion for her own career ambitions, not a passion for justice.

Soon after they were married, she'd accepted a promotion to Assistant Special Agent in Charge of IRS Criminal Investigations, placing him directly in her chain of command—a big no-no for spouses. She'd never even asked him before taking the job. And his only choice had been either a move to a desk in another division or joining forces with another federal agency.

When he chose the latter, she'd grown distant and spiteful about his prolonged absences and the perceived greater prestige of his new job with the FBI. Then he'd left for his long-term deep cover assignment with the Reapers. It took months before the divorce papers finally reached him. He couldn't totally blame her—not like he'd fought very hard for their marriage.

All this passed between them as they held each other's gaze. Hers was sharp, a stiletto balanced on its tip. He waited to see which way it would fall. Then she smiled and took a drink of water. "Tell me what you have on BioRegen."

"So you have a case open on them already?" Interesting. It took a lot more to open a case with the IRS's Criminal Investigations than it did other law enforcement agencies. Which meant Caitlyn's instincts had been right. Again.

"Not really," Lynn said, eyes narrowed as she dissected his expression. "A guy over in the Taxpayer Advocate Service opened a file last year but got nowhere. Their work is a bit unsavory, given its nature, but he couldn't find anything actionable. Then you called. Which of course made me suspicious."

"Did you bring the file?"

"Better. I brought the case agent. Had him reassigned to me. Temporarily. Until I see how this all plays out." Typical Lynn, manipulating pawns to achieve her own endgame.

In the years since he'd left the IRS, Jake had forgotten how convoluted its approach to law enforcement was. Just to get a preliminary investigation approved, it had to go through three layers of management before an agent could move forward.

Checks and balances, they called it. More like red tape with the potential to strangle a case before it even started, giving the bad guys time to cover their tracks and escape.

"Great. Where is he?"

"Hang on. I need a guarantee that if you find anything, we make the arrest. We handle all the press." Right, so she could add to the vaunted IRS "highest conviction rate of any federal law enforcement agency" statistics. Easy to get a conviction when you only go after the cases that were a sure thing.

"And if we don't find anything?" he asked.

"Then I had nothing to do with it." Translation: she was willing to sacrifice the poor slub who'd opened the case in order to protect herself from any political fallout. "This was just another FBI case gone horribly awry. And you were just another renegade FBI agent, out of his league."

Ouch. "Is that what you believe?"

She gave him a sad smile and shook her head, not a hair falling out of place. "Jake, haven't you learned by now? It's not about what anyone believes. The only thing that matters is how it appears to the public."

"And you're okay with that?"

"Of course." She waved a hand, and a light-skinned African American man left the counter to join them. "Tyrese Shapiro, this is Jake Carver."

Shapiro was maybe five-eight, muscled, with the kind of build that would have had the wrestling coaches back home in Kansas lined up to recruit him.

Lynn slid out of the booth and grabbed her bag. "You boys play nice now. And be sure to keep me in the loop."

With that, she was gone. Jake hadn't realized how tense he was until he released his breath. He'd really thought she couldn't get to him anymore, but ten minutes with Lynn made him want to volunteer for another ten months undercover.

Shapiro slid into the seat Lynn had vacated, plopping a worn briefcase onto the table. "So you and the ice queen. What was that like?"

Jake chuckled. "About what you'd expect. Hey, everyone's entitled to a mistake or two."

"Well, whatever it took, I'm glad to be out of taxpayer advocacy and on the enforcement side of things. Hope to make it permanent, you know what I mean."

"I won't stand in your way. In fact, we'll get along just fine if you keep interagency politics out of it. All I'm interested in is anything that can help me track down a missing girl."

"Missing girl? I thought this was about BioRegen."

Jake filled him in on Maria and her parents' strange behavior. "Tell me about this complaint you received on BioRegen."

"Complaints. Thirteen of them, last I counted. From every agency in the alphabet soup. After folks learned I was interested, they all get sent to me."

"Really? And there was nothing there?"

"Nope. Shady as far as ethics, but everything totally legal."

"Walk me through it."

Shapiro glanced at his watch. "How about if I show you in person? We should just about have time."

"Time for what?"

"A funeral."

CHAPTER FOURTEEN

Shapiro drove a Prius. Smart car for the D.C. gridlock, although Jake preferred the freedom and maneuverability of his bike. They headed across the river and down to Alexandria.

"Nice car, Shapiro," Jake said as they idled silently at a red light. He couldn't help the uptick in his voice on the agent's name—guy looked nothing like a Shapiro.

"What do you get when you cross a St. Louis beat cop with a junior high math teacher?" Shapiro chuckled. "An IRS agent who hates paperwork and loves doughnuts." He aimed a thumb at himself. "Don't worry, I've heard all the jokes. That's why I really want to hang on to this criminal investigation gig if I can. And I just know there's something going on with Bio-Regen."

"How long have you been investigating BioRegen?"

Shapiro made a face. "Last year, they first came to my attention. One of those cases that reminded me of my mom's stories from her days working crimes against persons. Did an internal review, nothing to reach the level of an audit, just a gut feeling that something was off. My supervisor shut it down, told me to make better use of my time and paper-shuffling skills, but I kept my eye on them. Spread the word that I was interested. Nothing much popped until a few months ago. Since then there's been over a dozen complaints, all over the country, all with BioRegen's name mentioned."

"Complaints against the company?"

"No, that's the problem. They farm out the dirty work, so the complaints were all against mortuary services and hospitals. But they all lead back to BioRegen." They pulled into the crowded parking lot of a funeral home. Stately red brick, white columns, tasteful flowers on either side of the front doors. "I even put the local mortuaries on notice to contact me if they had any problems with a BioRegen transaction. Hoping maybe I could find something solid enough to build a case with. This place called me in yesterday." They left the car, Jake wishing he'd worn something nicer, and approached the entrance.

Several women gathered in the front hallway, all black, all ages. Children ran up and down the wide corridor, dressed in their Sunday best, their cheerful voices a welcome contrast to the somber decor. The only men Jake saw were a few sullen teens slouched against the back wall, all wearing gang colors.

One of the women, dressed in a tasteful black jersey dress that went all the way down to her ankles, mid-forties, holding a handkerchief, rushed toward them. At first, Jake thought she was going to kick them out, but then she grabbed both Shapiro's beefy arms. "Mr. Shapiro, you came back."

"I promised I would, didn't I?" He wrapped the woman into a quick hug. "How are you all holding up?

Is your grandma doing okay after what happened yesterday?"

The woman shook her head. "Doctor said she should rest at home today. Too much stress." She looked at Jake with a question in her eyes.

"Excuse my manners," Shapiro said. "Deidre Thomson, this is Special Agent Jake Carver with the FBI."

Jake forced himself not to flinch at the use of his real name out loud, in public. Reminded himself that he wasn't living the undercover lie anymore. He stretched a hand out to Thomson. "Nice to meet you, ma'am. I'm sorry for your loss."

"The FBI? Mr. Shapiro, you brought the FBI? So you really think you can do something, stop this from happening again?"

Shapiro stretched himself tall, which brought the top of his head to Jake's ear. "We're sure going to try, Ms. Thomson. I thought, if it wouldn't be too much trouble and with your permission, I could show Agent Carver the extent of the problem?"

She hesitated, looked over her shoulder at the older women behind her. "Yes, but would you mind going alone? I just don't think I can take seeing that—I mean, what they did to poor Vincent . . ." Tears crowded out her words.

"Of course, of course." Shapiro patted her arm. "We won't need but a minute."

"Take your time. After what happened yesterday, when we realized—well, instead of a graveside service, Mr. Decker agreed to cremate Vincent, no extra charge. So we were all just leaving—oh, but you're welcome to come to the wake." She nodded at Jake, including him. "Both of you. If you have time."

"Thank you, Ms. Thomson. That's very nice of you.

I'm afraid Agent Carver and I have a long day ahead of us. But we do very much appreciate the offer."

"Okay. Please, let us know if there's anything more we can do to help."

"Of course, of course. And tell your grandma that she and the entire family are in my prayers." Shapiro grasped the woman's arm and nodded solemnly.

A few minutes later, they were sitting in the funeral director's office. "That was quite a show," Jake told Shapiro as they waited for the mortician. "Very diplomatic."

"No show about it," Shapiro replied. "Vincent Thomson was a victim of a drive-by. Shot eleven times, caught four of them in the face. Kid was fifteen—Deidre's great-nephew. His mom's locked up, dad's out of the picture, you know how it goes. Anyway, had to be a closed coffin, but Deidre and her grandmother—Vincent's great-grandmother—came yesterday to place some special items in the coffin with him."

"And there's a federal case in there somewhere?"

Before Shapiro could answer, an overweight black man who could have masqueraded as a melancholic Santa Claus came into the office. He was dressed in a conservative black suit, black shirt, black tie. "Agent Shapiro, I heard you were back. What can we do for you now?"

Shapiro stood and glared at the undertaker. "My partner here, FBI Special Agent Carver, wants to see the evidence for himself, Mr. Darrow. Before you cremate it. And I need to see those records you couldn't produce yesterday."

The man returned Shapiro's glare but it was all bluff, Jake saw. After a moment his shoulders slumped and feet turned toward the exit.

Shapiro saw it as well. "Now," he ordered with none of the gentle regard he'd shown the family outside.

"Of course. Come with me." Darrow led them down a back hallway to a room marked CREMATORY PREPARATION. NO ADMITTANCE. He unlocked the door and they were in a small room where several stainless steel wheeled tables waited. On top of one of them was a man-sized cardboard box.

On the opposite wall were two heavy doors marked CREMATORIUM. AUTHORIZED PERSONNEL ONLY. A young man dressed in hospital scrubs entered through those doors. "We're ready for him."

"Just a moment," Darrow said. "These investigators need to see the body one last time prior to its final disposition. If you could assist them?"

The cremation tech shrugged. "Sure. Whatever."

The funeral director nodded to Shapiro. "I'll have those records ready when you're done."

Shapiro gave him a fake smile. "Thanks." Then he turned his back on the director and nodded to the tech. "Open it."

No way Jake was going to tell Shapiro, but his experience with dead bodies was pretty much limited to animals back home on his family's dairy farm. Yeah, there'd been a ton of fights and blood and shit with the Reapers, but no corpses.

He tried to act nonchalant even as he was glad he hadn't had time to order breakfast when he met with Lynn earlier. His stomach clenched as the tech removed the top from the box, revealing the body of Vincent Thomson.

Vincent was dressed in a navy suit. His hands were folded across his stomach, arranged to hold a football. His face was wrapped in dark gauze, hiding the damage.

Jake had been expecting a lot worse. He glanced at Shapiro with a raised eyebrow.

"Yesterday as the aunt and grandma arrived to place Vincent's football in the casket, they jostled the table."

The cremation tech looked away.

"And?" Jake prompted.

"And Vincent's foot fell off. The old lady about had a heart attack."

"Hey, it wasn't my fault," the tech protested. "Besides, I fixed it. See?" He pulled back the pants' cuff, exposing the top portion of Vincent's foot. Attached to a length of PVC piping where his leg bones should be, held in place by two very large screws.

CHAPTER FIFTEEN

Caitlyn was fuming by the time she arrived at the Cozumel airport. What kind of game was Alvarado playing, ditching a U.S. federal agent as if she were hired help? Did it mean he'd really found Maria on his own, safe and sound in the warm embrace of "distant" relatives—or that she was in even greater danger than Caitlyn feared? Maybe he'd gotten a ransom demand and thought he was protecting his daughter by going alone?

Too many questions and no answers unless Carver came up with something while she was stuck in transit.

She made her way through security—thankfully the officer manning the special services line spoke English—and headed toward the international departures area. Only to see a familiar figure as she passed the small bar inside the terminal. She almost didn't recognize Maria's mother. Although she was dressed in a designer suit, Sandra Alvarado's hair was pulled back in a simple ponytail, and she wore dark sunglasses as she sipped at a Bloody Mary.

"Mrs. Alvarado. I thought you and your husband had already left." Caitlyn hid her irritation and anger, knowing they wouldn't help her get answers. "Your message made it sound as if you'd be joining Maria in Guatemala. Is she with your family or your husband's?"

Sandra stared at her a beat too long. As if she had to unravel the lies before answering.

"Hector's family. He took the jet and is sending me home—they couldn't even upgrade me, I have to fly coach." Her tone made it sound like it was the biggest insult yet. Far worse than fearing your child lost in the jungle a thousand miles away from home.

Then Caitlyn got a closer look at her face. Thick makeup hiding sagging wrinkles and dark circles below her eyes. "You spoke to Maria?"

"No." She swallowed hard. "Hector did. Such a silly girl, she only wants attention, you know. Chasing after Mayan ruins. It's a good thing Hector's uncle was able to find her." She shook her head in disdain. Obviously Maria's mother still thought Maria had slipped away from the cruise to join an archeological expedition.

Or that's what she wanted Caitlyn to think. Hector and Sandra had such a low regard for the FBI, not only did they think they could order them around like servants but they also seemed to think that Caitlyn wouldn't uncover the truth.

"Actually, I have some bad news about that." Caitlyn explained about the professor. "So, you see, wherever Maria is, it's not at an archeological dig. Or with Hector's family."

Sandra raised her glass to take a drink, holding it between herself and Caitlyn. Caitlyn didn't give her the chance to regroup with more lies. "Why did you call the FBI in the first place?"

Sandra clutched at her throat, her diamond ring sparking in the overhead lights. For the first time, the mother appeared her real age as she frowned in earnest.

"You don't understand. We didn't know—we thought we needed your help, that something had happened to her on that ship, that the cruise line was covering up—"

Right. The FBI would have the ability to investigate a cruise ship crime, even in a foreign country. "And now that we know Maria left the ship voluntarily, you don't want me involved anymore? Mrs. Alvarado, I can find your daughter. If you and your husband stop blocking me from doing my job."

"But . . . Hector said we couldn't tell anyone— especially not the FBI."

"What happened?"

She shook her head. "His old army squad will help. He'll save Maria; he'll bring my daughter back to me."

"Let me help him. Mrs. Alvarado, let me help Maria."

She hesitated, torn. "No. Hector knows what he's doing. He said not to involve outsiders."

"That's too bad. Because I'm already involved. And, no matter what political strings you pull, I'm staying involved. Do you want me barging in, risking your daughter's life, because I don't have all the information I need?"

Still Sandra resisted. Caitlyn remembered the way the couple had appeared so in synch when she'd first met them. Even with Maria's life in the balance, Sandra still felt compelled to trust her husband's judgment over anyone else's.

"Here's what I think happened," Caitlyn continued, refusing to give the woman breathing space. "You didn't hear from Maria or any distant relatives. Instead, you received a ransom demand."

Her shot hit its target. Sandra sagged against the bar, her face crumpling. "I told him it wouldn't work." She looked away, gaze unfocused in the distance, then returned her focus to Caitlyn, her expression determined.

"Hector got a message. They have Maria, want to meet at Santo Tomás."

"Who has Maria?"

"He said they were guerrillas he fought against during *La Violencia,* the civil war."

"I thought the civil war ended twenty years ago—"

"It never ends," she said scornfully. "Generations lost. I won't lose my Maria to it as well."

"You mentioned army friends of his?"

"Yes. My Hector, he was in the Kaibiles. *La mano dura.* It's the elite guard of the Guatemalan Army. The best of the best. He's called his old squad to meet him at Santo Tomás. From there, they'll head out to find the guerrillas, rescue Maria."

"Does he know where she might be?"

"No, but we have an old friend, Dr. Otto Mendez Carrera. He also used to be in the army with Hector. He doesn't live far from Santo Tomás. Hector hopes he might know where the rebels are based."

Caitlyn took note of the names. More keyboard work for Carver while she was en route to Guatemala. Hopefully he'd have answers by the time she arrived. Even better would be if she arrived in time to meet up with Hector.

"What did the rebels ask for a ransom? When is the drop?" she pressed.

"They didn't ask for anything. Said they'd only discuss the details with Hector in person. He knew what that meant—they want him as a hostage as well. That's why he can't negotiate with them."

He was right. Kidnap and ransom cases often turned into long-term extortions with the hostages moved around, held in primitive conditions for months or even years. Or killed outright as soon as their usefulness ended. If the guerrillas had Hector, they wouldn't need both Maria and Hector to extort their demands from Sandra. One of them would be expendable, executed in a brutal manner to end any resistance.

"When and where is the first meeting to take place?"

Sandra frowned. "I don't know. They just said for Hector to go to Santo Tomás and they'd contact him there."

Hector was obviously counting on his old army buddies and this Dr. Carrera to get him intel that would help him find Maria before the guerrillas started negotiations in earnest. And he was using himself as bait to give them time.

"You know Dr. Carrera as well?"

"Of course. He arranged—" She faltered, checked herself. What was she hiding? "He's our business partner in Guatemala. Our main procurement site outside of the USA."

"So he provides tissues for BioRegen?"

"Highest quality. It's such a blessing being able to help so many people, don't you think, Agent Tierney?"

Caitlyn thought the whole thing was creepy as hell, but what did she know? Maybe BioRegen was saving lives, helping researchers to unlock the secrets of the human body. All she cared about was finding Maria and getting her home safely.

"I can't understand why all this is happening to us." Sandra sniffed, holding back tears. "We're good people. We save lives with our work. You need to help us, please help us." She clutched at Caitlyn's arm with both hands. It felt like the first honest emotion Caitlyn had seen from the woman. "Don't let them take my husband and daughter."

They called Caitlyn's flight. She stood and grabbed her bags. "If you speak to Hector, tell him I'm coming. He needs to take my calls."

"He doesn't trust you. A woman, a foreigner who doesn't understand our country, our past—not even our language. He thinks you'll get Maria killed."

"Then what do you want me to do?" Caitlyn asked, exasperated.

"I don't know," Sandra wailed.

The second call for Caitlyn's flight sounded overhead. "I have to go. Call me if you hear anything."

Sandra took her glasses off to wipe her tears. She didn't look at all like the regal, elegant woman Caitlyn had met yesterday.

"Please save them," she whispered.

"I have to go." Caitlyn ran for her gate, leaving Maria's mother behind. Something told her she'd need every second she could get to save Maria.

The flight to Punta Gorda was a creaky outdated commuter jet with no Wi-Fi, so Caitlyn spent her time jotting down notes, trying to create a coherent story that pulled together all the various threads. A former army officer targeted twenty years after he retired. The elaborate scheme to draw his daughter back to the land of her birth. Lost Mayan temples and treasures.

It made no sense. Not if Hector was the true target. It would have been so much easier to target him through his business interests in Guatemala or the United States. Anyone who'd met the man would know his company was worth as much to him as his daughter.

Maria as a target didn't make sense either—she had no worth except as a hostage. And surely there were easier ways to take her? Yes, Hector and Sandra were overprotective parents, but anyone sophisticated enough to set up this subterfuge could have gotten to the Alvarado family in Florida. Plus, why wait two decades if this was to settle an old grudge?

She drew a rough map. Florida. Mexico. Guatemala. Traced the cruise ship's itinerary. Traced Hector's route. Marked the route Maria would have taken from the port to the site of the supposed archeological dig. All roads leading to Santo Tomás and none of them making sense.

As soon as the plane landed, she called Yates. "It has to be something from the father's past while he was in the army. Something big enough that it would be worth pursuing now."

"Twenty years—he's had time to become a multi-millionaire. If it's money they want, their patience has paid off."

"But why drag everyone back to Guatemala? Especially as Hector still has friends in the military there. Seems unnecessarily elaborate—and dangerous."

"I'll have Carver dig deeper. State is *concerned*"— she could hear his finger quotes around the word— "about negotiations they're in with the Guatemalans. They're trying to gain cooperation with drug interdiction and don't want you to do anything to upset things."

"What are they going to do, keep me from entering the country?"

"No, nothing like that. If you can rescue Hector and Maria without any—er—commotion, it would actually help their case."

"But if there is a commotion—"

"Let's just say they'd like to avoid that at all costs. So they're going to send a translator to meet you at Santo Tomás."

A "translator." She knew what that meant. A baby-sitter. Under orders from the State Department. Probably CIA with a nonofficial cover position in the Embassy.

"Great. When can I expect them?"

"We've booked you on the next ferry to Santo Tomás.

You should arrive by one o'clock. The translator will meet you at the dock."

Which wouldn't give her any time to find Hector and cover her tracks. But no way in hell was she letting the CIA or State call the shots—not when protecting their negotiations could trump saving Maria's life.

"Sounds good," she said brightly. Yates knew her well enough, he'd read between the lines. "Have Carver call me as soon as he knows anything."

"Tierney," he said, a warning in his voice. "Keep me posted. And don't do anything I wouldn't do."

One thing she'd learned about Yates—the main reason why she didn't mind working for the man—was that he had real-world law enforcement experience before he joined the FBI. He understood the need to put a girl's life ahead of politics.

"No, sir, I won't."

CHAPTER SIXTEEN

When Maria woke again, the sun was above the mountains outside her window, sending ribbons of light across her bed. How long had she been asleep?

Prescott! She tried to sit up, but her wrists were bound to bed rails with soft Velcro restraints. An IV flowed into one arm, its fluid chilling her veins. White sheets covered her and she wore a white cotton nightgown.

"Hello?" she called, trying not to panic as she flailed her arms, straining against the Velcro. "Is anyone there?"

The room was painted a cheerful yellow; a large crucifix hung on the wall directly across from her, surrounded by brightly colored paintings of the lake, waterfall, mountains, and flowers. The artist had a way with color, bringing the scenes to life with a childlike exuberance that made her smile and calmed her fears.

The windows weren't windows but French doors leading to a wrought iron balcony, she realized. They were open, allowing a fragrant breeze scented with a jasmine-like perfume to rustle the gauzy white cotton curtains. Beside her was a door leading into a bathroom, a small clothing cupboard, and a nightstand with a pitcher of water and a glass on it. There was a wooden chair near the main door with a newspaper lying abandoned on it.

"Hello!" She shouted this time. She had to get help to the professor.

Footsteps came running down the hall outside the door. A middle-aged woman in an old-fashioned nurse's uniform, complete with cap and white hose, entered. "You're awake," she said, her English colored by a heavy German accent. She stepped out into the hall once more. "*Herr Doktor,* she's awake."

A few moments later a man in his early sixties joined the nurse. He was tall but had a stooped posture, as if he spent most of his day bent over, and his gait was jerky, stumbling. Although he didn't use a cane, Maria thought maybe he needed one.

"My dear, how are you feeling?" His smile was kind, although his eyes were dark with sorrow. He raised her hand in his, his fingers settling over her pulse. His hand had a faint tremor and she wondered if he had Parkinson's. "Nice and steady, yes."

"Please, untie me." Maria hated the fear that strained her voice.

"Of course, of course. Helda."

The nurse glanced at him, a question in her eyes. He nodded. She rushed over and removed the restraints, then began to take Maria's vitals.

"You were dehydrated and you swallowed some water into your lungs," the doctor said. "You kept fighting us. Required sedation. I gave you fluids and antibiotics. Some of those scratches and bites are infected; you'll need several more days of treatment."

Free from the restraints, Maria pushed herself up in bed. The arm with the IV hurt when she bent it, so she rested it along the railing. "Please, I need to speak to the police. Something terrible has happened. A man was killed and more might be in danger."

"Yes, Maria. We know." He patted her hand reassuringly. "You told us about your friend when you first arrived. You don't remember?" He glanced at the nurse, then back at Maria. "Don't worry, dear. It's the sedative, it often causes a bit of amnesia. I'm Dr. Otto Mendez Carrera, and this is one of my nurses, Helda." He narrowed his eyes, assessing her. "Don't you remember anything?"

She thought hard. There was a fuzzy memory of men talking about her, something about protecting her. Nothing specific. Her strongest memory was of Prescott's face, covered with blood, and the sneer on the face of the man with the scar. The man with the gun. She remembered running into the jungle, thirsty, tired, aching, hungry, cold . . . then jumping . . . had she really done that? Jumped off a cliff into a lake at night?

"The police—the professor, they need to save him."

"Calm down, calm down. Such a brave girl, isn't she, Helda?" The nurse nodded and beamed at Maria. She was younger than the doctor, in her forties, but the way she looked at him reminded Maria of when her high school friends "fell in crush." Maria had often wished she'd felt like that about a guy—she did, kind of, about Prescott. But she barely knew him, so maybe it didn't count.

Now he was dead. She'd never get the chance to know him. She blinked back tears and failed. The room blurred and she grabbed on to the bed rail, trying to steady herself as the events of the past few days swamped her. It was over. She was out of danger. She was safe.

"My dear, my dear," the doctor tried to calm her. His left hand jerked with a spasm that he hid by shoving it into his coat pocket. "You saved them. You were so very brave. Swimming through the darkness to shore before collapsing. Thankfully my men found you. You wouldn't let me treat you until you told us all about the men and the professor. I sent my guards to rescue him, and the police have been here—you were asleep, so I told them to come back when you were feeling stronger."

Maria looked up at him. Tears made his chiseled features blur into a rainbow halo with each blink. "They caught them? The man who killed Prescott, did they get him, too? He had a scar down the side of his face."

"Everything is taken care of, don't worry. The professor came himself to thank you this morning—you were talking to him about some lost treasure, do you remember?" She shook her head, hating the confused blanks in her memory. "No worry. He'll be back again. Since he arrived last month, we've begun a friendly competition. He enjoys chess and none of his students are any good at it, so he comes here to play with another old man." He squinted at her. "You're the girl who discovered the temple for him?"

She nodded. The feeling of giddy anticipation that she'd felt arriving at the port had been swallowed by the events since. "Yes, that's me."

"Amazing." He made a clucking noise that was part way between disapproval and admiration. "Well, I guess only time will tell."

Tell what? If her discovery was worth Prescott's life? Maria slumped back onto her pillow, drained by the brief conversation.

"Helda, let us get our patient something to eat. Perhaps broth and eggs? Gentle food, we don't want to upset her stomach."

"That would be nice," Maria said. "So everyone is okay. I'm so glad." Then she thought of her parents. They would know she was gone by now. She'd planned to call them once she arrived at the dig, but—"Could I use a phone? I need to call my family, let them know I'm okay."

Her father was going to kill her. She squeezed her eyes shut for a moment, trying to think of what she'd tell him.

Dr. Carrera saved her. "Your mobile phone was destroyed—the water. I'm afraid the latest storms left our phones out of commission for the time being. I'm surprised the thunder and wind didn't wake you even with the sedation. But I did speak to your father yesterday before the storm hit. He said he's coming. He should be here by tomorrow, the next day at the latest." He frowned at her like a stern grandfather. "He didn't sound very happy with you, young lady."

At least she was spared her father's disapproval for a few more days. By then she'd be feeling better, strong enough to show him the temple and convince him to let her stay and work with the professor. If the professor still wanted her, that was. "Did Professor Zigler say, I mean, will he still be working on the dig? Can I join him?"

"Of course he'll be working. This is his life's dream. As for you joining him, not until you get some more rest and we have this infection under control." She opened her mouth to protest but he wagged a finger at her. "Doctor's orders. Now, rest. Let Helda take care of you. Everything will be just fine, I promise."

CHAPTER SEVENTEEN

Jake couldn't take his eyes off the grotesque marriage of human flesh with PVC pipe. Strung together with screws. Then covered by a sock. Macabre. "Was his leg taken off by the gunfire?"

"No." The tech laughed. "That's how all the chicken nuggets look." With a flourish he pulled back the other pant leg—the slacks were slit down the back to make the corpse easier to dress, Jake realized—and revealed the PVC pipe traveling from the foot up to the pelvis.

"Chicken nuggets?"

"Sorry, that's what we call them once they're through being processed."

"You did this?" Jake asked. He forced himself to look at the horrific amalgam of hardware and flesh, reminding himself this was once a boy. The reasons behind Shapiro's obsession with this case were becoming clear. This was wrong. So very wrong.

The tech casually realigned one of the PVC pipes so Victor's foot sat straighter. "Us? Hell no. Usually it's in the hospital. Once or twice crews come here if the body got to us first. They asked if we wanted to learn how, said it's a thousand dollars a body, but Mr. Darrow, he said no. He might be a crook, takes no mind to fleecing grieving loved ones, but even he ain't no body snatcher."

"So this is BioRegen?" Jake asked Shapiro.

"Not quite. They get the tissue eventually but the folks who procure it are all independent contractors. Kinda like how you go give blood at a neighborhood donation center but then they send it to the blood bank and then it's the blood bank that sends it to the hospital."

"This is more than a little blood." Jake nodded at the boy's missing legs.

"They use the skin for burn grafts," Shapiro explained. "The fat for plastic surgery. The muscle, I'm not sure about. And the bones and joints they use for implants, tendon repairs, even carve special screws and replacement parts from them."

Jake raised an eyebrow at the IRS agent. Shapiro had gone above and beyond in doing his research. Felt like he was more than a little obsessed by BioRegen—something the IRS would frown upon.

"Oh, yeah, they love them bones. But this ain't nothing," the tech said, warming to the subject now that he realized he wasn't the one in trouble. He gently removed Vincent's football and lowered his hands—exposing more gleaming white PVC pipe above the wrists. Then he drew the boy's shirt up.

The abdomen was stripped of flesh, leaving only red muscle behind. The ribs had been laid bare and the bottom half of the rib cage was missing, the chest cavity a gaping hole.

"They leave the gizzards after they take the skin." The tech pointed to the abdomen. Jake's stomach heaved. He'd never done well with the sight of blood—a fact that had led to endless teasing from his brothers growing up on the farm back home in Kansas. "But they take some ribs and they use the heart for valves and stuff. Since this kid was a closed casket to start, they went ahead and took the ears, jawbone, and eyes."

Jake stepped away from the body, choking down bile. He'd seen enough. "All this is legal?"

"Sure," the tech said. "We get copies of the paperwork—the families sign a release donating tissue to medical science. They don't get no money, but they get the satisfaction of helping others, and they still get a body to bury. Of course, they don't know what the vultures do to it before they give it to us. We earn every penny on prepping these guys, let me tell you."

The tech began covering Vincent back up. Jake was glad to see that he showed some deference, gently tugging the clothing back into place and arranging the football between the boy's hands. At least someone around here had a little respect for the dead.

"They've been doing this for how long?" he asked Shapiro.

"I've only been getting complaints about the body mutilation for the past few months. I think before then, they must have had another source for their tissue but something happened to it, it dried up on them."

"Another source? You mean they were passing non-human tissue off as human?"

Shapiro shook his head. "No, at least not that I've heard of." He motioned to Jake and they left the crematory prep area and headed back down the hall. "But you have to understand, none of this tissue trade is regulated. No one can trace where Vincent's bones or heart valves or skin went to. Dozens of patients could end up with his tissue and we'd never know."

"And how much does BioRegen make off a body?"

"If all the tissue is usable, about two hundred

thousand dollars. And demand for tissue is increasing exponentially. This is what you call a boom business—by this time next year, they might be able to double that if they can keep up with the supply."

The director had the copies of the tissue donation forms ready for them. He seemed relieved when Jake and Shapiro left, kept shaking his head about Bio-Regen and their damn body snatchers ruining his business.

Back in the car, Shapiro started the engine and turned to Jake. "You up for one more house call?"

Jake was surprised. IRS agents, especially the ones assigned to consumer complaints and the Taxpayer Advocate Service, never left their cubicle unless it was to get a Band-Aid for a paper cut. It was one of the reasons why he'd leapt at the chance to join Criminal Investigations and then the FBI. But Shapiro had obviously invested the time to keep this case alive long after his supervisors told him to move on. "You're taking this seriously?"

Shapiro nodded. "You meet some of these families—like the Thomsons. Good people, thought they were doing the right thing, helping others even in their time of pain. You can't help but take it seriously."

"So where we off to?"

"The first people who filed a complaint about Bio-Regen. They filed with us, the FTC, Better Business Bureau, AMA, tried to bring a civil suit, pretty much called everyone in the blue pages of the phone book. I'm the only one who listened."

"They were upset about how a family member's body was treated?"

Shapiro didn't answer right away. "They're upset that their daughter is dying."

* * *

Jake took a moment to study Shapiro after his dramatic announcement, not sure about Shapiro getting so emotionally wrapped up in things. Then he remembered the reason why he'd resented Lynn when she forced him out of Criminal Investigations.

He didn't work his cases just to save Uncle Sam a few pennies. He hated the idea of people, companies, thinking they were beyond the law. That they could do anything they wanted, stealing from the government and their own stockholders, and walk away scot-free.

It was that passion that had gotten him through a year and a half living undercover with the Reapers, his life at risk every moment of every day. Maybe he and Shapiro weren't so different after all.

"What happened?" he asked as Shapiro steered them out of Alexandria and south to Rose Hill.

"You ever hear of a disease called kuru? Cannibals used to get it."

"I remember reading about it when I was a kid. You get it from eating brains and then you go crazy and die. It's related to mad cow disease." He remembered being fascinated by the exotic disease when he'd read about it in *National Geographic*. And a few years back, when there'd been a mad cow scare across the border from his folks' farm, every dairy farmer in the state had researched the strange family of diseases, desperate to find ways to protect their herds.

"The real name is Creutzfeldt-Jakob disease. There's no good test for it until after it's too late, no cure, and you might not even see any symptoms for weeks, months, years, or decades. Because of that, there are regulations limiting blood and tissue donation from certain countries."

"So this girl, she got tissue from one of those?"

Shapiro turned into a driveway of a modest ranch

house. "That's the problem. No one knows how she got it. Or where the tissue came from."

Didn't sound like there was much of a case at all, much less one involving the IRS.

Shapiro continued, "Once you have it, it can kill you fast or agonizingly slow as it turns your brain into Swiss cheese and you go psycho. Julia's taking the slow path. Her symptoms began last year. But the way she's going downhill lately, the end can't be far." He sighed. "It'll be a blessing, really. You'll see."

They got out of the car and approached the house. Instead of ringing the doorbell, Shapiro knocked gently, as if afraid of waking a sleeping baby. A few minutes later a petite blonde in her mid thirties opened the door. "Tyrese, thanks for calling. It's been too long."

Shapiro gave the woman a friendly hug, then introduced Jake. "Valerie, this is FBI Special Agent Jake Carver. He's helping me with the investigation."

"Really? So nice to meet you, Agent Carver."

"Jake, please."

Valerie ushered them inside to the living room. Jake was surprised to see that although there was plenty of space, the only thing inside was a sofa. No other furniture or decorations. The light came from an overhead fixture, there were no end tables, no coffee table, no lamps or knickknacks. No sharp edges or corners. And nothing breakable.

It reminded Jake of when his big brother had his first kid and got OCD about baby-proofing.

"Can I get you coffee or water?" Valerie offered. Both Shapiro and Jake declined.

Shapiro settled himself on one corner of the sofa, obviously at home. Valerie took the other end, curling her legs up under her. She wore knit pants and a long-sleeved sweater, no jewelry other than a wedding ring.

"So," Valerie said, eyeing Jake, who stood just inside the door. "The FBI. Does that mean something's actually going to happen?" She sounded like someone who'd been disappointed more than once. Skeptical and weary.

"I can't promise that," Shapiro said, matching her tone. "But you know I won't give up on you or Julia."

She gave him a tired smile. "You're about the only one. The doctors are talking hospice. But no one can take her, not the way she acts out on her bad days. They're used to people fading quietly. You know Julia, she's a fighter."

Shapiro blinked and swallowed hard. "Where's Tom?"

Valerie gave a one-shouldered shrug. "Gone. Bad enough he was driving, all the guilt with that. He couldn't bear to watch . . ." She trailed off, looking away into the shadows crowding a far corner of the room.

Jake turned to follow her gaze and saw the only photo in the room, placed high up on the wall. It showed a smiling, happy family: Valerie, a man her age, and a little girl about six years old with pigtails and a missing front tooth. Christ, when Shapiro said daughter, he'd been picturing a teenager or college kid. Not a little girl.

He tore his gaze from the photo. How could she look at it, day after day? Be constantly reminded of everything she'd lost? "Can I ask—?"

Valerie turned to Jake. "Oh, of course, I'm sorry, I thought Tyrese would have filled you in."

"Thought it was better he hear it from you," Shapiro said.

She nodded. "A year and a half ago Tom and Julia were driving home when they were in an accident. No one's fault really, it was raining hard and foggy. Tom was knocked out, had a concussion and broken wrist.

But Julia's side of the car took the brunt of the damage."

Her gaze went back to the picture. "That was taken a few weeks before. It's the picture we gave the surgeons so they'd know how to put her face back together."

The mom's voice was clear, as if she were talking about someone else's baby girl. It was Shapiro who made a small sound in the back of his throat like he was choking down something nasty.

"It took two months and six surgeries, then another month in rehab, but finally we had our little angel back." Valerie shifted, turning her back on the family portrait. "For a few months, at least. It started slowly. Muscle spasms here, a twitch there, problems with her coordination, falling a lot. At first the doctors thought it was nerve or brain damage from the accident. But when they did the MRIs, they found—"

She squeezed her lips together, closed her eyes, her composure vanished.

"They found holes in her brain," Shapiro took over the narrative. "Spongiform encephalopathy, the doctors call it."

"Not from the car accident?" Jake asked.

"No. A variant of Creutzfeldt-Jakob. It has one hundred percent fatality. Usually within a few months of the symptoms appearing."

"What caused it?"

Valerie stood, not looking at either of them, and left the room, her hand covering her mouth. Jake watched her go, wondered what he could do—nothing except listen and see if there was something to Shapiro's suspicion that BioRegen was behind her daughter's illness.

Frustrating. He didn't have experience with dealing with victims of a crime—if this was indeed a crime. His entire career had been as an investigator, winnowing out bits of data that grew into airtight cases. And his life undercover hadn't prepared him for facing the family of a dying girl. He saw the look of compassion on Shapiro's face and wondered if the IRS agent had chosen the right career.

"It's transmitted by a small particle, a piece of protein called a prion that gets twisted into your DNA and cells," Shapiro explained, revealing his obsessive research tendencies again. "Usually it's transmitted by direct contact with brain tissue, sometimes blood or things like cornea transplants."

"And Julia?"

Shapiro shrugged. "She had a lot of blood transfusions but the blood supply was screened. No corneal transplants but tons of other tissues used by the surgeons. After reading her records, my bet is on a graft used by the neurosurgeon when he stopped some bleeding in her brain. But none of the tissue is traceable."

"Not even to BioRegen?"

"Hospital records and invoices show that they supplied the kinds of tissues used—as well as two other vendors. But the quantity supplied by BioRegen was three times the others combined."

"Not good enough for a court of law."

"Not even enough to pursue an official case," Shapiro admitted. "My supervisor didn't even bother taking it up the chain."

And yet, the IRS agent had taken the time to learn more about the rare disease than most doctors probably knew. A man on a mission.

"Why isn't the FDA all over this?" Jake asked. "Or the product safety commission? It's their job to protect consumers from this kind of thing."

"Overworked, underfunded, plus any fix would cost millions—can you imagine asking every physician with an outpatient clinic, every hospital, every surgery center to begin inventorying and tracking hundreds of thousands of pieces of tissue? Not to mention the costs of monitoring compliance, creating standards and guidelines, and licensing the providers."

Jake jerked his head up at that. "You mean BioRegen and the other companies doing this aren't even licensed?"

"There *is* no license. No one polices this industry. Hell, the government can't even decide who would do the job if they had the money to do it."

He thought of the hollow PVC pipes screwed onto Victor's feet, thought about mothers like Valerie suffering as they watched their children die. Outrageous indignities—multiplied by a government's apathy. He glanced at the father in the family portrait. The guy looked normal enough, one hand on his wife and the other on his child, his posture one of protectiveness.

And he couldn't do a damn thing to save his daughter. Neither could Jake. But maybe he could help nail the bastards behind it.

CHAPTER EIGHTEEN

Valerie returned, pushing a high-backed wheelchair. In it, her head strapped between two cushions, was the little girl from the photo. Her face revealed no signs of the trauma from the car accident except for a small scar crossing into her right eyebrow and another on her cheek.

Jake couldn't say that about the trauma from the Creutzfeldt-Jakob. The disease had left Julia emaciated, her limbs flailing with spastic contractions, and obviously had devastated her mentally. Her eyes circled in their sockets without focusing, her tongue lolled from her mouth, and as Valerie restrained one hand, she slapped herself in the face with the other. Her hair, once long enough to be in pigtails, was cropped close to her scalp, large patches of it missing.

"She's having a pretty good day," Valerie said, wiping spittle from Julia's chin with the bib that hung around the girl's neck. "I thought you might want to see her. One last time."

Shapiro got to his feet, his steps as he crossed the room a bit wobbly, but he crouched beside the chair and patted Julia's free hand, ignoring her attempts to scratch him. She made a noise like an animal, at first it was a moan of frustration, then as he kept up his rhythmic movements one of contentment.

"Remember me, Julia?" he crooned in a calming singsong. "Sorry I didn't bring you anything today. I know how much you like your fuzzy socks."

The only sign Julia gave that she understood him was kicking her heels against the padded footrests of her chair. She wore purple fleece socks with monkeys on them. The kind Jake's eight-year-old niece loved to mix and match with wild results. "Because life's too short, Uncle Jake," she'd say. "This way I can have twice the fun!"

Jake had been able to distance himself from Valerie's pain while listening to Julia's story, but now, seeing the devastated little girl, seeing those socks . . . it was too much. He had to turn, pretend to be looking out the window as he blinked away tears and swiped his cheek dry with the back of his hand. He felt guilty—he had no right to this grief, it belonged to Valerie and her family. But he couldn't help being moved by the sight of the once beautiful child now turned into an empty wraith.

Valerie joined him as Shapiro continued his one-sided chat with Julia. "He's so good with her," she said, glancing over her shoulder at the two of them. "The only one who took us seriously, who even bothered to look into our case. Not that it could ever do her much good, but at least maybe no one else . . ."

Her voice trailed off. They stood there in silence, studying the view: a patch of brown grass, a few brave azalea bushes daring to flower despite the March chill, a cracked sidewalk. "Are you really going to investigate BioRegen, Agent Carver? Or are you just here to tell a mother what she wants to hear? Because I don't need empty words or promises. I lost Julia a long, long time ago—it's just taken a while for her body to catch up. But that smiling, happy girl, my baby, she vanished when she couldn't remember who she is or who I am or how to feed herself or even what food is. What's left, well, that's not Julia. Hasn't been her for a long while."

Jake liked the spark of anger in Valerie's voice. Fought the impulse to tell her that she'd need that—who was he to offer her advice?

Instead he turned to her. "I'll do my best," he promised.

She nodded, brushed her hands together as if she'd completed a grueling task. "Okay, then. What's the first step?"

Shapiro answered from behind them. "I was thinking maybe Jake could take a trip to Guatemala."

Jake spun around. "Guatemala?"

"Yeah. I think I may have a connection between your missing girl and BioRegen."

"What's that?"

"Until a few months ago, BioRegen's main supplier was a private clinic in Guatemala. The Clínica Invierno. Given the timing, if the tissue that infected Julia did come from BioRegen, it would have come from there. You could see if there's anyone down there with symptoms of Creutzfeldt-Jakob."

With Valerie standing there, looking so hopeful and yet also totally beyond hope, Jake couldn't argue with Shapiro or question his conclusions. Which, of course, was exactly the way Shapiro had planned it.

Jake hated being played for a sucker. But then Julia squealed; this time it sounded almost human, came close to laughter. He stood, his gaze riveted on the little girl trapped in her body and her mind. All he could do was pray that there weren't more Julias out there.

God help the people who set this chain of events in motion. Because if he did find them—

Shapiro gave him a nod and Jake realized he had both fists clenched, ready to hit someone. "All right," he told the IRS agent. "I'm in."

State had cleared Caitlyn's way, making customs in Belize a breeze—it also helped that everyone spoke English. She was worried that her lack of Spanish would be a hindrance in Guatemala, but other than downloading an app to help out, there wasn't a lot she could do about it in the short time she had.

On the taxi ride over to the dock, she took advantage of decent cell service and dug up as much info on Hector's former army squad as she could. It wasn't good. Apparently the Kaibiles were the equivalent of Delta or SEAL Team Six. Worse, maybe. Their training was brutal. According to one article, each incoming class had a dog as a pet—and their final assignment to graduate was to butcher their class pet and eat it. Raw.

Ugh. She understood the need to harden men fighting in a civil war that often employed brutal tactics, but it sounded like the Kaibiles were more sociopaths than soldiers.

She tried calling Carver but it went straight to voice mail, so she updated him with the names Sandra had given her and Hector's connection to the Kaibiles. Although, knowing Carver and his seriously geeked-out intensity when it came to ferreting out arcane details, he probably not only knew that already but had also researched the origins of the death squad's name and knew its creed, emblem, and marching song. The thought made her smile. She was terrible at remembering small details; having Carver around was better than her own personal Google.

But, lacking Carver, she did her own search for any major incidents involving Hector and his squad twenty years ago. There were references in the legitimate media to possible "atrocities" involving "rebel sanctuaries" and a short piece that mentioned the squad in conjunction with a prison that sounded like the equivalent of Guantanamo. Nothing specific and certainly no evidence that anyone associated with the Kaibiles had ever been charged with any crime.

Twenty years was a long time. Plus, after the peace accord, the government would have purged as many records as possible in order to keep its tumultuous past buried. In the name of protecting the precarious peace, of course.

But someone cared enough to draw Hector back to his homeland. There had to be a reason why. If she could understand that, it might lead her to Maria.

The taxi drew up and stopped near the water. She shielded her eyes against the sun bouncing from the bright blue of the Caribbean. Of course she'd lost her sunglasses somewhere along the way. As usual. The water reflected the cloudless sky. A good day to take a boat trip.

The driver pointed her to the ferry. Instead of a ship built to hold vehicles as well as passengers, the boat he indicated looked like a refugee from a Disney ride. It rode low in the water, rows of seats beneath a sagging canopy, two outboard motors in the back.

"That's the ferry to Santo Tomás? There must be some mistake."

"No mistake." He took her money and drove away.

People were climbing on board the tiny craft, the seats in the middle already filled. Caitlyn looked out over the water. It was a hour trip across the Caribbean to Santo Tomás.

Hoisting her travel pack onto her shoulder, she approached the boat. The boy manning the dock nodded and confirmed that they were going to Santo Tomás and eagerly took her American dollars. He crouched and held the side of the boat steady as she ducked below the canvas and stepped on board, climbing over and around the passengers already seated until she found herself a spot against the side of the boat with room to shove her pack beneath her feet and hold her smaller messenger bag on her lap.

"You like the water?" the woman sitting beside her asked. She was dark skinned with a Spanish accent.

"Sure, why not?" Caitlyn used to be a guide on the New River's white water rafting trips during her college breaks. This boat couldn't be any worse.

The woman smiled and nodded. "*Bueno. Muchos toques.* Many splashes."

As the boat filled, people now jammed hip to hip on the benches, it sank lower in the water and Caitlyn realized what she meant. Even sitting still at the dock, each wave sloshed water over the sides onto Caitlyn. She slid her messenger bag into her travel pack, made sure all the zippers and gussets were closed tight. Her laptop and phone were as protected as much as possible inside plastic bags; unless she fell in, they should be okay. She hoped.

The boy—their captain, she realized—climbed on to the back of the boat and lowered the engines into the water. With a puff of smoke and gasp of diesel fumes, they started and the rickety craft pulled away from the dock, heading out into the Caribbean, chopping across the waves.

Caitlyn clutched the railing and was glad she didn't

get seasick. At least she never had before. She tried to think of Maria, excited as she'd headed off on her adventure.

Maria's mother hadn't mentioned if the kidnappers who contacted Hector had provided proof of life. Was Caitlyn racing to save a corpse?

CHAPTER NINETEEN

After eating some eggs and broth, Maria fell asleep again. This time when she woke, the restraints and IV were gone. A cool breeze rustled the curtains at the open doors leading onto the wrought iron balcony. Beyond them the sky was a brilliant cloudless blue.

She got to her feet, wobbly at first and aching in every muscle. But that was nothing compared to the wicked itching from the insect bites covering her skin. She raised a hand to scratch but remembered the doctor telling her they were infected and lowered it to her side, fingers curling into a fist as she fought not to think about it.

Her travel pack was at the foot of the bed. The police must have brought it. Nothing inside appeared to be disturbed. She used the bathroom, showered, and felt better with fresh clothing. As she combed her hair in the mirror, she was surprised that she looked like the same old mousy Maria as always. The girl no one ever noticed.

Funny. She didn't feel the same. Would her father see that she'd changed? Or would he still treat her like a silly child who couldn't think for herself?

She set her jaw, scowled at her reflection. No matter what he said, she wasn't quitting school, wasn't giving up on her dream. He could kick her out, cut her off from his money, she didn't care.

Except she did. Not the money—although she had no idea what kind of job she'd be qualified for. But how he felt about her. The worst punishment he could ever give her when she was a child was the silent treatment. She might be grown up now, but she still needed him, needed her father's love.

Was a little respect thrown in with the love too much to ask?

After scaring him to death and making him fly a thousand miles to rescue her, maybe it was.

She sighed and turned away from the mirror. She repacked her bag and made the bed, then turned around the empty room, restless. Maybe the phone was working again and she could call her parents. Well, maybe not her parents—she wasn't quite up to facing them yet—but at least Linda and the others, let them know she was okay.

The door opened onto a wide corridor with high ceilings and old-fashioned hand-carved cornices and crown molding. At one end were glass French doors, at the other was a staircase, and in between were five more doors like hers, three on each side of the hall. The house resonated with an old world elegance that surprised her, given its remote location. A woman, Helda, sat in a wooden chair outside her room, reading a magazine.

"Hello, there," she said brightly. But she wasn't smiling. Instead she glanced at her watch as if Maria were unfashionably early for a party. She brushed invisible wrinkles from her nurse's uniform and folded the magazine into a crisp bundle that she tucked beneath her arm. "You look better."

"Thank you." Maria wasn't sure of the protocol. She was a guest and owed these people her life. Somehow she felt like they were waiting for something more than mere thank-yous from her. What could she offer them?

Helda didn't give her a chance to say anything. The nurse took Maria by the arm and ushered her down the hall. "I think you need real food," she said, her German accent thickening. "Come, lunch is almost ready."

She led Maria to the end of the hall and down a wide set of beautifully carved wooden stairs. Every wall was filled with paintings done by the same artist whose vivid colors had brought a smile to her face when she first woke.

"Did the doctor paint these?" she asked. They didn't seem to fit Dr. Carrera's level of sophistication. Instead they felt as if they'd been painted by someone younger, less constrained by rules and convention. Someone trying to break free of invisible boundaries, just like Maria.

Or maybe she was simply projecting her own feelings onto the art.

"*Doktor Otto? Nein,* he did not paint these." Helda gestured with a sweeping motion, indicating there were many more paintings. For the first time her smile was genuine. "Michael. *Herr Doktor*'s son. He is our artist. Our ray of sunshine."

"He is very talented." Maria stopped to admire a large canvas on the foyer wall at the bottom of the stairs. It was positioned to receive the light from the windows above the massive mahogany front doors. Despite its size, the painting depicted one small vibrantly green leaf splashed with a drop of rain. The motion, the rainbow of color in the water, the hint of sunlight, all combined to create a powerful although simple image.

Maria smiled again, raised a finger to trace the path

the raindrop would have taken as it fell, touched the leaf, and bounced back into the air. Hope. That's what the painting said to her. Life is hope.

"Maria." The doctor's voice boomed through the foyer as he crossed a spacious living room to greet her. He always seemed so exuberant, passionate. Must be nice to live so far from civilization, devoting himself to his patients. "I see you found our resident artist's work."

"Yes. They are quite lovely." Maria almost laughed at the way she found herself mimicking the doctor's formal speech patterns. Her parents had taught her how to do that when she was a child and they'd introduced her to their friends at cocktail parties. The art of blending in—she was a master. "Helda said your son painted them?"

The doctor pulled up short, his expression going from sunny to cloudy and back again in a blink. "Yes. Michael. You'll have a chance to meet him. Come, come, you must be famished."

Helda left and he led Maria into a large dining room, his steps jerky, as if his balance was off. A waiter held out her chair for her at a massive mahogany table that could have seated twenty. The room was elegantly appointed with European style: heavy velvet drapes; crystal chandeliers; thick, hand-woven rugs.

It reminded her of her parents' club back home. Only instead of overlooking the golf course, here they overlooked a vista filled with the jungle climbing up into mountains tinted blue purple on the horizon, their peaks reflected in the lake below the house. No signs of other humans as far as the eye could see other than a glimpse of the corner of the large building behind the house. All she could see from here was bright yellow paint and a row of windows covered with ornate wrought iron grates. The main hospital building, she assumed.

Given its expensive décor, she decided the clinic must be more of a spa than an actual working hospital.

"It's lovely," she said, nodding to the view. "After lunch, perhaps I could go for a walk?"

"My dear, the jungle is no place for a lovely girl like you." He sounded just like her parents—overprotective to a fault. "And we can't risk infection setting in with those nasty scrapes and bites of yours."

She blushed under his attention. "You said Dr. Zigler might be joining us?"

"Oh, my dear, I'm so sorry. Zigler is an, how do you Americans say it, early bird? He's been and gone already. In a rush to get back to his beloved gold and jade."

"So he's already found the treasure?" A twinge of disappointment colored her voice. She'd been hoping to lead him there with the data she'd gleaned from her research.

"Bits and pieces washed out when the river changed course after the earthquake. Enough to make him paranoid about security—I've had to lend him most of my men to help out. If he's not careful, he'll become obsessed. Gold fever, the local Maya call it." He laughed at her frown of dismay. "I'm joking. The treasure itself is meaningless to Zigler. It's the history behind it that he's fascinated with. Wants to share with the world." The way he talked made Dr. Zigler come to life, exactly as she'd imagined from their correspondence. An old-fashioned gentleman-scholar. A cross between Richard Leakey and Albert Schweitzer.

"I can't wait to meet him." Then her shoulders sank. "Oh. I forgot about Prescott. Have they found the men who killed him?"

He patted her arm reassuringly. "No, but the police are working on it. They have all the roads blocked, asked us to stay put for the duration. Another reason for you not to venture out alone."

She remembered the killer's final words to Prescott, implying that the grad student had wanted the treasure for himself. She hated to think that about him—she'd liked Prescott. A lot. He was the main reason why she'd broken all the rules to come here now instead of waiting for the summer.

"I think I know where the treasure is," she blurted out. Damn, she'd wanted to keep that as a surprise for Professor Zigler. But he and the doctor had obviously become close friends since the professor's arrival. And the doctor talked as if the treasure was common knowledge to the locals. "I ran a computer simulation based on the ground-penetrating radar readings and compared them to the hieroglyphs he's uncovered. The temple is devoted to the rain god, Chaac. There's a cistern deep at its heart with hidden tunnels funneling rainwater down to it. I think the treasure is down there, at the bottom of the cistern."

He looked surprised. Then clapped his hands in delight. "Brilliant *and* beautiful! Zigler is going to love you, my dear."

She blushed at his words. She wasn't beautiful—not like her mother, a true Spanish beauty. Maria didn't share her mother's delicate features or golden complexion. The only features they had in common were their dark hair and eyes. Maria's cheekbones were higher, her face and forehead broader, her skin darker. Longing for some part of her mother's beauty, she'd once asked if she was adopted. Her parents had laughed and chided her for silly imaginings.

A whirling noise came from the direction of the hall. Helda escorted a young man who sat in a large electric wheelchair. The back of the chair was stacked with equipment connected to the man with tubing and wires that emerged from under the T-shirt he wore. He was about Maria's age, dark hair, high cheekbones, features a lovely mix of Maya and Spanish.

"Ah, perfect timing." The doctor rose from his seat and went to the man, speaking to him in rapid Spanish that Maria caught only bits and pieces of. He turned and gestured to her with a flourish. "Maria Alvarado, may I present my son, Michael."

Michael pushed himself out of his wheelchair despite Helda's gesture of protest. She hurried to unhook a small bag from the back of the chair and he slung it across his chest like a messenger bag. A thick power cord still tethered him to the battery on the back of the chair, but he had room to maneuver as Helda followed behind him with the chair.

"Nice to meet you, Maria," he said with a smile. His English was perfect, with a fluid Spanish cadence underlying it. Made him sound like a movie star.

He took a few steps to reach Maria and offered his hand. Helda stepped forward then back again, her hands fluttering with worry. Michael knew it, Maria saw. His grin filled with mischief.

He kissed her hand and she couldn't help but blush again. With him close beside her, she could hear a faint ticking from the machine in the bag across his chest, like a grandfather clock ticking the seconds. Underlying it was a high-pitched hum as if someone were vacuuming in another room not too far away.

"Michael, please," his father protested. "Sit down. You shouldn't exert yourself."

"I feel fine, Father. Better than I have in months."

"Then sit, if only for my sake and Helda's. You'll wear us out with worry."

Michael relented and took the seat beside Maria's.

Helda immediately positioned the chair behind him, then pulled some sanitary wipes from her pocket and began to clean his hands. Scrubbing away any contagion from shaking Maria's hand.

Suddenly Maria was worried. Dr. Carrera had given her antibiotics, but he did say her cuts and bites were infected. But surely he wouldn't risk his son's health if Michael was immunocompromised?

Dr. Carrera shook his head. "Really, Michael—"

"What's the point of having an artificial heart if I don't get the chance to enjoy it?"

"It's only a temporary measure. We can't risk anything going wrong."

"You see a blue sky and fear a drought. I have extra batteries, the chair isn't four feet away, and for the first time in weeks I haven't been tied to a damn oxygen tank. Why shouldn't I enjoy my freedom?" He turned to Maria with a grin that made her heart speed up. "Not to mention a pretty girl to share it with."

She smiled back. No one had ever looked at her like that before. As if she were the reason for his happiness.

"How long are you here for, Maria?" he asked.

Thoughts of her parents and how angry they would be chased her smile away. She focused on the fish the waiter had just deposited onto her plate. "I'm not sure. Hopefully through the summer—I'm working with Professor Zigler."

Michael nodded absently as he dug into his own food. He ate like someone who hadn't had solid food in a while. His clothing, a plain white T-shirt and jeans, hung as if he'd lost weight, and despite his dark complexion, he appeared pale.

"Can I ask?" She nodded to the bag that the tube from his chest ran into.

"LVAD," he answered, his mouth filled. He swallowed. "Left ventricular assist device. It keeps my heart pumping. Until a few weeks ago, I was a candidate for the last rites, heart failure from a virus. Father here was ready to measure me for a casket."

"Michael," Dr. Carrera cut in, his knife clattering to the floor. A waiter hurried forward to retrieve it and place a clean one beside him. "That's not funny. And not true. I'd never give up, you know that." Concern etched his voice, and a shadow passed over his face.

"I know, Papa." Michael smiled at his father with the same intensity he'd bestowed on Maria. Despite his illness, it seemed his sunny disposition was difficult to overcome. "But it feels so good to be free of that bed and able to move around again."

"So, your artificial heart, it's cured you?" Maria asked, hoping she wasn't being rude. But she'd never met anyone who almost died before. And she couldn't help but wonder how the LVAD worked—when her father got here, he'd know. Maybe it would distract him from being so angry at her.

"No," Dr. Carrera answered. "It's just a stopgap measure until we can find a donor heart. But it's given us the gift of time." He frowned at Maria. "As long as Michael is careful and doesn't strain himself."

"What better gift could anyone ask for?" Michael patted his breastbone as if proving his fitness. He turned to Maria, studying her again with that intense gaze that warmed her body more than the sun ever could. "I'm going to paint you before you leave. I warn you, I've never been good with human subjects, but there's something about you. . . . Please, will you do me the honor?"

How could she say no? She nodded shyly, unable to meet his gaze.

Michael clapped his hands like a little boy, the gleeful sound making even Dr. Carrera smile. "Good. We start right after we eat."

CHAPTER TWENTY

The ferry arrived forty minutes late; it was almost two o'clock by the time they docked between two cargo ships on the industrial side of the port at Santo Tomás, and Caitlyn's stomach wasn't too happy about it. She nibbled on a protein bar rescued from inside her bag—where everything was nice and dry, despite the drenching she'd taken during the ride from Punta Gorda—as she followed the other passengers onto the cement pier. The only sign she saw for any kind of customs agent was an abandoned stand near an empty stretch of dock obviously meant for the cruise ships with its brightly canopied tour kiosks and signs painted on the concrete pier directing visitors to a bus parking lot and sightseeing guides.

No one else seemed bothered by the lack of border control, so she shrugged her pack higher on to her shoulder and walked past men shouting at each other as they gestured to cargo containers, others checking clipboards and yelling back. At the far end of the row of containers stacked four high was a short balding Hispanic man, the kind of man no one would notice in a crowd.

Caitlyn noticed him right away. His gaze ranged over the passengers streaming from the ferry, stalled on her bright red hair, finished examining the others, and returned to her. Made her wonder about the CIA's field training if he was their idea of covert.

She decided to challenge him—after all, no way she could hide her presence here, a tall white redhead—and strode up to him. "Ready to go?"

He shrugged and laughed, didn't seem at all upset. "*Sí, sí.* This way. Can I call you Caitlyn?"

His accent was a funny combination of melodic Spanish and fast-talking New Yorker. "Of course. And you are?"

"Juan Carlos Romero. Everyone calls me Romero." He made it sound like he was inviting her into his inner circle of close friends.

"Where are you from, Romero?"

"Brooklyn. My mother is Puerto Rican and my father's father was Cuban." He lowered his voice and glanced around dramatically. "He, my grandfather, worked for the CIA way back when. So I guess you can say it's in my blood."

"I gather you don't do much fieldwork, though?"

He shrugged. "Nah. I wish. It's mostly handholding and translation. Sometimes I get to ride along with the DEA guys, but since we pretty much screwed the pooch here back in '54, the CIA I mean, starting the civil war and all, I try to keep a low profile. But a chance to meet Hector Alvarado? No way I could resist that. The man is legendary."

They reached a mud-splattered white Land Rover. Caitlyn settled her pack in the back and climbed onto the passenger seat. "Has Hector arrived?"

"In style. Flew in on a helicopter. Private charter.

Pilot's one of his ex-army buddies. They had a few more guys with them."

Great. Hector brought his own private militia. "Weapons?"

He nodded as he honked at two mopeds riding abreast, slowing traffic. They waved good-naturedly without increasing their speed. "He's camped out at the El Atlantico hotel while his men wait in the helicopter. It's parked in an empty lot behind the *mercado*."

He pointed to the building they were passing. The *mercado* was a bright yellow cinder block building beckoning to tourists off the cruise ship, its walls painted with murals promising local artisan crafts, fine handmade jewelry, and many other TESOROS ÚNICOS.

"Have your people heard anything?" she asked. "Rumors of a plot to exact revenge on Hector for something in his past? Or maybe a plan to kidnap Maria for ransom? Someone took a lot of time and trouble to put this all into motion."

The two mopeds turned off and he gunned the engine only to hit the brakes again as a man pulling a cart crossed the street in front of them. "I put out a few feelers, but no one's talking. Definitely no signs of Maria being taken out of the country—not that the borders around here don't leak like sieves. My money would be on someone from Hector's past. I dug around unofficially, and the stories I heard about what he and his unit did—let's just say there's a damn good reason he fled the country as soon as the government starting talking peace with the guerrillas."

They pulled into a parking space across the street from the El Atlantico. Romero led her into a small café, where they found seats near the window and drank strong coffee.

"What about this Prescott kid?"

Romero frowned. "Best I can figure, given what little time I've had, is that he might be an actor brought in on a work visa last week. Name of John Kandlass. Description fits and he listed an address here in Santo Tomás. Wasn't there when I checked."

Caitlyn pulled out the photo of Prescott. "This him?"

"Yeah. Matches Kandlass's passport photo."

Great. The plot had gone past thick to impenetrable.

A school-aged girl with a basket on her arm entered, gesturing to Caitlyn. She was dressed in a white peasant blouse over a colorful tiered skirt and wore a bright woven shawl over her shoulders.

"She wants to sell you chocolate," Romero translated. Caitlyn took a look in the basket. Irregular chunks of dark grainy chocolate were wrapped in plastic. "The locals, they harvest cocoa and grind it, make the chocolate themselves. It's a little bitter for my taste, but very rich."

"I don't have any money except American." There'd been no place or time to exchange currency during her rushed travels today.

"One dollar, one dollar," the girl gushed, handing Caitlyn the largest piece.

Caitlyn couldn't resist and pulled a dollar bill from her pocket. Romero stopped her, speaking to the girl in rapid Spanish. The girl looked down at her feet, scuffed her toe. Caitlyn thought she was about ready to cry.

"What's wrong?" she asked.

"For a U.S. dollar, you should get pretty much the whole basket."

"No, that's not right, not if she and her family went to all the trouble to make it themselves." Caitlyn smiled at the girl, who looked back up, shyly. She held up two fingers. "*¿Dos?* One for me and my friend? *¿Mi amigo?*"

The girl beamed and nodded. Then carefully selected the smallest piece and set it daintily in front of Romero, as if bestowing a great honor on him. Caitlyn laughed and handed her the dollar.

"Gracias."

"Sucker," Romero said. He shooed the girl out the door while Caitlyn unwrapped her chocolate. It was hard, but when she dunked it into the hot coffee, the melted section was delicious.

"Tell me about Hector and his war buddies."

After Shapiro dropped him off at his bike, Jake headed to the Washington Field Office to grab some time on a computer. He was tempted to start with the Guatemalan clinic and any outbreaks of Creutzfeldt-Jakob, but instead he began with the basics.

First, a routine check of other missing persons reports from Guatemala, focusing on foreigners who disappeared near Santo Tomás. Not much—most of the crime against outsiders involved assaults and armed hijackings of tourists. But there was a Canadian who went missing from a town named Livingston six weeks ago.

He glanced at a map. Livingston was very close to Santo Tomás, just up the coast from it. According to the report released by the Canadian officials, Kevin Cho was a surgeon who'd just finished a medical mission. He'd planned to drive across the border to Belize and return home via Punta Gorda but had never made his flight.

Another look at the map. Not a whole lot between Livingston and Punta Gorda in the way of towns, but a lot of Mayan ruins and some nature preserves. Looked like rugged country, easy to get lost in.

He tabled the doctor's missing persons report and began on background checks on Hector and Sandra Alvarado. Caitlyn had texted him some other leads:

Alvarado's old army squad, the Kaibiles, and his friend, Dr. Otto Mendez Carrera.

Soon Jake had over a dozen windows open on the machine as he built a history of Alvarado and BioRegen. A pattern was emerging, one that he didn't like. He made hard copies of the important files, grabbed an elevator going up, and dodged Yates's administrative assistant as he barged into the Assistant Director's office.

"You need to pull Caitlyn out," he told Yates, who had a tuna salad on rye in one hand and was typing on his computer with the other. "Or get her some backup."

"You must be Carver," Yates said after he swallowed. His assistant poked his head inside the door with an apologetic shrug, but Yates waved the man away. "You do know that this field office has a dress code?"

Caitlyn had said Yates was a stickler for rules when he wanted to be. Also said he was a good guy who'd used to be a boots-on-the-ground law enforcement officer. Unlike so many of the suits populating the Department of Justice.

Jake detected amusement flickering across Yates's face so skipped any excuses for his informal attire and cut to the chase. "Does Caitlyn know about Alvarado's past? Why he fled Guatemala?"

"I sent her everything we had, little that it was. Mostly redacted by State and our cousins over in Langley. She's good at reading between the lines—and can Google as well as anyone. Why? Did you find something?"

Helping himself to the director's spare chair without asking permission, Jake leaned forward. "Maybe. I think I have an idea why someone might be targeting Alvarado."

Yates returned the favor by continuing to munch on his sandwich and type while he waited for Jake. But this was too important. Jake wanted the man's full attention.

Finally Yates turned away from his keyboard. "An idea? No proof?"

"No proof."

Doubt filled Yates's face, but he relaxed in his chair and templed his fingers. If a low-ranking agent like Jake dared to barge in on his lunch because of an idea, it had better be important, his attitude said. "Okay. Let's hear it."

"You know that Alvarado and his squad were in charge of a secret prison, code-named U4?"

"According to media conjecture. The government has always denied it, and no witnesses or other proof have been found."

"Conjecture from the media and the Catholic church and the UN's commission. And of course they deny it. If half the things they're accused of are true, it makes Gitmo look like a trip to Baskin-Robbins."

"That's all ancient history. What's it got to do with a missing college student?"

"I think that in exchange for their cleaning up the mess, Alvarado and his second-in-command—a Dr. Carrera—were allowed to keep the prison. And the prisoners, plus whoever else they dragged in or that the government wanted disappeared."

"You think U4 is still in existence? Without a word? After twenty years?"

"Only it's not U4 anymore. It's now the Clínica Invierno. I think Alvarado fled here to the U.S. and set up his biotech firm to take advantage of the one thing U4 had plenty of—too much of, in fact."

Yates frowned. "What's that?"

"Body parts."

Yates bounced forward in his chair. "Wait a minute. You think the U.S. government gave Alvarado entrance to our country so he could get rid of the evidence of his war crimes? And he made a fortune doing so?"

"Think about it. BioRegen has been the forerunner in the business, always able to meet the demand of medical researchers and hospitals without any problems. Until recently, at least. Most of the tissue they use can be stored for years under proper conditions. He and his second-in-command, this Dr. Otto Mendez Carrera, were sitting on a fortune. All they needed to do was slice and dice and set up a legitimate front here in the U.S."

"You've got to be kidding." Yates thought hard. "Although, it would explain the lack of forensic evidence when the UN investigated the Kaibiles. So you think U4 is still functioning?"

"I think the whole thing has been whitewashed. Changed into a psychiatric clinic run by Alvarado's former second-in-command and medical officer. Dr. Carrera. Who better to continue to supply the parts they need than psych patients who can't defend themselves and no one would believe if they ever talked?"

"What you're describing, it's something out of a science fiction novel—no, a horror movie."

"Soylent Green is people, I know. But look at the Kaibiles' training—they were taught that nothing stood in the way of achieving their objective. That anyone not a Kaibiles was inferior, inconsequential. Look at the atrocities they've been accused of. Almost a quarter of a million people vanished. Other than a few mass graves, no trace at all. Makes the Nazi's SS look like a bunch of Girl Scouts in comparison."

"I still don't understand why someone is targeting Alvarado and his family now. Why wait twenty years?"

"I don't think it's someone from his past in Guatemala. I think it's someone from his present. Someone who received tissue tainted with Creutzfeldt-Jakob. Or more likely, a loved one who had to watch them die."

Jake explained about the disease and its cannibalistic origins and the devastating consequences. Yates considered. "This Julia, you said her dad was out of the picture, could he be behind this?"

"I haven't been able to track him down. The CDC says there have been a few more cases than usual of CJD. It's one of those diseases that's always cropping up here and there sporadically, so it's hard to know for sure when to worry. They said it hasn't reached the level of clinical significance yet, but promised to follow up."

"You're not here to ask for the resources to track down each of those patients and their families." Yates made it sound like a statement, not a question.

Caitlyn had said Yates was no dummy. "No, sir. I'm not. If someone's after Alvarado, he's already in Guatemala."

"Tierney can take care of herself."

"Yes, sir, she can." Jake waited.

Yates tapped the tips of his fingers together. "Reading between the lines and given how easy it was for him and his family to gain citizenship, Alvarado was probably a CIA asset."

"Then, if I'm right, State and the CIA will try to cover all this up. Leaving Caitlyn out there with no one watching her back." Jake stood. "There's a direct flight to Guatemala City from Dulles. I can be there by dinner."

"And from there to Santo Tomás?"

"I've got a few ideas." Not exactly regulation travel plans—the Assistant Director was better off not knowing the details.

"All right, I'll push the paper through. You can go. *If* the U.S. Attorney approves it. Last thing I need is more grief from Justice."

"No problem, sir. Already taken care of," Jake lied. He reached across the desk and shook Yates's hand. "Thank you, sir."

"I'm going to tell you the same thing I told Tierney. Whatever shit comes down, I need the Bureau to come out smelling like fucking roses. I don't care if you have to leave Alvarado and his daughter behind—it was his decision to go there and ditch Tierney, we can spin that. But I can't spin two agents getting blamed for creating civil unrest in a country we're trying to forge a partnership with. Sometimes the past is best left buried."

CHAPTER TWENTY-ONE

Lunch was sumptuous, and Maria ate with what her mother would have labeled unladylike gusto. Michael didn't seem to mind; she caught him watching her several times during the meal. And his father smiling at both of them.

After the plates were cleared, Dr. Carrera insisted that Michael return to the wheelchair. Michael rolled his eyes but cheerfully obeyed.

"Maria, let me show you the sights," he said, steering the chair into a tight 360 that made Helda jump back.

"Only the house, Michael," his father cautioned. "No further than the courtyard."

Michael and Maria left the dining room, the wheelchair humming as it crossed the terrazzo floors leading down the hall to the rear of the house and out into a courtyard in the center of the U-shaped complex. There was a pergola style roof overhead, supported by columns covered in beautiful exotic flowers, a cheerful fountain at the center, and a view of both the mountains and the lake. The far side opened onto a garden, and beyond it she could see more of the large clinic building.

It was three stories tall but very long and sat at an angle to the main house. Despite its cheerful yellow paint and many windows, all with wrought iron scrollwork covering them, it seemed forlorn. Maria was glad when Michael positioned her with her back to it.

"This is where I do my best work," he said. "I missed it so much during the months I was trapped inside."

"I'm sorry you were so ill," Maria said cautiously. She'd been lucky; she'd never been seriously sick, and neither had her parents or any friends. Once she had a teacher who left school early in the year because she had cancer—the kids had a fund-raiser and made T-shirts and a video for her. That was the closest brush she'd ever had with mortality. Until seeing Prescott killed.

"And I'm sorry you've had to witness such awful things since you arrived here. I wish I was healthy enough to take you on a true tour of our secluded paradise." He waved a hand to indicate the mountains looking down on them.

"I just hope Professor Zigler will still let me work with him. I discovered the most amazing thing, analyzing his satellite images. I still can't believe that there's an entire temple hidden by the jungle. And no one's ever found it before."

He looked at her, confusion in his eyes. "The temple? It's not far if you take the trail through the mountains on this side of the river."

"But—I thought it was lost. . . ." She stumbled over her words in her confusion.

"Not to us. Or the Maya who live here. The jungle has overtaken it, so it's hidden from outsiders. But we've always known about it."

She frowned. Why hadn't the doctor told anyone? An educated man like him would understand the potential, the importance of such a discovery.

"Please, don't frown," Michael said, spinning his chair again and making a clownish face until Maria smiled once more. "There, that's better. I wish my father would let me take you there, to the temple. There are stone heads taller than me on either side of the path leading to the entrance. And where the water broke through after the earthquake, you can find shards of jade and even gold. Oh, and there's this beautiful mural painted on the inside walls in shades of the most fantastic turquoise blue and scarlet and brilliant yellows—"

She sat down on a stone bench. "Why haven't you and your father shared this with the world? Think of the history we could preserve. It could be the key to unlocking secrets lost by the Maya centuries ago."

"That's what I tell my father. But he insists the temple is holy and should be left alone. In fact, ever since the earthquake when I found those shards of jade and gold—and even some bones, I think they were human—he's forbade me from returning."

"But your father is a man of science. Surely he understands the value of a site like the temple."

"He'd argue that its value to the Maya who live here is more important. After all, who is this professor of yours that he can suddenly come and ransack their sacred temple?"

Maria jerked her chin up at that even though Michael's tone wasn't angry or rebuking—more as if he enjoyed debating. "Professor Zigler is world-renowned. And the government gave him a permit—"

"That's not the same as permission from the people who live here."

She squinted into the sun, staring at the jungle that she'd come through during her flight for her life. "Those men. The ones who killed Prescott—could they have been Mayans? Upset by the dig?" Her lip quivered. "So, if I never found the temple and told Prescott and the professor about it . . ."

Michael left his chair to sit beside her, placing his arm around her. "Maria, don't. You can't blame yourself. Please, don't cry. Maybe it's fate. Finally time for the world to see the secrets buried at the temple. That wouldn't have happened without you."

He held her for a long moment until she pulled herself together. She was glad her father wasn't here to see her break down. Finally she sniffed and sat upright. He tilted her chin up high.

"There. That's better." He returned to his chair, watching her and instructing her to shift her body as he composed his picture.

"Do you have any paintings or photos of the murals inside the temple?" she asked, longing to see the treasure she'd worked so hard to find.

"No. I went back to school and then got sick soon after so I never had a chance to sneak back on my own." He smiled at her again. "But for a pretty girl like you, I would. All you'd need do is just ask."

She looked longingly at the mountain. If she crossed her eyes, she could just about convince herself there was a trail there. "Could you show me how to get there? On a map, I mean. The least I could do after all the trouble I've caused is to go and help the professor out, even if it's only for a day."

"Of course. It's too late for you to go today—but tomorrow I'll ask my father to assign one of his men to go with you, if the roads aren't open yet." He twisted in his seat and pulled out a notebook from his bag. Quickly he sketched a map for her. "Once you find the trailhead, just always bear right at any fork—if you get lost, simply go downhill to the river, you can always follow it back, although it will take longer than the direct route." With a flourish he signed his name and tore the paper off, handing it to her. "Now, you must let me paint you before we lose the light."

His fingers brushed hers as she took the piece of sketch paper. He didn't pull away and neither did Maria. She tried to decide what the right move would be—she'd never had a boy flirt with her as Michael did. But he was so cultured, so worldly, he probably wasn't flirting at all, he was probably just being nice.

Helda bustled out, carrying an easel, canvas, and a toolbox of art supplies. She cleared her throat and stepped between them, breaking the spell. After setting up the easel for Michael, she planted herself on the bench beside him, glowering at Maria. Their very own Teutonic chaperone.

Michael quickly took care of that, telling Helda, "Your shadow, Helda. I'm afraid you'll need to move. That chaise in the corner, if you don't mind."

The nurse huffed and glared at Maria, but finally took a new seat, out of earshot.

At first Maria was self-conscious, stiff, didn't know how to hold her chin or her hands or where to look. But Michael kept talking to her from behind the easel and finally she relaxed. She realized he hadn't been flirting with her—he spoke to Helda the same way he did her. He was just a genuinely nice, charming guy. Handsome, too.

Good thing he hadn't been on board the cruise. Maria would never have gotten close to a guy like him. Not with all the beautiful girls on the ship.

"Where did you learn to paint?" she asked.

"Art was required in my boarding schools. I spent most of my childhood abroad," he explained. "With my mother dead, and my father so busy with work." She couldn't see his body, but the shrug was implied by his inflection. "It was nice to see the world. I went to schools in Geneva, London, even a year in Paris."

"I've never been anywhere except Florida." Her parents traveled all the time for work, so they only wanted to stay home during vacations. And they had no family to visit.

"You're here now," he said brightly. "Seeing the world."

So far she'd seen a cruise ship, a man get killed, and the jungle where she'd run for her life. "Where are you going to college?"

"Yale." For the first time, his voice faltered. "Well, I was. Until I got sick last year. Everyone had the flu, no reason to think what I had was any different. But they got better and I got worse. Woke up in the ICU. A virus had attacked my heart."

"I'm sorry," she said, knowing it sounded lame. "You were alone, so far from home? That must have been awful."

"Like I said, I've never really had a home—only came here during a few school holidays. And my father, well, I'm sure you noticed. He can no longer travel."

She nodded. Dr. Carrera's muscle jerks and tremors must be symptoms of something much more serious if it prevented him from going to his son when Michael was in the ICU. "Is it Parkinson's?"

"Something like that. He doesn't like to talk about it. It's gotten a lot worse the last few months—" His voice filled with guilt. "The stress of taking care of me, I'm sure."

"He loves you very much," she said, wishing she could reach his hand, let him know through a touch that none of this was his fault.

Michael cleared his throat and his voice returned to

normal. "They stabilized me enough to get me home so my father could care for me. According to the doctors, I should have died months ago, but they don't know my father or how stubborn he is. And at least I've had the chance to finally spend time with him. I missed that growing up."

Maria looked down, regretting her own childish thoughts about how much she wanted to get away from her parents and their overprotectiveness. Maybe Michael had gotten to see the world, but he had to almost die in order to get close to his father.

"The hardest part is, before the LVAD, my only hope was waiting for someone to die. To get a transplant. But now, I feel so much stronger. And I've read reports of some people living with the LVAD for years, if they take care of it. So maybe no one has to die after all." He looked at her from around the side of the canvas. "Wouldn't that be wonderful?"

CHAPTER TWENTY-TWO

"You know what the Spanish called Guatemala centuries ago?" Romero began. "*Tierra de guerra.* 'Land of war.' Because they could never defeat the Achi Maya. Things haven't changed much since. What do you know about the civil war?"

"Not much," Caitlyn admitted. She'd been more concerned with Maria and her family here and now, not ancient history. "I know it ended in the '90s, and right after that Hector and his family emigrated to America."

He sniffed and rolled his eyes. "Wars like that don't end. They mutate."

Romero ordered a beer for himself and something for Caitlyn that turned out to be a delicious fish dish. "You know what started it all? Fruit. In the 1950s, the U.S. fruit companies were worried that the leftist regime here would seize their properties. So the U.S. in its infinite ignorance decided to muscle a new regime into power. As is often the case, they backed the wrong horse."

"The CIA instigated a coup d'état, right?" She finished

her fish and dared another entrée, this one chicken wrapped with spices in a fried tortilla. Delicious.

He nodded. "That was 1954. Way before my time, of course. But that's when it all started, with Colonel Carlos Castillo Armas. The first of many. Until after a few decades, a few more coups d'état and rigged elections, and entire Mayan communities wiped out, it became virtually impossible to separate the army from the government. That's when I first got here, back in the mid-'80s when the Reagan administration sent us in to help secure a legitimate election. I was just a kid, a grunt in the marines, first time out of the country."

Caitlyn nibbled on the rest of her piece of chocolate while waiting for him to finish.

"Reagan called the election a tribute to democracy. And we left, off to take democracy to other shitty parts of the world whether they wanted it or not. But of course, one election couldn't cure three decades of chaos. The military regained control, and there were assassinations, extrajudicial executions, and thousands more disappeared." He shrugged as if the numbers were so overwhelming, it was difficult to see the people behind them.

"Until the peace accord in '96," Caitlyn finished.

He gave her a crooked smile and a nod that felt patronizing. "Right. Until the peace accord."

The waiter brought their check, and Caitlyn paid for it with U.S. dollars, glad for the chance to get some of the local currency in case she needed it.

"Just leave the centavos for the tip," Romero said, indicating the coins the waiter left as change. "They're pretty much worthless anyway."

Caitlyn left a U.S. five-dollar bill instead. Romero did the eye-roll thing again as she scooped the mound of coins and slipped them into the side pocket of her cargo pants. She didn't care. This was her first trip outside of the United States and she wasn't going home without something to show for it.

Then Romero tapped the table and nodded to the window. "There he is. Hector's leaving."

Hector had changed out of the designer suit Caitlyn had last seen him wearing and into black fatigues. No insignia, but his new ensemble included a pistol in a holster strapped to his leg. He moved with military precision, his features chiseled into an expression of barely contained fury. As soon as he reached the curb, a black SUV pulled up to him.

Caitlyn and Romero ran for their Land Cruiser. Romero followed the SUV, keeping his distance. "Damn, he's headed to the helicopter."

He parked at the entrance to the *mercado* as Hector's vehicle continued around to the back. "We're sunk. No way to follow him now."

Caitlyn hopped out of the truck and grabbed her pack. "That's what you think."

"Wait! You can't—he'll never let you."

"What's he going to do? Throw me out of the helicopter?" She didn't give him a chance to reply before she dashed up the steps to the entrance to the *mercado*.

The shortest way through to the rear of the *mercado* was cutting through the large open-air sales area. As soon as Caitlyn saw the bustle of eager salespeople and crowds of tourists, she began to doubt if shortest meant fastest. No time to go back, so she plowed into the crowds, jostling her way past men barring her path, their outstretched arms filled with beaded belts, women calling to her to try their jewelry, and even children like the girl she'd met in the café who ran through the place with baskets of chocolate and small trinkets.

Her pack came in handy. Swinging it quickly cleared the aisles as merchants rushed to protect their wares and tourists dodged. She made it through the back exit and ran down the steps until she reached a cracked concrete loading bay. Beyond it was the vacant lot where the helicopter was waiting.

Hector and his men were gathered together, examining a map spread out on the trunk of the SUV he'd arrived in. They all had AK-47 machine guns slung over their chests and carried extra magazines.

"What's the plan?" she asked brightly, trying to disguise how out of breath she was, as she joined them.

"The plan is for you to mind your own business." Hector scowled at her. She grinned back. Slid the map closer to her. It was the same area where Maria's temple was located, only the spot Hector had marked was farther north, upriver from the temple.

"Sorry, Hector. No can do. Not since you made Maria's safety my business." Again with the piercing stare. Like that was going to stop her from doing her job? "Did you get a ransom demand?"

"My men have intel on a guerrilla outpost not far from here. We're going to—" He shifted the AK. "—investigate it."

Right. And she was Mary Poppins. "You're not in the Kaibiles anymore. You can't go in shooting and killing civilians." What was the phrase Romero used for it? Extrajudicial executions. Not on her watch.

His men alerted at that. Now there were four men glaring at her.

"You won't do Maria any good if you're locked up in a Guatemalan prison," she added.

"That would never happen. I still have friends in high places. Here as well as in the United States."

"Right, right. Then think of Maria. Go in shooting

and they could shoot her—or she could get caught in the crossfire. She might not be held there. What if news of your 'investigation' reaches her captors and they kill her in retaliation? What if the kidnappers try to find you here while you're out on your little expedition?"

"We have rules of engagement." His men blinked in surprise, one of them shrugging as he exchanged glances with another. "This is a simple reconnaissance mission. No firing unless we're first fired upon. And the guerrillas' last message said they'd contact me in the morning. That gives us all night. Satisfied?"

No. It was still an idiotic move. One she couldn't let him make alone. Someone had to be looking out for Maria's safety. "Fine. Let's go."

"You're not coming. You have no standing here."

"No. I don't. But I have a lot of standing with the U.S. government. Including the IRS, the FDA, and the FTC. All of whom might have a sudden, intense interest in your company if you piss me off." She didn't bother with a stare-down, instead she turned her back on him and brushed her hands together. Done deal. "Oh, nice helicopter. What is that, a Bell Ranger?"

They climbed on board, Hector's men giving Caitlyn a wide berth and staring at her as if she were a zoo specimen. Hector sat up front with the pilot, but Caitlyn grabbed one of the radio headsets and continued her argument against lethal force.

"You know I'm a trained hostage negotiator," she told him. "Use me to make contact with these guerrillas. Send a man to interpret. Let's make sure Maria is even there before we commit to anything."

"This is my daughter. My only child. Do you think I'm going to trust her life to anyone but myself?" Despite the noise of the helicopter's engine, his voice crackled over the radio louder than in person.

"Okay, fine. You and me. Leave the others behind as backup. Who are these guerrillas? What do they want? Why did they chose Maria?" She knew narcoterrorists used the country to cross from Colombia into Mexico, but this plan to get Maria and now Hector back to Guatemala was much too elaborate for a bunch of drug smugglers trying to stay below the radar.

"They're animals," came his answer. "Animals who will stop at nothing to destroy me and everything I hold dear."

Sounded pretty damn personal. Caitlyn remained silent, hoping Hector would keep talking.

"Leftist pigs," he continued. "They want the land and everything on it for themselves. Think because they were here first, it's theirs to do with what they want. Even if that means sitting on it while the jungle devours it and everything goes to rot and ruin."

Wait. "This guerrilla group is Mayan?"

His men listening in swiveled their faces and bodies, complete with their AK-47s, in her direction. She kept her face neutral, realized the guerrilla forces weren't the only men with guns she'd need to negotiate with tonight.

"If they're Mayan, that gives us an edge," she continued, ad-libbing. "There's no way they can stand against your squad, not with your superior training." The men relaxed. A tiny bit.

By the time they took off, the sun had set. The helo left the lights of Santo Tomás behind to fly over complete blackness. Not a single light to reveal any evidence of civilization could be seen as far as the horizon. Caitlyn hugged her pack tighter against her chest. If anything went wrong out here—if she died—no one would ever know.

"One problem," she told Hector. "It sounds like they

don't want money. And there's no way you can give them their land back. Do you know what they do want?"

There was a pause before he answered. "Me," he finally said. "They want me. Dead."

CHAPTER TWENTY-THREE

The helicopter descended into darkness. Caitlyn assumed the pilot was using forward-looking infrared radar and night vision to guide their landing but decided it was best not to ask. Sometimes ignorance was bliss.

The helo landed with a thump, shuddering as the rotors slowed their movement. Hector's men jumped out and vanished into the darkness. Caitlyn debated leaving her pack on board but decided that despite its weight, it was better to keep it with her. Hector had already abandoned her once. Best not to trust him too far.

She climbed down from the passenger compartment and, keeping her head bent low and eyes squinted against the rotor wash, made her way through knee-high grass to the front of the craft, out of range of the blades.

Hector met her there a moment later. "Where to?" she asked.

He didn't answer but instead began moving through the darkness, leaving the clearing where the helicopter sat and heading toward the trees. Caitlyn followed, pushing her stride a little to stay at his side. His men were behind them, but when she turned to look, they had vanished into the shadows.

Suddenly shouts came from in front of them. Caitlyn couldn't understand what the men were saying but she was damn sure they weren't friends of Hector's. Gunfire echoed through the darkness. Hector raised his AK-47. Caitlyn drew her Glock, scanning the shadows for danger.

A light blinded her, stabbing her in the face. Then more lights. From three directions. A man shouted in Spanish. Beside her, Hector straightened and for a moment Caitlyn thought he was going to fire on the unseen men surrounding them. But he simply unslung his weapon and laid it on the ground.

The man shouted again. "Drop your weapon," Hector translated.

Caitlyn lowered her gun, raised her hands, empty.

Men rushed them. They took Caitlyn's pack and service weapon, Hector's knife and pistol as well as his AK-47 and ammo, then bound their hands behind them with cord and pushed them forward to form a line, single file into the jungle. Caitlyn counted five guerrillas but didn't see any signs of Hector's men. Were they dead?

As soon as they entered the cover of the jungle, an explosion rocked the ground. She stopped and glanced over her shoulder.

The helo was engulfed in flames.

The day passed quickly and after an elegant dinner with the doctor and Michael that lasted until late into the night, Maria was exhausted. She returned to her room, only to realize that somehow she'd never gotten the chance to ask again about the phones. Despite her trepidation about facing her father's anger, better to do it now long-distance than to have to face it all when he arrived.

Besides, if she wanted to be treated like an adult, then she needed to take responsibility for herself. Spending a day with Michael and watching his unflinching embrace of life and his own mortality had emphasized that.

She returned downstairs to the doctor's private study where they'd sipped cognac after dinner. The doors were closed, but she could hear raised voices beyond. She stopped, listening yet not wanting to listen, unsure of what to do. Wait until morning? But her parents would probably be on their way here by then.

"You can't do this!" Michael shouted. Maria flinched at the anger in his voice. "I won't let you!"

"Calm down." The doctor raised his voice to be heard over his son's.

"No. I won't. It's outrageous. Insane. It's, it's—"

"It's necessary. There's nothing more to be said."

"I have no say in the matter? It's my life, after all."

The voices dropped to a murmur muffled by the wood doors. Maria decided the best she could do was to leave now, maybe try again first thing in the morning. She crept up the steps, reaching the top just as the study door below her banged open.

"Michael, don't do anything stupid. Stay away from that girl!" the doctor shouted.

Was he talking about her? Why would he warn Michael to stay away from her?

"You do what you want, Father." Michael's voice made the term of endearment sound like a curse. "I guess you always have. What I want is meaningless."

"Don't talk like that. Everything I do, I do for you. You must believe that."

Michael said nothing as his wheelchair whirled

toward the elevator beside the staircase. Maria pressed back against the wall, hidden out of sight of anyone at the bottom of the stairs.

"Michael," his father called as he boarded the elevator. "Everything will be all right. I promise. I won't lose you, son."

The elevator doors clanged shut and it began its journey up. Maria ran down the hall to her room but didn't shut the door the entire way. She watched through the crack as the elevator stopped and Michael wheeled out. He made it to his room, across the hall and two doors down from hers, but paused before continuing down to her door.

She flew back across the room and onto the bed, pretending to be reading Helda's discarded magazine when a tentative knock came. "Maria, are you awake? May I come in?"

"Yes, of course."

He pushed the door open and came inside. To her surprise, he then shut the door behind him.

"Michael, are you okay? You look awful." His face was flushed and he seemed short of breath. "Should I call your father or Helda?"

"No. I'm fine." He didn't meet her eyes. "And he's not my father. Not really. Not anymore."

She sat up on the bed. "What do you mean?"

"I don't know who my father is, but it's not that man." He wheeled the chair forward until his feet almost touched hers. "I told you my mother died when I was a baby."

"Yes."

"Dr. Carrera adopted me. He's always treated me like the son he never had, so I never really think about it much. But now . . ." His voice faded as he searched the shadows below the bed for inspiration. When he finally looked up, his face was dark with fear and regret. "Maria, I'm so sorry. I never realized—the kind of man he is, what he was capable of."

She laid a hand on his arm. He was trembling. "Michael, you're scaring me. Tell me what's wrong."

Footsteps sounded out in the hall. He jerked upright. "There's no time. You have to leave. Tonight." He fished a folded piece of paper from his pocket and pressed it into her hand. "This will explain."

He toggled the chair, steering it away from her and toward the door. Maria left the bed. "Michael, what are you talking about? Why do I need to leave? Where would I go?"

She knew some heart problems caused decreased blood flow to the brain—was he experiencing a mental lapse because of a malfunction in his LVAD? Or maybe a stroke?

Helda's voice came from the hall. "Michael? Where are you?"

Maria ran to the door, ready to call to the nurse, but Michael grabbed her arm, hard. "You're in danger," he whispered. "Terrible danger. Run, Maria. Now. Don't let him find you."

She started to protest, but the look on his face stopped her. Fear filled her as she began to believe. She shouldn't—it was ridiculous, outrageous. And yet . . . Slowly, she nodded. He nodded back.

"Wait for me at the loading dock behind the clinic. I'll steal his keys, come for you. I'm so sorry," he said. Then he opened the door. "Helda, I'm here." He shut the door behind him and she realized he was giving her time to escape.

Escape what, she had no idea. Why would Dr. Carrera

want to hurt her? She'd never even met the man before last night—when he'd saved her life. But Michael, he'd been truly frightened. For her.

Maria remembered the look on Michael's face and didn't hesitate. There was no time to do more than grab her jacket from the chair and flee out the balcony and down the wrought iron steps to the courtyard.

The cold night air was an abrupt change from the warmth she'd felt earlier, basking in the glow of the sun and Michael's attention. The only lights in sight came from the house behind her and a faint glow from the second floor of the clinic building across the courtyard and past the gardens. The only sounds were the waterfall in the distance, the faint howls of monkeys, the screech of birds, chirp of crickets, and a shrieking noise that brought out goose bumps all over her body. Nothing human.

The door from her room opened above her. Maria pressed her body against the cold stone of the wall beneath the stairs, holding her breath as if that would keep the shadows from fleeing and exposing her.

As soon as the presence above her moved back inside the building, she sprinted into the darkness, panic surging through her as Michael's words repeated through her mind: *Run, Maria, run now. . . .*

CHAPTER TWENTY-FOUR

Jake's flight to Guatemala City was the easy part. Getting from there to Santo Tomás got a little tricky. But one good thing about spending a year and a half undercover working an outlaw motorcycle gang, you got to make tons of friends in various other parts of the federal alphabet soup. A few well-placed friends in the DEA were able to sweet-talk Jake a spot on a drug-interdiction training mission's helicopter.

He hadn't been able to reach Caitlyn, but had gotten ahold of her CIA contact. The news wasn't good. Apparently she'd gone off into the jungle with Hector Alvarado and several of his former army buddies. The CIA officer, a guy named Romero, had no idea where they were or when they'd be back. He'd been less than enthused to hear that Jake was already in country and on his way to Santo Tomás.

The helo was crowded with two DEA guys and a squad of Guatemalan soldiers who seemed a stern bunch, said nothing during the ride. But the two DEA FAST team members more than made up for it. And once they learned Jake was here not just for a case, but mainly for a girl, and that he was putting his ass on the line with the AUSA to get to her, the chance to help a fellow fed screw the system and potentially his girl was too tempting to pass up.

"If she comes to her senses and kicks your ass out of bed, tell her to give me a call!" one of them shouted as they dropped Jake off at Santo Tomás and took off again to patrol the coastline. Jake saluted with his middle finger, tossed his small rucksack over his shoulder, and grabbed his phone.

"She's out of range," a voice called from the shadows. Headlights snapped on and a man stepped forward. He was short, bald, and at least ten years older than Jake. Had the bland look of a man who could play many roles—and had. Jake knew that look: you got it after spending a long time undercover.

"You must be Romero." He stepped forward and offered his hand. The other man nodded and shook it. "I'm Jake."

"So I guessed. Still not sure why you're here. My bosses are not very happy about having two feds running amok, not when they're trying to negotiate with the Guatemalans."

"Don't worry about it. My bosses aren't happy about it either. But everything I dug up about Alvarado's company led back here, and when you said Caitlyn took off with Maria's dad, well, I just had to follow my gut."

Romero gave a snort, his gaze moving from Jake's face down to his belt and back up. "Gut? More like your dick."

Jake doubted Caitlyn had let the CIA officer get away with talking like that. Of course not. Being a spy was a lot like being undercover. What you said and did wasn't about who you really were. It was all about who the person you were with was and what you wanted from them.

He didn't miss that part of being undercover. By the end of his time with the Reapers, he'd hated lying to them, had been sorely tempted to just say, "Hey, guys, tell me who the bad guys are and we'll call it a day, go have some beers." But of course, he hadn't said that. Not even to men who'd opened their homes to him, treated him better than family.

No way in hell could he imagine living his life like Romero. A chameleon changing colors based on the whims of his boss and what the politicians safe back home in D.C. wanted. Everyone he met, he might eventually have to betray.

"What did you hear from Caitlyn?" Jake asked.

"Nothing. But twenty minutes ago, there was an explosion near her coordinates. About the size of a Bell Ranger helicopter."

Jake stopped. He whipped around, anger and fear colliding. He wanted to slap Romero's nonchalance off his face. "What the hell we doing here? We need to get there. Now."

Romero gave him a sad smile. "You don't understand anything about this country, do you? 'There' is halfway up a mountain in the middle of the jungle. The only getting there involves several hours of travel over nonexistent roads that are near impossible to navigate in the middle of the day, much less at night. There's no getting anywhere until sunrise."

Jake whirled on Romero. "You mean to tell me that a helicopter could blow up and nobody is going to search for survivors? What kind of country is this?"

"The kind where people believe secrets should remain buried. Hector pulled a lot of favors to get that helo and those men; he still has friends here and his company provides an important revenue stream. But there's a damn good reason this is his first time back to Guatemala in twenty years. He should have remembered that his enemies have a long memory."

"You think the helo was blown to assassinate Hector? And Caitlyn just happened to be on it?" Jake scrutinized the CIA officer. Yes, it was a plausible explanation, especially after what Jake had learned about Alvarado's work with the Kaibiles.

Maybe a bit too plausible? Besides, Romero didn't know Caitlyn. It'd take a lot more than a downed helo to kill her. A helluva lot more. He grabbed a map from the glove box and smoothed it out on the dash. "Show me where."

"I'm telling you, it's no good."

"Where did they go down?" Jake insisted.

Romero leaned forward and finally pointed to a spot on the map labeled Cubiltzul. "There's nothing there but an abandoned Mayan village. It's halfway up a mountain, rugged terrain. Middle of the jungle."

The more Romero tried to convince him to give up on going after Caitlyn, the more Jake resisted. Not only for emotional reasons—at least that's what he told himself. No, Romero was hiding something. Didn't want Jake to go into those mountains to reach Cubiltzul. The name rang a bell—one of the Mayan villages Alvarado's squad was accused of destroying, massacring the population. No survivors, no witnesses, no bodies, the UN Historical Clarification Commission's reports had said. Which meant it never happened, at least not according to the history as rewritten by the post–peace accord government.

"How long have you been here, Romero?" Jake asked. "You must know everyone who is anyone."

Romero relaxed at the change of subject. "Oh, yeah.

I've been here decades—not always in Guatemala, not always for the Company. Honduras with the Marines, Nicaragua, a stint in Colombia, but mostly here in Guatemala. Do you want me to pull in some favors, see if I can get a rescue mission started in the morning?"

"No. I want you to tell me why you're lying to me." Jake slid his Glock from his pocket and aimed it at Romero. "And while you're at it, start driving. We're not waiting for morning."

CHAPTER TWENTY-FIVE

The darkness in the jungle was different from any other darkness Caitlyn had ever experienced. She had hunted and camped in the woods a lot as a kid—not so much since she began her career with the FBI—but this wilderness had little in common with the Appalachian forests of her childhood.

The air was thicker, more than humid; walking through it felt like pushing through an unseen force field that left a sticky residue clinging to her skin. The smells were sharper, more acrid, a strange mix of spices, rotting fruit, and the tang of decay. And the sounds. High-pitched squawks of unseen birds, gentle rustles of small animals on the ground and racing up tree trunks, chirps and cricks and chugs popping through the air creating a cacophony of chaos.

But the worst was the howling.

It sounded human. Cries of pain and despair echoing from every direction. Some near, some far away. Monkeys, she knew intellectually. But every primitive reflex alarmed, disagreeing with logic.

The path was steep at times and she knew they

must be partway up one of the mountains. Remembering the satellite images of the area, there was a village that had appeared abandoned, not far from Maria's temple. Down the mountain from it were irregular patches of land where the jungle foliage had been burned to clear it for farming. They must have landed in one of those.

She could hear the river but the way the night distorted sound, couldn't be sure how far it was. It was her best chance at escape—follow it downstream and she'd reach the clinic she saw on the map. Near that lake that started with an *I*, she couldn't remember the name.

A short time later, they emerged into a clearing that was dimly lit by starlight and a faint moon. Jagged skeletons of buildings surrounded them and Caitlyn realized that this was the village she'd seen on the satellite images. All she'd been able to make out was a ragged church steeple and part of a caved-in roof as well as several patches of stone foundation. There hadn't been any signs of inhabitable buildings, but maybe they were hidden by the jungle.

Could this village be one of the ones Hector and his squad were accused of destroying?

He'd also been accused of genocide, she reminded herself. But her job wasn't to investigate crimes from twenty years ago; it was to save Maria.

Their guards motioned for them to halt. Flickering candlelight appeared at the gaping void that used to be the entrance to a building. The old stone church, Caitlyn realized as the person holding the candle drew closer.

Hector shouted something in Spanish—Caitlyn caught Maria's name but nothing else. Whatever he said, the guards didn't like: one of them butted him in the back with his rifle, sending Hector to his knees. He kept talking, not stopping even when the guard raised his weapon, prepared to smash it against Hector's head.

"Stop!" Caitlyn shouted, taking a step toward Hector and his guard. Her own guard hauled her back, bruising her arm with his grip. She shook free. "Please, we're here asking for your help in saving a girl's life. Please listen."

She had no idea if any of them spoke English, could only hope that Hector would translate her words. But his guard lowered his weapon and looked to the person holding the candle.

The woman raised her candle high, closer to her face. She was shorter than Caitlyn, with the high cheekbones and deep eyes of the Mayans. She wore a simple white blouse and jeans, appeared to be in her late thirties or early forties, and had thick, dark hair wrapped around her head in a braid.

Hector spit on the ground at her feet. "I'd hoped you were dead."

The woman smiled. "Sorry to disappoint, Colonel Alvarado." Her English was melodic, barely any accent but a cadence that was exotic. "And you are?" she asked Caitlyn.

"FBI Supervisory Special Agent Caitlyn Tierney."

"FBI? You have no jurisdiction here."

"I know. Which is why we need your help. We believe Maria Alvarado, a nineteen-year-old girl, has been abducted and is in danger." Caitlyn threw every bit of sincerity into her words.

The woman fingered a small cross she wore on a chain around her neck. The gold glinted in the candlelight. Finally she nodded to the guards, turned, and headed back into the burnt-out church.

"Who is she?" Caitlyn whispered to Hector as they fell into step with their guards and followed.

He said nothing, his lips pressed together tight, gaze centered on the woman. She wondered where his men were and if they had a plan. Every rule in the book said not to allow your captors to force you into a vehicle or building, but this entire encounter was already breaking all the rules.

She was glad she'd convinced Hector not to come in hot and heavy with a tactical strike. *If* he'd conveyed her opinion to his team and *if* they followed his instructions.

Although she counted only five guards and the apparently unarmed woman, she sensed that there were many more along the perimeter and in the shadows of the burned-out buildings. If Maria was here, a firefight would probably get her killed—not to mention her father's squad as well as Hector and Caitlyn.

The stone arch entrance to the church still stood upright, although the walls behind it had fallen into a pile of rubble with small bushes and a tree growing out of them. The woman followed a path twisting between the debris, and crossed another threshold, this one with part of the roof remaining, casting it into deep shadows. Then she disappeared.

As their guards nudged them forward, below the roof, Caitlyn saw more candles lighting their path, leading down a set of steep stone steps. They were made of a different material from the rest of the church and appeared older. Much older.

Hieroglyphs chiseled into the wall confirmed her suspicion: ancient Mayans had built the stairs and the tunnels they led into. They traveled deep underground, heading into the mountainside, so deep that the air turned chilly and a crisp ozone scent replaced the jungle's humidity. The candles flickered and there was the reflection of water, although Caitlyn couldn't hear it.

The place felt different from a modern church—still reverent and awe-inspiring, but somehow more calming. Maybe it was the low ceilings and narrow passages or perhaps it was the way even their footsteps were muffled by the thick stone surrounding them as they burrowed into the mountainside. Caitlyn stumbled and couldn't catch herself with her hands tied behind her, but her guard pulled her back onto her feet.

The stillness and impenetrable blackness triggered a wave of claustrophobia—never a problem before for Caitlyn, but she'd also never been trapped belowground in ancient Mayan catacombs. Finally they traveled down a final set of stairs and the tunnel opened up into a larger cavern.

There was a pond at the center, several families gathered around fires surrounding it. Caitlyn could make out bedding and cooking areas. "You live down here?"

"Only when we're being hunted," the woman answered. She nodded to Caitlyn's guard and made a slashing gesture with her hand. At first Caitlyn imagined the worst, but she met the woman's gaze and saw no malice there. Instead of panicking, she raised her wrists and bent forward. The guard cut her bindings and her hands were free.

"Who are you?" Caitlyn asked, wondering about both the woman and the group as a whole.

"Tell me again about this girl you seek."

Caitlyn moved her hand to her pocket. The guard stepped forward, his gun raised. "Just a photo." The woman waved him off. Caitlyn handed her Maria's picture as well as Prescott's. "This is Maria Alvarado. She's nineteen, a sophomore at University of Central Florida, studying Mayan archeology. She was lured here to Guatemala by this man who went by the name of Prescott Wilson. Have you seen either of them?"

To her surprise, the woman's hand trembled and she dropped Maria's photo. Before Caitlyn could retrieve it, the woman scooped it back up and clasped it to her heart. "She's turned into such a beautiful girl."

Caitlyn stepped back and watched. The woman wasn't talking to Caitlyn; she was speaking to Hector, who reluctantly looked her in the eye and nodded. "She is."

"Tell me, Colonel. Is she happy? Have you given her that, at least?"

"Yes. She's happy. Please help."

The woman's eyes narrowed, her hand closing into a fist. "You came here to ask me for help?"

"I'm here because I'd do anything for my daughter." There was a hint of rebellion in his voice.

Silence for a long moment, the woman and Hector in a staring match that condemned everyone else to oblivion. The woman whipped her head around, staring at Caitlyn. "You asked who I am. I am Itzel Ytzab Tamay. Maria is *my* daughter. Stolen from me by this man."

CHAPTER TWENTY-SIX

To Jake's surprise, Romero merely grinned, ignored the gun pointed at him, and put the Land Rover in gear. "Okay, have it your way. No guarantee we'll make it in time. Or in one piece. There's more to these jungles than you can see, even in broad daylight."

"Then why'd you let Caitlyn go?"

"I didn't. Thought we were all set to wave Alvarado bye-bye when the damn fool jumped out of the car and ran after him."

Sounded like Caitlyn. Jake scrutinized the CIA officer for a long moment. Clearly the only side Romero was loyal to was his own. "How long have you and Alvarado been working together?"

Romero's demeanor changed. No longer jovial, he considered his words. A true chameleon. Or sociopath. "I wouldn't put it that way. I wasn't his handler or anything like that. But yes, sometimes he and his squad needed assistance with missions that had the potential to be mutually beneficial. And occasionally we needed a group like his that would ask no questions to take care of—well, let's just call them nuisances. Altogether a profitable enterprise for both parties—and all government sanctioned." He glanced at Jake. "Unlike your and Tierney's escapades. Although many of our joint ventures could potentially be embarrassing if allowed to surface from where they're buried in the annals of history."

"So your job now is to help him as long as he keeps quiet."

"All he asked for was transportation and a diversion for a certain tenacious FBI agent."

The pieces fell into place. "You don't care if Hector gets killed."

"Dead men tell no tales."

Jake wondered if the ransom demand Caitlyn had told Yates about was genuine. Maybe luring Maria here to Hector's homeland had been simply to bait the trap that would end in Hector's execution? "What about Maria and Caitlyn?"

"Outside my mission parameters." Romero shrugged. "The thing about this business is you can't make personal attachments. Because sooner or later everyone gets burned. It's just the way the cookie crumbles."

"Want to see what a forty-caliber Glock can do to a cookie?" Jake said, mimicking Romero's carefree tone. "Or maybe to your head?"

Romero drove on in silence. They were on a narrow double-lane road with uneven pavement. But at least it was paved, so they made decent time. From the map, it looked like they'd soon be turning onto unpaved roads that went from a solid line to barely perceived squiggles as they headed into the mountains toward Cubiltzul. There was no other traffic to slow them. If they were lucky and the road didn't deteriorate, they should make it in another hour.

If they were lucky. Jake hadn't survived a year and a

half living undercover by depending on luck. But right now he had no choice.

As the roads got worse, Jake was glad Romero was the one doing the driving. The CIA officer didn't seem at all bothered by being taken at gunpoint—it was as if this was all a big game to him. Reminded Jake of some of the hard-core 1 percenters he'd met while with the Reapers. True sociopaths, focused only on their next hit of adrenaline.

"You know about the Kaibiles?" Romero asked, making casual conversation about Alvarado's old death squad.

"I've read about them."

"Take what you read and multiply it by ten. Those SOBs were crazy, did what they wanted, when they wanted. Hector was the worst of the worst."

"How the hell did he end up running a biotech company of all things?" Jake asked, although he had his suspicions.

"Oh, well, that was kinda like fate stepping in. After a decade of his squad terrorizing the country, they suddenly found themselves in the spotlight once the peace talks began. They'd annihilated a village, Cubiltzul, massacred all the guerrillas—"

"I read there were no guerrillas there. Only innocent civilians."

"Depends on who's writing the history, doesn't it? To the government back then, anyone blocking their seizing of land, any natives refusing to move into the city and become assimilated, they were all leftist rebels. Anyway, Hector had real bad timing. Fresh blood of hundreds on his hands—including a Catholic priest, a no-no regardless which side of the war you were on—and a public outcry. So the government promoted him."

"Of course." Typical.

"They put him in charge of their top secret prison at Lake Invierno."

"U4."

"You have done your homework." Romero sounded both impressed and condescending. "Hector and his second-in-command, Dr. Carrera, they ran the place. Torture, interrogation, rape, murder, you name it. The prison had both male and female prisoners and Hector found a nice little sideline—he'd sell any babies the women had to fine, upstanding government-approved families. Or to rich Americans desperate to adopt."

Jake sat up at that. He'd heard of the stolen infants in Spain and Argentina—many were taken by the Catholic Church, their leftist mothers told that they'd died in childbirth. But this? Raping prisoners in order to sell their children?

And the man behind it was with Caitlyn right now. She had no idea whom she had at her back. "Drive faster."

"Told you Hector was no choirboy. Don't worry, I doubt he'll risk touching Tierney. Not unless he can destroy any evidence. Did I mention what happened when the peace talks began and the government had to shut down U4 before the UN inspectors came? Hundreds of prisoners vanished. No trace of them or their bodies."

"Do you know what happened to them?"

Romero shrugged. "No idea. But they whitewashed the prison, turned it into a clinic specializing in unwed, troubled mothers. Most of them just kids on the street, many prostitutes, addicts, considered unstable, insane by society's standards. Until our Congress did something that changed everything."

"Wait. *Our* Congress? The U.S.?"

"This was the mid-'90s. Stem cell research was going to heal the crippled, save little kids with cancer, help us all live forever. Then Congress outlawed the use of federal funds for work with embryos, the source of the researcher's stem cells. Scientists panicked. While Hector and Dr. Carrera saw opportunity. Because the other place you can get stem cells, outside of embryos, is from umbilical cord blood."

"Harvested from their pregnant prisoners." Jake blinked hard. He thought he'd seen everything, but . . . "So Alvarado set up BioRegen in the U.S. while the doctor collected the stem cells."

"Then came the cosmetic surgery boom and surgeons were crying out for more tissue to squirt into Hollywood stars' cheeks and lips and asses. Suddenly having access to a captive population that no one else cared about turned into a treasure trove. Carrera spread the word that he was repenting his past by opening his clinic, free of charge, to any unwed pregnant woman who needed a safe haven. Soon he had more patients than ever. Homeless, cast out by their families. Unwanted and, most importantly, unnoticed when they vanished. Invisible."

"No one ever questioned what happened to them?"

"They're only women." Romero shrugged. "Who'd bother?"

Jake knew he didn't really want the answer to his next question, but he had to ask. "Did Carrera kill them all for the body parts?" He swallowed hard, remembering the sight of Victor's mutilated body back at the funeral home. "How many? BioRegen has been in business for almost two decades."

"Not sure if we'll ever know. I'm also not sure if they were all killed." He turned to glance at Jake. "After all, you can harvest body parts and tissue without killing the donor."

Jake fought and failed to keep the horror from his

face. Romero chuckled, delighted by the response to his macabre story.

Maria hid in the fragrant shrubs that created a border between the courtyard and the garden. She was confused and scared, and half her mind was trying to convince the other half that Michael was wrong, there was no danger, except maybe in his imagination.

But she hadn't imagined the anger she'd heard when he and Dr. Carrera had been arguing. That she couldn't deny. As much as she wanted to.

Should she trust Michael? Wait for him behind the clinic like he asked? Or should she try to escape on her own? If she could make it over the tall brick fence that surrounded the compound and follow the drive around the lake, she'd reach the road. No, that was the first place they'd look after they searched the house.

Michael had mentioned a trail across the mountains that led to the temple—but even with the help of the map he'd drawn her, there was no way she could find it in the dark. Did she even have the map? She patted her pockets frantically. Yes. She had it and the other paper he'd given her before telling her to run. There wasn't enough light to read either by, so she folded them carefully into her jacket pocket and zippered it shut so she wouldn't risk losing them.

The tiny triumph settled her nerves. She might not know what she was running from, but at least she now had a plan. Or at least the start of one. All she needed was a place to hide until daylight. Somewhere close to the loading dock Michael had mentioned—that way she could make sure he wasn't followed. She'd decided to trust him. After all, he had no reason to lie and had seemed truly frightened, plus he'd diverted Helda's attention so she could escape.

She turned to the other building in the compound. The clinic. Three stories high and half a football field in length—no way they could search it quickly. And there should be plenty of hiding places. Even better would be a working phone. She could call for help, rescue both her and Michael.

Skirting the trees and bushes, she jogged through the gardens to the clinic. The main entrance was dark, no lights outside to welcome staff or patients, no lights showing at all on the first two floors. She tried the door. Open.

Inside, she waited for her vision to adjust. The building didn't smell like a hospital. It stank of human waste and decay. Worse than the jungle, because here there was an underlying subliminal scent of terror.

Maybe it came from her. She gathered her thoughts, trying to focus. Her father was coming, the doctor had said. Was that a lie as well?

She had to assume it was all lies. Which meant he must be working with the men who killed Prescott. And that the police hadn't really come, they weren't protecting the archeology site. If the professor was still alive, maybe she could still get help to him. A phone. She needed to find a phone.

Fear rattled through her veins in a staccato drumbeat. Even though no one was here, she kept holding her breath, which only made her dizzy and breathe harder and faster. Focus. She needed to focus.

She crept across the dark foyer. This first floor felt empty—felt as if it'd been empty for a long, long time.

The entrance was at the center of the long side of the building. Inside the doors, there was a wooden desk on the other side of the reception area. Behind it a short passage lined with doors, their windows glinting in the faint glow of an EXIT sign at the far end. On either side, two more halls, stretching out the length of the building. Somewhere there must be staircases or elevators leading up to the patient floors, probably more corridors of offices and exam rooms, but she couldn't see them in the dark.

She circled the receptionist's desk. No computer. Just a datebook, a cup with pens and pencils, a stack of stationery with its corners curled by age and humidity, a newspaper, and—yes!—a rotary dial phone. She raised the receiver—something scuttled away, making the newspaper crackle—and listened. Nothing. The line was dead.

A woman's scream cut through the silence. Maria dropped the phone and jerked up. The sound had come from one of the upper floors. Several more quickly followed—not just screams but howls of anguish and high-pitched laughter.

More than one woman. Patients? But where was the staff? Maria rummaged through the desk, found an empty pack of cigarettes and a box of wooden matches. Crouching down behind the desk, she lit a match. With its illumination she saw that the newspaper was dated yesterday. Then she spied the logo across the top of the stationery: CLÍNICA PARA LOS DELINCUENTES PSICOTICOS.

Psicoticos? Even she knew what that meant. This clinic wasn't the spa she'd imagined. It was a hospital for the criminally insane. Another howl of laughter crackled through the building.

Deciding it was best to avoid the inmates, she crept behind the desk to the hallway. Administrative offices, a staff lounge with a couch that stank of mold and decay, and a clinical area. There might be supplies she could use in there—a knife, bandages to protect her infected cuts and bites, antibiotic ointment. She pushed open the door. Recoiled against a strong odor of bleach.

She stared into the shadows, making out a form of a person. There was someone in the room. On the exam table. There was no movement. Were they tied down as she'd been earlier? Sedated?

"Hello?" she whispered. No response. She crept inside, silently closing the door behind her. "It's okay. I'm here to help."

The person on the table didn't move. The silhouette appeared large like a man's, but the shape wasn't quite right. Shielding her hands from the windows in case the light could be seen, she struck a match.

And understood why the man wasn't moving. Both his legs had been amputated at the upper thigh. There was a gaping hole in his chest cavity, as if someone had wrenched his ribs apart and reached inside to pull his heart out.

Images of ancient Maya human sacrifices danced through her mind—something her brain could grab on to, rather than the macabre sight before her. She wanted to run but her feet were rooted to the spot.

The flare of light danced in her hand, casting shadows against the corpse's contorted face. It was Prescott! His eyes had been removed as had his lower jaw.

Maria's gasp blew out the match. She stood frozen, panic disorienting her, choking back the scream that clawed at her throat.

CHAPTER TWENTY-SEVEN

This woman who had captured them, Itzel, she was Maria's mother? Caitlyn looked to Hector for confirmation.

He lunged forward, almost escaping his guards. "Tell me where she is, you—" Spanish words that Caitlyn couldn't understand spat from him at a rapid-fire pace. Itzel replied in kind as her men restrained Hector.

The shouting match continued for several minutes, echoing through the dimly lit cavern. The families gathered near the water huddled closer together, looking on in fear. More than fear: terror.

Their encampment looked fairly permanent, each area swept clean, kept tidy. Not many possessions but there were sacks of corn and crates of food. No one looked like they were starving. But to live underground like this, what had Itzel said? They were hunted.

Why? Surely not just because they were Maya? Maybe because they refused to give up this land even after decades of being terrorized by the government forces? Caitlyn hadn't been able to see much on the trip here, but she certainly hadn't seen anything special, worth dying for.

Other than it was their home. Which also meant it was worth killing for. Perhaps that's why the ransom demand had led Hector here? Who would have more reason to kill him than the woman whose baby he'd stolen?

"Stop it!" Caitlyn's yell surprised Itzel and Hector. Both stopped mid-word and turned to stare at her. She focused on Itzel. "Is Maria here?"

The woman fingered her gold cross, lips moving as if in silent prayer. "No."

"Do you have any idea where she is or who took her?"

Itzel shook her head. "No."

"You're lying," Hector said. "You told me if I ever wanted to see her alive again, to come here with money."

"No, I didn't." Again with more Spanish between the two of them.

Caitlyn turned to Hector and interrupted again. "How did you know the ransom demand came from Itzel?"

He glowered at Itzel, ignoring Caitlyn. "She used to have a special curse word for me. She used it in the ransom demand she texted to my phone. No one else would have known. That's how I knew to look for Maria here rather than waiting in town like a chained dog. I will not sit helpless while my daughter is in danger." He shouted at Itzel and the room at large. "Tell me where she is or you all die!"

The words echoed through the cavern and returned empty of meaning.

Itzel straightened. Her regal calm diminished Hector, made his fury seem childish. "I did not send any message. Certainly not a text message—look at us, we have nothing, our only phone doesn't work here, away from the city."

"Then you sent someone into the city to send it. Now, stop lying and give me my daughter!"

"Quiet," Caitlyn commanded. "Itzel, please. Release him. Keep the guards if you must. But we need to work together, share what we know, if we're going to find Maria before it's too late."

Itzel stared at Caitlyn long and hard, then nodded to her men. One of them pushed Hector to his knees again and held his wrists up while another slashed through his bonds. Hector climbed to his feet, posture straight, pride and arrogance intact despite the weapons trained on him.

"She's lying," he said. "That's all these animals do, lie, cheat, steal, and murder."

"It was you who murdered and stole. You massacred an entire village, claimed our land for your own, tortured and raped, and then stole our children." Itzel's voice wasn't loud but the force of her passion gave it strength. And despite her being shorter than Caitlyn, some trick of the light made her seem as tall as Hector. "But I have long ago accepted that it is not me but God who will punish you, Colonel Alvarado. My concern must be for the living, for the few who survived your reign of terror."

Caitlyn was now certain that the ransom demand was a diversion. A ploy to distract Hector, waste his time, maybe even get him killed. Which meant Maria was still alive. Why? What did her kidnappers really want?

She pulled her well-creased map from her pocket and sank down to sit cross-legged on the cool stone, her abrupt movement drawing both Itzel and Hector's attention. "If you're done wasting time . . ."

The other two sat down across from her as Caitlyn spread the map onto the stone. One of Itzel's men brought a lantern, a clever inflatable device, clear, flexible plastic like a beach ball, with LED lights inside and a solar panel on top. "Show me where we are."

Itzel and Hector both moved, their fingers almost colliding at a point east of the coordinates Maria had been looking at. Caitlyn marked the location of the village. "Maria was tricked into believing she was helping an archeology expedition who had found a temple hidden in the jungle here."

Itzel nodded. Hector leaned closer to look at the last point—it was a little more than two miles into the mountains from where they were now.

"As far as I can tell, that's where Maria was headed." She didn't mention that there was no way to trace Maria if her captors had taken her elsewhere in the country or even beyond its borders. All Caitlyn could do was work the clues she had.

Hector leaned back from the map, his gaze distant.

"Maria was going there?" Itzel asked in a puzzled tone. "No one goes to the Temple of Chaac. There are certainly no archeologists working in the area."

"Someone must have known about it—enough to convince Maria, lead her right to it." And oh so cleverly, letting Maria do all the work of "discovering" the temple. Talk about the perfect bait.

Another reason to believe Maria was still alive. If her captors wanted her dead, a bullet to the head back in Florida would have been cheaper and easier. No, they wanted her healthy, couldn't risk her being injured, and they needed her here, in Guatemala.

But why? Caitlyn hated that she couldn't figure out the answer to that basic question. Understanding the kidnapper's motives would be the key to saving Maria, she was certain.

Itzel shook her head. "No. None of my people would speak of the temple or tell anyone in the outside world. It's a place of death."

"You mean some ancient superstition?"

"Not superstition. Real. The temple was built over a cenote. A natural cistern like this one," she gestured to the small lake beside them. "A bottomless pit leading to the underworld. Chaac was the rain god, necessary for crops, so in times of drought, sacrifices were made to him. Human sacrifices. Two years ago, after the earth-quake, part of the temple collapsed, temporarily dam-ming the river. It flooded everything upstream. All that remained at the bottom of the cenote at the temple were bones. Thousands upon thousands of bones."

Wouldn't make the temple a big tourist draw for Caitlyn, but it was the kind of thing that would bring in scientists and looters. "How can you be so sure that no one would go there?"

"No one would dare to disturb them—it would be like looting one of your cemeteries. That temple and those bones are sacred, to be protected at all costs."

Caitlyn conceded the point. But someone who knew of the temple had used it to lure Maria here. She pointed to the only other location on the map: Clínica Invierno. It was about four miles away from the temple in a straight line, twice that distance if you followed the river, a little farther going by road. "What about this place? It's a hospital? Is there anyone there from your past, Hector? Someone who would use Maria to hurt you?"

Hector remained stone-faced, not even glancing at the map or the two women. His posture was rigid, a soldier at attention despite his sitting on the ground. Itzel, in contrast, made a small gasping noise and her hand clutched at the cross around her neck. She also said nothing but kept shaking her head as if trying to deny the possibility.

"No," she finally choked out. "Why would he want her?" She turned to Hector. "Why would you let that monster have my daughter? Haven't you both taken enough from me?"

Hector stood and, ignoring the guards trailing him, stalked to the other side of the cavern, leaving Caitlyn sitting on the floor with Itzel. Itzel's demeanor had totally changed. Gone was the calm, confident leader. Instead she cowered, arms wrapped around her head, face down, not making eye contact, shivering.

Caitlyn touched her shoulder and Itzel flinched as if she'd struck a blow. "What's at the clinic, Itzel? Who are you afraid of?"

Finally she raised her head. She didn't look at Caitlyn; instead she stared at Hector. He wasn't doing anything—a fact that disturbed Caitlyn. He was a man of action, a man used to controlling every situation. Yet, here he was, held captive underground, far from his men, and he was content to simply stand and do nothing.

"I was young, seventeen, I knew nothing except my village, my family," Itzel began, her voice sounding higher pitched, as if she were channeling the seventeen-year-old she once was. "The war, it had been going on for decades, since my grandfather's time, it was simply the way we lived. We'd work the fields, try to grow enough to eat, we lived, we died, but we were together. We had a priest and this church, but we also had our old ways, what we could remember passed down father to son, mother to daughter. We didn't have much, but we were happy."

"And then what happened?" Caitlyn asked when Itzel went silent.

"The soldiers came. They'd been here before, taking what little we had, leaving our home in ruins. But we always managed to survive. When we saw them coming, we'd hide. Sometimes down here, sometimes in the jungle, sometimes in the temple. But then one day they came again. And this time my people couldn't run—they had the village surrounded. They claimed we were guerrillas and that our land no longer belonged to us."

She choked and looked away as she rubbed her eyes. Her hands came away wet. "I was gone, meeting a boy. He never came. I heard gunfire and ran back and I saw . . . I saw . . ."

She couldn't finish. Caitlyn took her hand and squeezed it. Itzel had gone deathly cold. "They killed your people?"

Itzel nodded. "It went on for two days. They killed the men quickly, but the women and children—" She inhaled sharply as if it hurt to breathe. "I had nowhere to run, so I hid in the temple. Then I saw the smoke. I came back. They were burning everything. Our crops, our homes, this church. They dragged the bodies onto their trucks and drove away. I waited until I thought it was safe, came out from the jungle to try to search for anyone still alive, and that's when they found me."

"They took you prisoner?"

"Yes. To Lake Invierno." She practically spat the words.

"The hospital."

"Back then it was—" She closed her eyes for a long moment and without opening them said, "—hell. The worst prison imaginable. Anyone sent there never returned, would disappear forever. I was there for two years when I became pregnant."

Caitlyn shuddered, imagining the horrors Itzel had suffered during that time. "And you had Maria."

Itzel opened her eyes again. Seemed calmer, more in control at the mention of Maria's name. "By the time she and her brother were born, the colonel and his men had already taken all the men and most of the women. We never found out where. They just . . . disappeared.

The pregnant women, they kept us there. Threatened to kill our children if we said anything to anyone from the outside. They turned it into a hospital. Claimed we were all insane. Simply because we dared to live on land that had belonged to our people for centuries. That is what makes you insane in this country."

"But you escaped?"

She looked at the ground, her palms flat against the stone as if drawing strength from it. "After Maria was delivered, I was bleeding and they couldn't stop it. I passed out and then woke up in the back of a truck surrounded by other women. All prisoners, too sick to have children or work in the fields or be of any use to the soldiers. I realized they were taking us to execution— we'd disappear just like the men had. I jumped off—we were in the jungle, not far from here. I made it home, hid here until some Lutheran missionaries traveling with the UN inspectors found me. They nursed me to health, took me with them. I lived and studied at their mission in Cobán—that's how I learned English."

"Then you came back."

"I had to see—I couldn't stop thinking about what happened to the others, to my babies. But no one was left. I was the only one who survived. Who escaped."

"You said Maria had a brother?"

"Yes. They were twins. His name was Michael."

"What happened to him?"

"Before they were born, they'd told me I had to chose between my babies and my silence. The Butcher of Invierno, the colonel's second-in-command, Dr. Otto Mendez Carrera. He took my son. And the colonel took Maria for his own. I never even had the chance to hold them. They were hostages to my silence. I couldn't follow Maria, but after I escaped, I returned here to care for my people and watch over my son as best I could."

She shuddered and broke down again, fighting the tears she tried to hold inside. "Now the Butcher has Maria as well." Her eyes squeezed shut as she crossed herself and her lips moved in prayer. "Please help me. We must save her from that monster."

CHAPTER TWENTY-EIGHT

Romero slowed the Land Rover. The headlights reflected off the gravel surface of the single-lane road. Jake couldn't see anything else through the darkness except more darkness.

"Why'd you stop?"

"This road—" Romero pointed to the narrow road they were on that curved to the left. "—goes to Lake Invierno and the clinic. Which, if you're serious about getting to the bottom of Hector's company and where it gets its tissues from, is where we should be heading."

Ah. Now he knew why Romero had been so forthcoming about the clinic. Diversionary tactics.

"No. We need to go to Cubiltzul and find Caitlyn."

"Here's the problem. That is the road to Cubiltzul." He pointed to the right. All Jake saw was jungle. There was maybe a car-sized clearing through it, but he couldn't be certain. Two gleaming white globes glinted in the headlights, then with startling speed they moved into the air, straight up, disappearing from sight. The vertical leap was too high for a jaguar—at least Jake hoped so. Maybe a monkey?

"Then we go right," Jake told Romero.

"Be serious. That road is barely passable in broad daylight. It's almost two in the morning—why don't we head to the clinic, charm our way into the doctor's good graces for the night, check things out there, and then we can head into the jungle in the morning if Caitlyn hasn't checked in by then."

Logical. Reasonable. If you didn't give a shit about the person left with a sociopathic former leader of a death squad in the middle of the jungle facing God knew what.

"Get out," Jake ordered. He raised his own weapon to back up his words.

"What, you're not going to leave me? Here? In the middle of nowhere?" Romero shrugged and raised his hands in surrender with an exaggerated sigh and shake of his head. "You're making a big mistake, man. You'll never make it a hundred yards into that jungle without me. And unless you speak Spanish and Achi, you won't be able to sweet-talk your way out of any shit you get into. I know the land, I know the people, I know the politics. You need me."

Jake leaned forward just far enough to yank Romero's 9 mm from his holster. "Get out. Now."

Romero's lips twisted into a sneer. He handed Jake the phone and opened the door, climbing down to the ground. Jake didn't relax his aim. "You're dead, Carver. One more corpse the jungle's gonna swallow, and no one will be the wiser."

Jake slid over to the driver's seat and followed Romero out of the car. He couldn't risk leaving Romero behind the wheel of what amounted to a two-ton weapon, but the CIA officer was right: Jake needed him.

"Hands on your head," Jake ordered. Romero complied, not resisting as Jake searched him. No more weapons. But the sat phone's antennae was broken off.

"Insurance," Romero said. "If you can't call for backup, you have to keep me alive."

Jake used Romero's belt to restrain the man's hands before shoving him back into the Land Rover's passenger seat. Jake got behind the wheel and took off to the right into the jungle.

He drove over the rough terrain as fast as he could without risking losing an axle, hitting a hidden boulder, or getting stuck in one of the many washed-out ditches filled with mud and water. Probably could have walked it faster, but he liked the relative safety of being inside the vehicle, despite being trapped with a rat like Romero.

The CIA officer remained silent, his expression bordering on bemused, as Jake drove.

Jake hoped Caitlyn was safe inside somewhere. The jungle came alive at night—and not in a good way. Shrieks and howls like someone getting skinned alive echoed from all sides, trees shook and swayed despite there being no wind, and strange glowing eyes caught the headlights' reflection, appearing and disappearing.

Oh yeah, this Kansas farm boy was definitely staying inside the truck.

Then the rains came. One second the jungle was still, quiet; the next he was caught in a tsunami of rain, lightning, thunder, and wind fierce enough to bend trees. He stopped the Land Rover and sat there as the rain and wind buffeted it, the noise drumming into his head so loud, his teeth ached.

"How long do these storms usually last?" He had to shout to be heard over the thunder. Romero merely shook his head and shrugged. Jake had to resist the urge to pound the smirk off the CIA officer's face.

Caitlyn didn't have time for this. As soon as the storm eased to a mere hurricane force—at least that's how it felt trapped inside the Land Rover—he inched forward again. The road was even more treacherous now. Who was he fooling? It wasn't a road; it was a freaking river trying to sweep him off the side of the mountain. He hated to admit it, but maybe Romero was right. They should have gone to the clinic. It wasn't going to do Caitlyn any good if he was stuck out here in the middle of nowhere.

As suddenly as the downpour started, it was gone. Water flooded around the wheels as they skidded and lurched forward through the mud. Twice the Land Rover's tires lost their grip, spinning out, the vehicle tilting ominously as if it was going to tumble down the mountain, but both times he managed to regain control. Barely.

According to the odometer, he had only about half a mile to go to reach the area where the helo went up in flames—if the map and Romero's coordinates were at all accurate. He was exhausted, his shoulders tight with tension, hands cramped with fatigue from wrestling the steering wheel.

The Land Rover shuddered around a steeply banked curve. Just as Jake straightened the vehicle, heading up a steep incline, there was a loud crash. The entire vehicle shook. Jake hit the brakes, thinking he hit something hidden by the mud and darkness. Romero rolled under the dash. Another noise came, this time more of a crack.

Jake dived for cover as more shots followed, rocking the Land Rover, shattering the windows. He tried to gauge where they came from as he drew his Glock and kept his body behind as many layers of steel as possible. The bullets kept coming, giving him no chance to get a fix on the shooter's location or even raise his head high enough to take aim.

He was surrounded. He changed tactics, opting for a strategic escape instead of confrontation. He slid across the seat and opened the door on the side of the vehicle facing downhill. As soon as he pushed the door open, a man leapt forward and yanked him out of the Land Rover, throwing him facedown into the mud.

The man shouted something in Spanish as the barrel of his AK-47 dug into the back of Jake's neck. Jake kept his hands clear and in sight. The man grabbed Jake's weapons and phone. Then he finally switched to English.

"Who the hell are you?"

Without the match's light, Maria was totally disoriented. It was hard to breathe with her heart pounding in her throat, blocking any attempt to swallow. Logic told her she must be breathing; all she could hear were her own gasps. Her fingers and toes and nose were tingling. Why was her nose tingling? The stray thought only increased her confusion and panic.

She lurched toward the door. Slipped in something wet on the floor and fell down onto the concrete. Blind, she reached up to steady herself on the gurney, only to plunge her hand onto something that felt like raw meat.

This time she couldn't stop her scream. It echoed shrill through the room. She propelled herself forward, slammed into the wall, felt a door hinge at her side, and finally got the door open. Escaping into the hall, lit only by the red EXIT sign a few feet away, she collapsed against the wall.

Running footsteps sounded above her. Someone had heard her scream. She pushed off from the wall and ran for the steel door below the EXIT sign. It opened onto a stairwell filled with noise from above: shrieks and screams that came close to inhuman. Mimicking her own terror. Cutting through the noise was a man's voice, shouting in anger.

Not that way. She took the steps leading down. As she ran, she scoured the walls and ceilings and spaces between the water and steam pipes that shared the stairwell. No place to hide.

Just one small crevice, one overlooked alcove, that's all she needed. She found nothing except institutional cement walls. At the next floor she pushed through the door. The hallway here had its lights on, that was a relief. Until she glanced down and saw the blood glistening on her hands. Terror shot through her. She clenched her hands, hard enough for her nails to bite into her flesh as she tried to throttle her fear.

The walls were white tile and the scent of disinfectant was stronger. Solid wooden doors lined the hallway and a stainless steel surgical table with instruments on it stood outside one of them. A medical unit? If so, there should be plenty of supply cabinets and cupboards where she could hide.

The first room she came to was an immaculate operating room, ready and waiting for a patient. No place to hide there. She ran to the next room and opened the door.

Another operating room. This one not so immaculate.

Blood covered the corpse on the operating table, the floor, and the man holding a human heart in his hands.

Maria wasn't sure what kind of noise she made, it was drowned out by the roaring that filled her head. She wanted to run, her lungs already working hard and fast as if she were running, but her feet wouldn't move.

The man was a few inches taller than she was, a little older, maybe in his thirties, Asian, lean, muscular, with hair that looked scraggly and needed a trim. For some reason, that hair bothered her. She couldn't pull her gaze from it. The way it almost brushed the collar of his surgical scrub top. The fact that it was loose and not tucked into a scrub cap.

Of course, he wasn't wearing a mask either. Or a surgical gown. But he did have bright purple surgical gloves on—the color clashed horribly with the brilliant crimson of the blood seeping from the heart.

And the corpse—another nightmare, no legs, this time a woman, belly skinned so the muscles were exposed, chest cavity cut down the middle and held open with a stainless steel ring clamped into place. At least her face was covered with a drape.

Maria took all this in before she realized the man's mouth was moving.

"Help me," he kept repeating, his voice breaking as if he were ready to cry. "Please, help me."

He dropped the heart onto the corpse and lunged forward. She reeled back, slamming into the door behind her, fumbling blindly for the handle.

"No, don't go. Please, you've got to help me," he begged. He took another step and there was a rattling noise.

That's when she noticed the chain fastened to his ankle, bolted to a large pipe running up the wall.

He held his hands up as if surrendering. "My name is Cho. Dr. Kevin Cho. I'm a cardio-thoracic fellow at McGill. In Toronto."

His voice came fast, as if he needed to get the information to her before it was too late and he lost his chance. "I was here volunteering for a medical mission sponsored by Dr. Carrera, but on my way home, he kidnapped me. That was a month ago."

He gestured to the chain. "I've tried everything,

even using the rib cutters and a bone saw. Is there anything outside, any tools? If not, could you go get help? Tell someone, anyone I'm here? Please, he's going to kill me."

Hector still stood immobile, but Caitlyn could tell by his rigid posture that he'd heard Itzel's story. "Why would the doctor take Maria, Hector? What does he want with her—or from you?"

He spun on his heel as if making a decision. "Coming here was a waste of time. A simple diversionary tactic. He knew if I thought the ransom demand came from her"—he nodded to Itzel—"that I would come here. Probably thought she'd kill me or that we'd kill each other."

"What is Dr. Carrera trying to divert you from, Hector?" Caitlyn persisted. "Why take Maria?"

He shook his head, his eyes narrowed as if seeing into the distance—or the past. "He's been irrational, unpredictable these past few months. Since Michael got sick—maybe even before . . ."

"You've stayed in contact with him?"

"He's my business partner. In BioRegen. I haven't seen him in two decades, but we talk on the phone. Lately he's been fixated on the past—our past. Talking about penance and redemption. As if Michael's illness was his fault and if he redeemed himself, he could save his son."

"My son," Itzel said, standing and facing Hector. He ignored her.

"How would he redeem himself for his war crimes?" Caitlyn asked, trying to assess how grave the danger to Maria was. Carrera sounded unstable at best. Maybe even psychotic.

"No one was ever able to prove any war crimes,"

Hector snapped. "She and the others who tried found nothing. We did nothing wrong except to defend our country from the likes of her."

Itzel didn't agree. "You murdered an entire village. Don't you dare call that nothing!"

"No one can prove it." His voice grew low, deadly.

"If the Butcher has both my children, if he harms either of them, then I will prove it to the world," Itzel threatened. "I know where the bodies went, Colonel. I know what you and the Butcher did with them."

Hector raised a hand as if to slap her, but Itzel's men stepped in, guns raised. Caitlyn rushed to disarm the situation. "Calm down. We all want to get Maria back unharmed."

To her surprise, Hector merely smiled and turned to face the wall, hands up, elbows wide. At first Caitlyn thought he was surrendering, but then realized he was pressing his hands against his ears.

He wasn't surrendering—he'd merely been stalling.

"Everyone, down!" she shouted.

Too late. The cavern filled with a flash of bright light and loud bangs that made the ground heave.

Women and children screamed as Hector's men swarmed inside, tossing a few more flash-bangs at the far reaches of the space, quickly dropping any resistance.

Hector grabbed a gun from one of the stunned guards, used it to head-butt the guard, and then shot the guard's partner. The man fell against Caitlyn, knocking her to the ground. Red flashes filled her eyes, she couldn't see, her ears rang with a high-pitched buzz, but Hector wasn't so affected.

Of course not. Bastard knew it was coming. He hadn't been standing there listening to Itzel or his conscience, he'd been listening via an earbud to his men prepare their entry.

She pushed the guard's body away and slowly sat up, her vision returning but balance still off. Hector's men quickly had the adults, including Itzel, in zip-tie restraints—the ones left alive. Children cried and ran to their parents, but one guard held them at bay, forcing them to back up until they huddled together on the edge of the cistern.

"Any problems?" Hector asked one of the men as he retrieved his sidearm and an AK-47 along with ammo.

The man shook his head. "No. But we found this one outside." He nodded to his comrades, who dragged in a man with long, sandy brown hair, his wrists and ankles in restraints. They threw him at Hector's feet.

He moaned and rolled over, exposing his face.

Caitlyn sprang to her feet, her hand going for her weapon—a weapon that wasn't there. "Carver!"

CHAPTER TWENTY-NINE

Maria should have run. She wanted to run. Everything that had happened since seeing Prescott killed collided in her brain, and nothing made sense. She couldn't trust anyone; she had to save herself.

The look on Kevin's face mirrored her own panic. Could she leave him behind? As she'd left Prescott?

Her fingers found the door handle and grabbed it, the cool metal jarring her from her stunned paralysis. She yanked the door open and fled back into the hallway.

To the right lay the stairwell and escape. To the left lay more rooms with who knew what horrors waiting behind their closed doors.

Her feet turned her body to the right. But she couldn't stop looking to the left.

Finally she ran. To the left. Searching for something to free Kevin. Then, together they could escape this nightmare.

The next room she came to was filled with large steel vats with thick gaskets, each plugged in to its own outlet. The room was freezing. When she brushed against a vat, cold burned through her clothing. Each barrel had a clipboard hanging near it. She glanced at one and cringed as she read it. Row after row, identifying donor tissue types of heart valves stored at 200 degrees below freezing.

She recognized the HLA tissue identification types from her parents' work. The histocompatibility antigen matches decreased the risk to recipients of organ and bone marrow transplants. One of the reasons behind BioRegen's success was that it had such a large tissue bank, it could provide tissues that had a high degree of HLA matching.

Her mother had explained to her that it wasn't important in most tissue use, but that anything to decrease tissue rejection would increase safety for the patient and allow BioRegen to charge more for its unique services. All Maria had wanted was some basic info for a biology project, and as usual her mother had reduced it into boring dollars and cents.

And they wondered why she wanted to study archeology.

Maria turned to the next vat. Umbilical cord stem cells. Another had tendons. A fourth, corneas. She remembered Prescott's body: they'd removed the eyes. For transplant?

What was Dr. Carrera doing here? Did he want Maria to blackmail her parents into helping him run some kind of black market tissue factory?

She spun in confusion, but forced herself to focus. There were no tools here that could help Kevin escape his bonds. Hugging herself against the cold, she left the tissue inventory behind and returned to the hall. The next room was a storage closet filled with surgical tools. She rummaged among the shelves, searching for something heavy enough to break Kevin's chain.

The best she came up with was a set of stainless steel chisels and an orthopedic mallet. She ran back to the operating room where Kevin was. He huddled on the floor as far away from the corpse as his chain would allow. He'd cleaned off most of the blood covering him, although red still streaked his blue surgical scrubs.

"You came back," he cried out when he saw her.

She couldn't help but smile. It felt weird, as if her face muscles had been stretched too tight, trying to hold back her panic. As terrified as she was, being able to help him, to do something—anything—to take control of the situation made her feel better.

"Of course I came back." She showed him the tools she'd found. "Will these work?"

A wide pair of handcuffs were fastened around his ankle and through the one of the chain's links. The other end of the chain was secured by a padlock. They decided the best spot to use the chisel was on the link connected to the cuffs.

Maria's hands shook so badly that with three tries, she still couldn't hit the chisel. Kevin took over from her, his steady surgeon hands able to hold the chisel in place while Maria stabilized the chain.

Kevin aimed the chisel at the joint in the chain link, and after a few hard blows a chink between the two ends of metal appeared. Maria looked up at him, feeling hopeful. But with the next blow the chisel cracked down the center, the hammer bouncing off the floor as Maria ducked flying metal.

"Are you okay?" Kevin asked, taking her hand in his. A small shard of metal stuck out from the flesh between her thumb and index finger. Funny, she didn't feel it until he drew her attention to it. "Hold still, let me."

He gently eased the shard out. It hadn't gone very deep and there was almost no bleeding, but still he frowned over the small puncture. "Can't let that get infected. We need to flush it out."

Kevin climbed to his feet and reached a hand out to Maria. She took it, letting him do the work of leveraging her upright, her legs suddenly feeling wobbly. He put his arm around her waist and led her to the scrub sink.

"Why were you taking her heart out?" Maria nodded over his shoulder to the corpse on the table.

"I wasn't taking it out, I was putting it in. Carrera has me practicing doing a heart transplant with only a rudimentary team—somehow he's gotten all the equipment, but the donor hearts he keeps giving me look like they were harvested by a gorilla and I can't do both the harvest and the transplant myself, not without losing precious time and cardiac viability."

"Wait. He kept you here to give Michael a heart transplant? Why does he need to keep you prisoner for that? Why not just fly Michael to a hospital?"

His hands soaped hers, his touch warm and comforting as he worked. "First he had me place the LVAD to buy time. But now with the LVAD working as well as it is, Michael won't be on the top of the transplant list. Plus, he has a rare HLA type. Usually we don't worry too much with cardiac transplants—there used to be no time to get HLA results before we needed to commit. But now we're realizing that it can make a big difference in organ rejection and with the newer tests—" He stopped himself, looked down at her. "You realize this is the first semi-normal conversation I've had in a month? I feel like I've fallen into some terrible B movie horror film. *Psycho* meets *The Texas Chain Saw Massacre*."

"You think he's crazy? He's just trying to save his son." She wasn't defending Dr. Carrera as much as she was Michael. She didn't want to see him die. Of course, that didn't give his father the right to murder people.

"The man is nuts. More than that, he has some kind of neurodegenerative disease. Huntington's, I'd guess, given the psychotic and delusional tendencies mixed with his muscular symptoms."

Michael had mentioned the doctor's illness growing worse—obviously whatever disease he suffered from had affected his mind as well as his body. "Do you think he'd really kill us?" she whispered.

"We know too much. Once I save Michael, I'm toast." He rested his hands on her shoulders and looked down at her. "But why does he want you?"

Hector's men shoved Caitlyn back from Carver, sending her sprawling until she hit the cavern wall.

"He's a federal agent. Release him," she ordered in her best command voice. She knew it was probably fruitless—it was clear Hector had his own agenda—but it was worth a try.

"Did you bring the charges?" Hector asked one of his men.

"*Sí.* What about the *federales*?"

Hector was halfway to the exit. He glanced over his shoulder at Caitlyn and shook his head. "I told you not to get involved."

The guards covered his exit; then they left as well. Caitlyn was torn between running after them—what good would that do, Hector would never listen to her anyway—and freeing Carver and the others. She went to Carver and, using a rough-edged carving knife from near where the women had been cooking, sawed through his ankle ties.

She'd just finished cutting him free when a tremendous boom shook the ground. And the ceiling. And the cistern. Chunks of rocks fell from the ceiling, water splashed over the side of the cistern, people screamed and cried out, the adults calling for the children who were dangerously close to the water. Smoke and dust clouded the air.

Caitlyn ran to the children, scooping up the smallest ones and covering them with her body as a second blast, this one even louder, rocked the ground. The sound of stones crashing shook the air, followed by a wave of compressed hot air that buffeted her like a tornado.

Her ears filled with pressure, then popped painfully, a small trickle of fluid warm against her skin on one side of her neck. The children were crying, she could tell from the way their bodies shook, but she couldn't hear them. She swallowed, it tasted of dust, coughed and choked on the thick air.

Stunned, she finally stood and looked around. The floor felt tilted beneath her feet, and she wasn't sure if that was reality or because her equilibrium was so skewed. She staggered across the space, glad to see that no one had been hit by any falling debris and everyone seemed okay. Jake had cut Itzel free. Together they worked to release the other adults from their restraints.

Caitlyn stumbled up the steps leading to the surface. It was dark here, all the candles and lanterns destroyed. She felt her way up one step, two, tripped on the third that was cracked, the fourth was filled with chunks of debris, and the fifth . . . the fifth was gone. As was the opening above it. Half the mountainside and what was left of the church had fallen to now occupy the space.

They were sealed in.

CHAPTER THIRTY

"I don't know why Carrera wants you here," Kevin said, holding Maria's hands in his and looking into her eyes straight on, as if they weren't standing in a den of horrors with a mutilated corpse beside them. He looked at her as if she was more important than the danger they faced or his own freedom. Maria felt a warmth creep up her throat but couldn't look away. "But whatever the reason, we need to get you out of here. Now. Before the guard comes to check on me."

"No. I can't leave you."

"You must. Breaking me free will take too long. Someone has to get help, tell the authorities what's going on here. These corpses he's bringing me to practice on, they're all women, all have suffered severe mutilations. The man is mad, a serial killer. Maria, you need to get out of here."

"We'll try again with your chain. The link opened the tiniest bit before the chisel broke—"

"The strongest chisel we have. I can keep trying with the smaller ones you found, but I'll need to do it slowly, it might take time. Too much time for you to stay here, in danger."

She hesitated, glancing from him to the door to the thick links of chain dragging on the floor, and finally back to him. His eyes were bloodshot with fatigue, stray flecks of blood stained his forehead, but she'd never seen a man more handsome. That wasn't why she made her decision. After all the running and panic of the past few days, for the first time, she knew the right thing to do.

"No. I'm staying. I'm not leaving without you."

She dried her hands, grabbed the next size of chisel, and they resumed work. Between hammer strokes, he kept arguing and she kept ignoring him. After all, it wasn't like he could stop her from staying. If they heard anyone coming, she'd hide behind the machine he told her was the heart-lung bypass pump. It was big enough that as long as no one moved it, it would conceal her from view.

The hammer blows rang through the room as they found their rhythm. He told her about Toronto and his work there, asked her about her studies. He seemed truly interested when she told him about discovering the temple and how the jungle had consumed so many important sites like the city of El Mirador, thought for generations to simply be a collection of forested hills until explorers discovered beneath the jungle growth a pyramid larger than any in Egypt.

He had his arm raised to swing the hammer when they heard footsteps. Close, very close. Maria gathered the tools and dashed for cover behind the bypass machine. Too late she realized that she'd left a trail of footsteps crisscrossing the corpse's blood. They had dried already, there was no way to erase them, and they clearly didn't belong to Kevin. Especially not the ones leading in and out of the room.

Kevin saw them as well. They both stood, scrambling to find a sheet to throw over the footprints. Too late. The door swung open.

It was Michael. He stood wide-eyed in the doorway, staring at first the corpse, then Kevin, and finally Maria. "Dr. Cho—I don't understand—" Then he saw the chain. "Oh my God, he's gone too far. I had no idea." He glanced over his shoulder down the hall and then entered and closed the door behind him. "Maria, are you okay?"

"I'm fine. But what the hell is your father doing?"

Michael didn't answer right away. Instead he ran to the pipe with the large padlock holding the chain in place. "I stole his keys. Help me find the right one. We have to hurry. Pablo will be here anytime now."

Maria didn't bother to ask who Pablo was—obviously someone she'd rather not meet. As Michael fumbled through the large ring of keys, he explained, "I had no idea he kept you, Dr. Cho. I never asked for any of this. And Maria—"

Kevin interrupted him. "She needs to go. Now. You and I can take care of this."

Maria didn't want to leave them—there was safety in numbers. "Michael, are you okay? Your heart—"

"I'm fine."

"With the LVAD, you should be able to do almost anything you want," Kevin said. "As long as the pump is connected to the batteries and you keep them charged."

Michael patted his shirt. Maria realized it was different from the one he'd worn earlier. This one was like a T-shirt but with two pockets sewn below the armpits. Both bulged with the outline of a battery and had wires connecting them to the small bag across his chest that contained the LVAD pump. "I think my father—the doctor—wanted me to stay in the house, so they kept me in the chair with its power supply for the LVAD. But I realized that if I could use the battery for short trips out of the chair, there was no reason I couldn't go farther. And I feel better than I have in months. Thanks to you, Dr. Cho."

"Get us the hell out of here, and I'll consider that thanks enough."

Maria moved to keep an eye on the door. "How long will your batteries last, Michael?"

"A few hours, give or take," Kevin answered.

"Then you can come with us."

Michael didn't answer. Instead he straightened, the open lock in his hands. "Got it."

Kevin unraveled the chain and slung it between his hands since they couldn't do anything about the cuff around his ankle. At least not anytime soon. "Let's get out of here."

Maria held the door for them. Kevin led even though Michael was more familiar with the floor plan. It just felt right to have him lead them. Maybe because he had the confidence of a surgeon or because he was older or because he had the length of chain to use as a weapon. Their only other weapons were the hammer and chisels that Maria still carried. She offered one of the chisels to Michael. He took it but held it tentatively, like it was a piece of charcoal to sketch with. She slid the remaining chisel into her jacket pocket and hefted the hammer.

"Which way?" Kevin whispered after they climbed up to the first floor and reached the door to the corridor where Maria had found Prescott's body.

Before Michael could answer, footsteps came from above. *"Alto!"* a man shouted. Maria glanced up. He held a machine gun on them. He climbed down the stairs and she saw his face.

A scar ran down the right side. It was the man who had killed Prescott.

Kevin raised the chain, but the stair landing was too cramped, he couldn't twirl it to use as a weapon, and the man had the high ground. Then the door to the corridor opened and Dr. Carrera appeared. Two men behind him raised their rifles, aiming at Maria and Kevin.

"Don't shoot," he ordered. "We need them alive."

CHAPTER THIRTY-ONE

"Is everyone all right?" Caitlyn asked as she came back down the steps, her voice much louder than it needed to be. Jake rubbed his aching head and wondered why she was asking him; he'd just gotten to this party and quite frankly he wasn't getting his money's worth. He didn't bother voicing the joke out loud. They had more important things to attend to.

What amazed him was how quickly the civilians responded. As if bombs and guns and hiding in caves were the norm.

The children had all been gathered together by one of the younger women while the others tended to the wounded. Yes, there were tears and frightened looks in the direction of the cave-in, but no hysteria. Just determination. They weren't going to let Alvarado beat them.

Caitlyn ran her hands through her short hair, clearing it of dust and debris. She seemed fine, just a few small cuts on her forehead. He followed her, wanting to check her out more thoroughly, but she waved him off as she dug her travel pack from the rubble.

"Itzel," she introduced him to the woman who was

obviously the group's leader. "This is Jake Carver with the FBI. He's here—Well, actually, Carver"—she looked up, a grin slicing through the dirt and dried blood on her face—"why the hell are you here? Not looking for another three-way, are you?"

And that's when Jake knew everything was going to be all right. He grinned right back at her, "You offering?"

Caitlyn winked, then turned serious again. "Sorry about the welcoming committee." She gestured to the cave in.

Jake shrugged and began collecting weapons and ammo and searching for anything that might help. A sat phone, radio, bazooka . . .

Caitlyn rummaged through her travel pack and found a small med kit that she handed off to Itzel. Jake returned her two Glocks and her cell phone, not that it'd be any good in here. He kept a revolver and an AK-47 for himself—their previous owners wouldn't be missing them.

He made sure Itzel was out of hearing range—without knowing the players, he didn't trust anyone except Caitlyn. "I came because it turns out Hector has a business partner, a Dr. Carrera, who's been helping him harvest body parts from prisoners here and selling them in the United States." There was more, but that was the main gist—not that his intel would help them escape. "Oh, and, that CIA guy, Romero. Definitely playing both sides."

"You mean his own side," she said. Should have known she'd see through Romero's bull. She looked past Jake. The others had triage and first aid well in hand.

"Is there another way out?" Caitlyn asked the woman, Itzel.

"There's a way through the caves, down the river. But it's dangerous."

"Show us."

Itzel handed them each one of the lightweight inflatable LED lanterns and led them around the small lake—well? Pond? Jake wasn't sure, the thing looked bottomless with its strange milky green water, and was a good twenty feet in diameter—and then back through a narrow passage leading deeper beneath the mountain.

"I never should have told him I have proof of his atrocities," she said. "If I'd kept quiet, he might have let us go."

"No," Caitlyn told her. "He wouldn't have. He can't afford to leave any witnesses."

"What kind of proof do you have?" Jake asked.

"After the earthquake a few years ago, part of the temple collapsed and flooded. It's a temple dedicated to Chaac, the rain god, and contains a cenote like ours." She nodded over her shoulder at the well behind them. "It must have developed a fissure, allowing it to drain. Once the water receded, we found shards of bones. At first we thought they belonged to our ancestors, human sacrifices to Chaac, but then we found modern-day clothing. Remnants of prison uniforms, women's skirts, shoes."

She broke off and pressed one hand against the cold stone wall, as if catching her balance, but the lantern light glinted off tears on her face. "They weren't all from twenty years ago, either. Some of the body parts still had flesh on them." She turned to them. "What did they do to them? The way they were butchered—"

Jake explained about what he'd found in D.C. and what Romero told him about the clinic. Itzel grew quiet, her fingers clutching her cross so tight, he was surprised she hadn't yanked the chain off.

"Maybe Romero was exaggerating," he finished. "Trying to distract me from coming here."

She shook her head. "There have been stories. But what could I do? I had Michael to worry about and my people—" She looked behind them to where they'd left the others. "I should have done more. Should have fought back. Found a way to stop them."

"It's not your fault, Itzel," Caitlyn said, laying a hand on the older woman's arm. "Right now we need to concentrate on getting out of here. Getting help. And finding Maria."

They continued through the narrow passage. Jake ducked his head, but still ended up banging it against the low-hanging rocks. The sound of running water came from below. They came out on a narrow cliff above another pool of water, this one fed by an underground stream that disappeared into the rock wall, tunneling beneath the mountain.

"Follow the current. You'll come out at some natural pools. We use them for fishing and bathing. There are several canoes there, take one downriver—there's a tall waterfall at the entrance to the lake, but if you get out on the north side of the river, there's a path that will lead you down the rest of the way to the clinic." Itzel paused, looked them each in the eye, reminding Jake of his third-grade teacher. She could look at you like that, know exactly who'd been naughty and who'd been nice— only much more scary than Santa Claus.

Last place Jake wanted to look was all that water rushing beneath the rocks, into absolute darkness, an entire mountain on top. He hated water. Had ever since he was a kid and his brothers threw him into the pond on their farm and he almost drowned. How the hell was he going to make it down a river and through a mountain?

Didn't matter. He would. He had to. He distracted himself by examining the cavern walls. The rocks were stained in a straight horizontal line almost at the top of the chamber. A water line.

"After the earthquake this cavern flooded," Itzel said as Jake reached over his head to touch the high-water line. "But over time the river has stabilized back to its previous levels."

Caitlyn bent down and tested the water temperature. "We just need to swim through there? Sounds easy enough."

Of course it did—to her. She'd spent her college vacations as a white-water rafting guide in West Virginia. Hell, plunging into an unknown underground river that traveled beneath a mountain was her idea of fun.

"Will you all be safe here?" Jake asked. What he really wanted to ask was, Isn't there another way out? But he didn't.

"Yes. There's fresh air, we have food, enough for a few days. If we need to, the adults can follow this way out, but the children—"

"Don't worry, Itzel," Caitlyn reassured her. "We'll bring back help before then."

Jake turned away from his examination of the cavern walls as he did the math. Something wasn't adding up here. "You said the temple had a partial collapse during the earthquake. That was when you found the bones and clothing? Did you find those here?"

"No. On the mountain below the temple."

"Do you still have them?" Caitlyn asked as they moved back into the chamber below the church. "We could use them as evidence."

Jake shook his head at her; she was missing his point. He was distracted as she went through her pack, pulling out anything they could use for the journey, shoving it into her jacket pockets. Passport, a knife, cell, wallet. She emptied her clothing from the plastic bags she had it packed in.

He'd forgotten about her obsession with water-tight storage—ever since she'd flown to Toledo last month and had been stranded in the sleet and rain waiting for a taxi that never showed. He'd teased her mercilessly every time she packed for a trip—but now her obsession might be their salvation, he realized.

She blew air into each of the plastic bags before sealing them, providing a cushion around the guns. Then she pulled out a plastic laundry bag, put the smaller bags inside, and began to blow it up like a balloon. When she finished, she'd turned the water-tight storage into a makeshift flotation device. He shook his head in amazement. God, he loved the way she thought.

"We returned the remains to the temple," Itzel answered. "With the others. I can take you there. After we save my people and Maria."

She still didn't realize the flaw in their plan. "Not if Alvarado gets there first," he told her.

"But surely he's gone after Maria?" Itzel asked. "He wouldn't abandon his daughter, adopted or not. He'll save her, right?"

Caitlyn and Jake exchanged a glance without answering.

Jake finally broke the bad news to Itzel. "He can't let the evidence of his genocide remain—not if Carrera is planning to tell the world about their crimes."

Itzel's eyes went wide. "You think the colonel will sacrifice Maria and go to destroy the temple instead."

"Doesn't matter," Caitlyn said firmly. She bent over, tucking her pant legs into her boots and lacing them tight. "We can't waste time chasing Hector. We have to save Maria, bring help back here."

"No. It's not about stopping him from destroying evidence," Jake explained. Both women looked at him with puzzled frowns. "If he blows the temple, it will block the river." He gestured above his head to where there was another high-water mark from the previous flood.

Caitlyn followed his gaze, her face growing pale, lips tightening. Then she turned to look at the families gathered by the cistern. Her eyes widened as she realized there was no high ground that would save them.

"This entire cavern will flood." She stared at Jake. "We have to stop him."

He nodded. "And we have to stop Carrera."

"No choice. Once we make it out, we need to split up."

He did not like the idea, but she was right. There was only so much ground they could cover, and with lives at stake . . . To hell with anyone else. He grabbed her by the waist, bringing her to him, pressing his lips against hers and not giving a damn about what anyone watching thought.

"I don't want to let you go," he murmured.

He loved the blush that colored her freckles and the way her eyes had lost their focus. Loved that he could do that to her—make her lose control.

Not for long. She pressed her palms against either side of his face and kissed him hard. "I'm not that easy to get rid of. Wanna bet I make it back before you?"

"It's a bet."

When she was young, Caitlyn had loved water. She and her dad fishing in the river below their home in North Carolina. Rafting the New River Gorge during summers off school.

All that changed last year when a serial killer tried

to drown her. He'd failed, but the man with her had died, sacrificed himself to save her.

As she pulled away from Carver, trying to keep her worry from her face, all she could think of was his face, floating below her in the dark water, as the current yanked her away. She had to keep Carver alive.

Her oath to protect and serve meant Maria and the lives of Itzel's people should take precedence over either her or Carver. In the past, she'd always put that oath and the lives of civilians first. But now, Lord help her, she knew in her heart that she could not bear to let another man die to save her. Not Carver.

She didn't care what it took. He was making it out of here alive. If that meant she was going to rot in hell, so be it. Because the only way she'd let any harm come to him—or Itzel's people—would be if she were dead.

They grabbed their gear and followed Itzel back into the rear cavern. Caitlyn took out her map of the area around the temple, and Itzel marked the best path for Carver as well as several dangerous areas where the earthquake had left sinkholes.

Caitlyn handed Carver the improvised flotation device she'd made with the bags filled with air as she zippered the whole thing inside her travel pack. "Strap it onto your chest," she told him. "It will help stabilize you if the current gets rough."

"What about you?"

"You weigh more than I do. Plus, my jacket will give me some buoyancy." She snugged the elastic cords at her wrists and waist as tight as they would go and zipped the jacket tight. She'd sealed her smaller Glock along with her personal items into the inside pocket. Her knife she kept in an outside pocket, where it would be handy.

Itzel handed them each one of the inflatable LED

lanterns. Caitlyn secured hers with a length of cording to the zipper pull on her jacket pocket so she wouldn't have to worry about dropping it.

Carver made do with tying his to his upper arm, where it would be out of his way. As he glanced into the water, she was surprised to see fear flit across his face. By the time he looked up at her, it was buried— the man was a consummate actor.

She hugged Itzel. "We'll get Maria," she promised, hoping it wasn't a lie.

"Stay safe," Itzel said. Then she hesitated. "Maybe I should go with you."

"No, you stay," Carver said. "Your people need you." With one last grimace at the water below them, he jumped in, Caitlyn right behind.

She swam to take the lead. The current quickly swept them from the pool and into the tunnel leading under the mountain. "Keep your feet up in front of you," she told him, shouting over the roar of the white water. "Don't try to walk until it slows."

He flailed a bit at first but finally leaned back and stopped struggling against the current. Their lights were bright beacons reflecting from the water and the limestone walls surrounding them. Caitlyn's attention was divided between anticipating obstacles and navigating their route ahead, and keeping track of Carver behind her.

The roar of white water thundered ahead of them. Caitlyn guided them to a boulder small enough that they could climb out of the water. "Let me try to see how big these rapids are."

"We don't have much time," he reminded her. No need. She was quite aware that at any moment they might be engulfed by floodwaters backing up into the caverns if the temple collapsed and dammed the river.

But until that happened, there was nothing to do but keep moving forward.

She crawled over the boulder, holding her lantern ahead of her. The river cascaded through a narrow crevice, barely three feet high—and only a third of that not filled with water.

There was no way to tell how far a drop it made or if there would be any room with air to breathe on the other side. Itzel had said the route was passable, but who knew what level the river had been at when her people used it before. Too many variables, too few answers, and no time.

She crawled back to Carver. "From the sound of it, there's a waterfall, but I'm not sure how high it is. Or how deep the water is below it—we could be crashing through to rocks. And I can't see if the water fills the passage or if there's room to breathe."

He swallowed hard but gave her a grin. "Why don't I go first? No reason you should hog all the fun."

Before she could stop him, he rolled off the boulder, into the water, and the current swept him into the darkness.

CHAPTER THIRTY-TWO

Dr. Carrera gestured, and the two men with him grabbed Kevin while the man with the scar rammed his gun barrel into Maria's back and took her arm.

"Stop it," Michael cried out. "You can't do this. I won't let you."

"Now, Michael," Dr. Carrera said in a voice more appropriate for scolding a toddler, "you need to listen to me. I know what I'm doing. Pablo, take Maria upstairs. She can wait in the isolation ward until we're ready for her."

The man with the scar prodded Maria up the stairs. She reluctantly climbed the first two steps, then looked back over her shoulder.

"Dr. Cho, let's get you back to the OR. I'd like you to do at least one more practice run before we begin. We can't afford any mistakes."

Kevin stood straight, glaring at Dr. Carrera. "I don't make mistakes. But you have. This will never work—you don't have the skills to perform the harvest."

"You let me worry about that," Dr. Carrera snapped.

"Let them go," Michael said. He raised his shirt and grabbed hold of the thick tubing running out from his belly. "Let them go now or I'll pull the LVAD."

The doctor tilted his head and shook it at Michael. "Now, now, Michael. I'm sure you don't want anything to happen to your sister."

Maria couldn't help her cry of pain as Pablo grabbed her hair and yanked her back toward him, his gun jabbing her between the ribs. He twisted his fist in her hair so that she had to contort her body, trying to relieve the pressure.

"No, stop!" Michael shouted. "Don't hurt her."

"That's better," Dr. Carrera said. The guards dragged Kevin down the steps back to the basement with its operating rooms while Pablo pushed Maria up. She craned her head to look down and met Kevin's eyes. Neither of them said anything—what could they say?

As they turned the corner on the landing, she saw Helda and Dr. Carrera escorting Michael through the door and into the main corridor. He looked terrified and called out, "I'm sorry, Maria."

Then he was gone. But a puzzle still remained. Had Dr. Carrera really said that she was Michael's sister? How could that be possible?

The questions helped to distract her from the sights awaiting her when they reached the third floor and Pablo unlocked a solid metal door and shoved her through it. The hallway was lined with doors more like prison doors than hospital ones: metal with small windows and an open slot in the middle. Behind the windows were women: all ages, mostly Maya, eyes wide with fear or insanity, she wasn't sure.

At the sight of Maria, howls and shrieks filled the air as if the patients were greeting her with their own language. Pablo hustled her past them quickly, but she caught glimpses of women missing a leg, some with eye patches, one lying on a cot facedown with her shirt pulled up, exposing angry red tissue on her back where her skin had been peeled off.

She'd been able to keep her panic under control while she was with Kevin, but the sight of these women, in pain, insane—or driven there by their captivity and the horrors they'd suffered—brought her own terror back in a wave that threatened to swamp her. She staggered but Pablo caught her. Before she could find her balance again, he threw her inside a cell. The door clanged shut behind him, and she was alone except for the anguished cries of her fellow captives.

The room had a cot with a thin mattress, no sheets or pillows, a sink and a toilet, and a window with ornate bars high on the outside wall. That was it. Except for a bloody handprint planted to the side of the door as if someone had been fighting to stay inside the cell and had to be dragged out.

Maria's breath came in short quick gasps that left her dizzy. She sank onto the bed, the springs groaning under her weight, and gave in to tears. What she wouldn't give to be back home in her boring life with her boring parents and their boring routines. Or on the booze cruise, watching drunken frat boys hit on her friends.

Her dream of exploring, finding adventure . . . what an idiot to think she could ever have a life like that. Way it looked now, this cell might be the last place she saw.

Pity drowned her with tears she couldn't stop. Her thoughts traveled back through the past few days, to the fun conversations she'd shared with Prescott—poor Prescott!—and the way he'd flirted with her, made her feel so smart and pretty and special. Michael had made her feel the same way—only not giddy like she wanted to get closer to him romantically, like she'd felt about Prescott, more as if he somehow knew and understood her.

Sister, the doctor had said. Michael's sister.

And earlier, Michael had said the doctor wasn't really his father.

She remembered the paper he'd given her when he warned her to run. She pulled it from her pocket and unfolded it. It was a printout from a lab test with her name on it. And Michael's.

She recognized the HLA tissue typing that her parents used at BioRegen. It wasn't mandatory, but they'd found that closer matches helped to prevent complications and so offered it as part of their "premier concierge" service.

Why would the doctor have tissue-typed her and Michael? And why did they match? On almost every marker.

She sank back, her fingers tracing the test results. Only close relatives had matches that close. Like brother and sister.

It didn't feel right—except it did. If her parents weren't her biological parents, it would explain so very much. Like why she didn't look like either of them or possess any of their grace and charm and poise.

The more she thought about it, the more it made sense. But then she kept thinking and looking at the HLA typing. Kevin had said Michael had a rare HLA typing. Yet she was a match.

A rush of cold surged out from her heart all the way down to her fingers and toes as the pieces clicked together. She ran for the door, stood on tiptoe to look through the tiny slit of a window, hoping to see someone who could help her, someone who would listen.

There was no one except the twisted grimace of the

wide-eyed woman in the cell across from her. Maria spun in a circle, not knowing what to do, just knowing that she couldn't just sit here and let it happen, let Dr. Carrera take her.

Because if Michael was her brother . . . and Kevin was a cardiac surgeon . . . and Dr. Carrera had him prepping for a transplant . . . then he'd want the perfect donor to save Michael's life.

Maria.

CHAPTER THIRTY-THREE

The cold water swept Jake into the darkness of the tunnel leading beneath the mountain. This was such a huge mistake, he thought as the current banged him from one wall to the other. The LED lantern was too bright to be helpful, creating a blinding whiteout of glare as it reflected from the water.

The water. Greedy bitch. It tugged and yanked and pulled him in all directions. Time blurred as he spun, smothered by water, then gasping, then drowning once again. Thanks to Caitlyn's crazy freezer-bag flotation system, he always ended face up.

Somewhere in the middle of the tunnel—he'd lost all sense of time or distance—the plastic protecting the LED lights ruptured. A few seconds later, the lights fizzled and died. Suddenly he went from an out-of-body, bright-light, tunnel experience to deep, cold, bleak, blackness.

His vision useless, he focused on his hearing. Not much help. All he could make out was a rushing and pounding that could just as easily have been his heart thundering as the water churned around him. Flailing, he fought to gain purchase against the wall—or floor, he no longer was totally certain which way was up.

The current grew stronger. Now when he was tossed above the surface, his hands scraped the tunnel ceiling mere inches from his face. Then he was spun around again, panic seizing him, and with good reason—this time when his hands struck rock, there was no air. Not in any direction.

He couldn't reach the bottom, couldn't find a space in the darkness where there might be air, couldn't fight the current and go back.

A stray thought lanced through his terror. He had to make it through—if only to shout a warning back to Caitlyn. He had to live that long—and he wouldn't if he used up all his oxygen flailing about like a idiot.

Calm overtook him. He forced his body to relax and let the current speed him through the tunnel. The bags strapped to his chest helped, they kept him face up so he could navigate with his palms pressed up, searching for any air pockets.

As he held his breath, his chest burning for relief, the pounding rush filling his brain increased to a crescendo. This was it. He couldn't hold on any longer. He was going to have to take a breath. . . . No, no, no. Stubbornly, he overrode all his primitive instincts. Kept his mouth closed tight, refusing to release the pressure that had grown unbearable in his chest.

The thundering noise grew and grew. Then, suddenly, he was flying through the darkness.

He gulped in surprise, arms and legs not sure which way was up; then he plunged back into cold, black water. Hit bottom and bounced back. The current wasn't so strong here, and there was the faintest light coming from somewhere above, creating gray on black on gray shadows. He kicked over to a boulder and pulled himself out of the water, flopping onto his back like a dead fish.

Not quite dead. The waterfall created enough ozone that he felt giddy as he hauled in a few deep breaths. Or maybe it was simply the joy of being able to taste oxygen again.

He sat up, ready to call out a warning to Caitlyn, but too late. A bright streak of light pierced the darkness above the waterfall, and then she was catapulted into the air beyond it, just as he had been. It was a lot more fun watching than living through it—maybe because she didn't look panicked at all, instead she pulled her legs together, arms to her sides, and actually managed to appear graceful as she knifed into the pool of water below the falls.

When she popped back onto the surface, she let out a whoop of pure, unadulterated joy. "Helluva ride," she called to him. "You okay?"

He just laughed and shook his head at her. "I am now."

She climbed up beside him. "Why didn't you let me go first?"

Pride didn't let him tell her the truth—that he didn't want to risk her seeing him panic. "Didn't want to slow you down. Besides, why should you have all the fun?"

She stood and used her lantern to explore the cavern. "That light is coming from up ahead—I think I see the path out."

Wearily he got to his feet, almost slipping on the wet rocks, but she reached a hand and steadied him. A lone lizard scuttled on the vertical rock face, proof that life could exist even here in this godforsaken hellhole— and he meant that literally. He could see why the Maya thought these caverns led straight to the underworld.

"Ladies first," he said with a gallant wave of his hand.

* * *

It was painfully obvious that Carver wasn't comfortable in the water. In fact, Caitlyn swore she'd glimpsed fear on his face, yet he'd put the lives of Itzel and her people first. As she held her hand out to him and they scrambled over the slick rock path together, she wished there were a way to let him know how proud she was to know a man like him.

But all she seemed to manage—all they either seemed to manage—was silly gallows humor. No matter. As daylight grew stronger and their path clearer, she knew he was going to get out of these caves alive. After that, it had to get easier.

She hoped.

They emerged onto a flat ledge, the silvery glint of dawn making the calm pool of water at their feet appear like a brilliant emerald. Dragonflies darted across the water, giving it a faceted appearance as their movement reflected in its still surface. Fish leapt and eagerly caught the insects, silver and gold scales like glitter.

"Paradise," she sighed, wishing they had time to enjoy the beautiful setting. But of course, there was none.

As they unpacked their weapons, Carver said, "Can't help but notice, there's no smell of napalm in the morning—or C-4."

"Hector would have reached the temple hours ago. What's he waiting for?"

"Maybe he went after Maria? The guy did come all the way here to find her. With a bounty on his head, no less. Seems like Hector's worth more dead than alive here in Guatemala."

"He wants it all."

"What do you mean?"

"I mean it's all about his pride. He and his wife wanting Maria back, upset that she'd disobeyed them and snuck off the ship, him making a preemptive strike against the people he thought were holding her hostage. He can't stand to lose."

"You think he has gone after Maria. And after he gets her, then he'll come back to destroy the temple?"

"And bury the evidence forever. Just like he thinks he's buried us and Itzel's people."

Jake shoved a magazine into his AK-47 and stood. "That wasn't even his first mistake. Guy doesn't stand a chance."

He reached his hand down to her and she let him pull her to her feet. Their kiss was quick but heated.

"So," she asked, hating that she had to let him go without her, "what was his first mistake?"

Carver brushed his hand against her check as if embedding its curve into his memory. "He pissed you off. I heard it on the phone that first night. Knew you'd never give up. Not until you save the girl."

Another quick kiss and he was gone, vanished into the jungle, heading for the temple. There was no time for regrets. Caitlyn climbed over the rocks until she reached the edge of the pool of water. The rocks formed a narrow gorge here—any increase in water flow in either direction, and the water would have no place to go but back into the mountain, flooding the underground chambers.

If she got to Hector first, Carver might not have anything to worry about—and neither would Itzel and her people trapped below the mountain.

If Hector already had Maria and was at the temple, then it would be up to Carver.

No one else she'd rather trust her life to.

She spotted two dugout canoes on the bank at the edge of the lowest pool. After emptying one of its fishing nets, she grabbed an oar and shoved off into the gorge and down the river. Just like the New River back home—except she hadn't scouted this river and was blind to what she'd be facing.

The current swept her away and Caitlyn remembered her mantra from her days of being a river rat. *Paddle, paddle, paddle. You don't fall in if you just keep on paddling.*

She fell into a nice rhythm but couldn't help but wish that Carver were here with her. Where she could keep an eye on him. Then she hit white water and couldn't think of anything except steering the canoe and staying afloat.

Maria paced the cell at least twenty times, searching for anything she could use as a weapon or to escape. The cot was bolted to the floor. Instead of springs or metal support bars to hold the thin mattress, it had woven ropes laced together to form a lattice. Which might have been helpful if she needed to climb out the window and down three stories to the ground, but she couldn't move the cot under the window and couldn't reach the window without something to stand on.

The door was strong, hinges on the outside, the lock not like any she'd ever seen—not that she knew how to pick one to start with, but at least it would give her something to do besides worry that the next sound she heard would be Dr. Carrera come to harvest her heart, still beating, from her body.

Calm down, calm down, panic would not help. Okay, not the door. What else, what else? The sink. Maybe she could loosen a length of pipe, use it to club the guards when they came for her? Better than hoping her little chisel was sharp enough to slice through clothing and flesh—which she sincerely doubted it was. The chisel she had was the thinnest one, and they'd pretty much ruined it while hammering against Kevin's chain. The edge was nicked and didn't feel sharp at all. But Pablo hadn't found it in her jacket, so at least she had something.

She tried to remove the drainpipe below the sink. It was heavy steel or maybe lead, she wasn't sure, it was so filthy. But whatever it was, it wasn't budging. Decades of grime cemented it in place.

Not the sink. The toilet? It wasn't like the toilets back home, just a seat over a wide drain hole, more like a latrine than an actual toilet. And goodness, the smell. She remembered hearing about prison escapes down the toilet drain and into the sewer system.

She rocked the toilet to see if she could move it from the drain. Like the sink, it was not budging, not even when she threw all her weight against it. After a dozen tries, she sat on the floor and leaned against the wall beside it, exhausted.

And, she had to admit, a little relieved. That stench would probably have suffocated her or made her pass out halfway down the pipe. What a way to go—trapped in a toilet drain.

She laughed. Okay, maybe it was a little on the hysteria side of the spectrum, but it wasn't like her father was here to tell her to behave herself. Not like she'd ever see either of her parents again. They might never even know how she died.

And what a choice. Death by toilet or death by mad scientist reenacting his own warped Mayan human sacrifice.

Finally her laughter petered out and she just sat there, drained, pressed against the wall between the toilet and the sink.

That's when she noticed the machine screws. Holding a steel plate in place. Plumbing access panel. It had to be. And that would run the length and width of the building. If she could get the screws off, she could slip inside the crawl hole beyond and climb down.

All she needed was a screwdriver. She pulled her old friend, her faithful companion, her chisel from her jacket pocket. Scraped away layers of paint and rust and dirt until the first screw was fully revealed. Then she raised the edge of the chisel.

Oh please let it fit, let it fit. Let it not be too big or too wide. Let it fit.

It fit. A perfect match. The screw was stubborn—it'd obviously been in place for a long, long, long time. But Maria kept at it, despite nicking herself with the chisel blade so many times that she had to wipe her palms every few minutes to keep the blood from slicking her grip.

It took a long time, but the screw turned. And then, finally, it fell into her palm. One down, seven more to go.

Maria wiped the sweat from her face and got started on the next. She was done hiding, done running, done being scared. No matter what happened next, at least she was fighting back.

CHAPTER THIRTY-FOUR

The small canoe handled the river's twists and rapids nicely. If there hadn't been so much at stake, Caitlyn would have enjoyed her swift passage down the river. When she drew close to the falls Itzel had told her about, she steered the canoe onto the north bank, where she was able to scramble over some boulders, and found a path leading out of the river's gorge.

Below was the lake, and on its north shore was the doctor's compound. There was a road leading to it on the far side of the lake. A tall brick wall created a boundary around the buildings.

Caitlyn grabbed her monocular to scout the best way in. There were two main buildings: a large mansion situated for the best views of the lake and mountains, and behind it the hospital building. Beyond the hospital were several smaller buildings that appeared to be barracks and storage facilities for vehicles and equipment. There was no movement on the grounds, no guards patrolling.

Had Hector and his men already been and gone,

leaving her wasting her time on a fool's errand? Or was the doctor simply complacent about security?

Given that Carrera had orchestrated Maria and Hector's journey here, she doubted he'd leave his compound unguarded. Which meant a trap.

The good news was that if it was a trap for Hector and his men, she might have better luck going in alone than they would going in as a force.

Bad news was, it was a helluva lot of ground to cover alone.

As she scrutinized the brick wall surrounding the compound, she realized that beyond the front of the compound, near the road, the rest of the wall was in disrepair. There were areas where the bricks had crumbled or were leaning, lopsided, and one place in the southeast corner where the jungle growth encroached upon the wall and had toppled a small section of it, leaving a gap.

Her entrance. She pocketed the monocular, grabbed her Glocks, and made her way down the trail and through the jungle. She was still debating whether to clear the house or the hospital first when the rattle of weapons fire came from the front gate. Hector had arrived.

That made up her mind for her. If he was attacking from the front, he'd be at the house first, leaving her the hospital.

She reached the wall. The tumbled bricks were covered with ferns and small palm trees using them to leverage more sunlight. She climbed over them and jumped down into the clinic compound, finding herself in an abandoned cornfield. Not much cover or camouflage and no time to belly-crawl a stealthy approach, so she sprinted across the overgrown field, past a better maintained garden, and around to the rear of the clinic building. There was an entrance halfway down the building. She ran to it, the door was solid metal, no telling who or what was on the other side.

Holding her pistol at the ready, she reached for the doorknob. Unlocked. Gave it a yank. It swung open with protest, off balance, so she had to wrestle with it. She didn't open it all the way, instead only cracked it wide enough to peer inside.

A stairwell. Empty as far as she could tell. She stepped inside, cushioning the door's closure to make as little noise as possible. Not that it would have mattered. Above her the cries and shouts of women echoed through the staircase like the soundtrack to a slasher film.

She checked the hall on the main floor. All the doors were dark, silence beyond them. Returning to the stairwell she debated: Up into bedlam? Or down into silence?

Maria was a valuable hostage. And Carrera would need to be able to quickly produce her once Hector arrived. Plus, the less people who knew Caitlyn was here, the better.

Down it was. She crept down the steps and through the door at the bottom. Noted the tables with instruments in the hallway. The medical wing. Where Carrera dissected women for their body parts?

A shudder ran through her as she opened the first door, braced to find a horror show to match the screaming from the floors above.

She pulled the door open, stepped through it, assessing any danger. It was an operating theater. Sparkling white tile and stainless steel. Instrument trays and equipment for a procedure were lined up along the walls. A surgical bed sat at the center, awaiting its patient.

And on the floor in the corner sat a man in surgical scrubs, handcuffed to the base of the sink.

* * *

Jake had hoped with the sun being up that he'd have the chance to get dry again. No such luck. Instead, the jungle's humidity clamped down and he felt as if he were moving while wearing body armor. Very thick, very heavy body armor. Armor that chafed in the most intimate places.

He decided he hated the jungle. Not just the humidity, also the terrain. Itzel had said there was a path, and indeed, there was a six- to eight-inch strip of bare earth showing through the layers of dead leaves, ferns, palms with wicked sharp spiky fronds, and tangled roots that grabbed at his ankles and tried to twist him up. He had to push through branches that scratched and sliced at his hands, vines—just like in the movies—and pine needles, which was a surprise.

He'd expected the jungle to smell nice, exotic, or at least clean after last night's downpour. Nope. It stank worse than his old high school gym locker. The only good thing about it was the noise. A constant barrage of birds chirping and screeching, frogs croaking and monkeys calling back and forth. No one would ever hear him coming, not over that din.

Of course, he also wouldn't be able to hear anyone either.

He broke through to the intersecting trail, the one on the north bank of the river that Itzel said to turn right on and it would lead him to the temple. He still didn't see how it was possible there was a temple here—all he could see were trees. Every shade of green and gold imaginable. Yes, there was a hill ahead, as if the mountain were shrugging one shoulder. He guessed maybe it had a kind of sharp peak, but nothing that looked man-made.

Then he rounded a bend and almost ran smack into

a human head. It was taller than he was, laboriously carved from limestone. Intricate symbols covered its cheeks and foreheads as if it wore tattoos.

His own tattoo itched and he ran his fingers through his hair to rub it. Suddenly the jungle had grown completely quiet. Despite the humidity, a shiver sprinted across his skin.

Feeling as if he was being watched, he stepped off the path, back into the jungle. Crouched down and listened. Hard.

Men. Talking in Spanish. Just ahead. He nodded thanks to the stone head. If Jake hadn't stopped to look at it, he would have stumbled right into Hector's men.

He crept through the undergrowth, cursing it even as he was grateful for the concealment it provided. A few yards down the path, he spotted them. Sitting on stone slabs near an opening in the mountain. No, not the mountain, no natural opening would have a triangular-shaped ceiling or such straight sides.

He'd found the temple. If he strained, he could make out faint horizontal lines in the foliage growing around it as well as the occasional glimpse of white stone. The men were relaxed, waiting for something, smoking cigarettes that he could smell even over the stench of the jungle. They carried sidearms and AK-47s, but he saw no signs of any explosives—had they already set them? If so, where?

He was trying to decide on the best move when he felt movement behind him. Someone was coming down the path from the lake and they weren't being too quiet about it.

Hurrying to retrace his steps, he made it to the curve, out of sight and hopefully hearing of Hector's men, when he spotted a man in his late teens coming down the trail. He wore a small bag across his chest and staggered like someone in a hurry but who had run out of energy, yet wouldn't give up. His face was flushed, eyes wide with the look of a wild animal fleeing a forest fire.

What the hell? Now he had to put up with a civilian stumbling into the middle of his action? Nothing to do but grab the kid and see what his story was.

Jake waited until the kid had passed him; then he stood, stepped behind the kid—still clueless and breathing too loud and fast to sense Jake—clamped his arm around him in a choke hold but instead of applying pressure, held the kid's mouth closed shut.

"I'm not going to hurt you," he whispered. The kid was too shocked even to struggle. "Do you speak English?"

The kid nodded. His breath came faster, panicked gasps, and Jake worried he was going to faint.

The kid had two hard rectangular slabs inserted into his shirt, beneath his arms, with wires going to the bag around his chest and another thick cord extending from the bag beneath his shirt. The slabs didn't feel like blocks of explosives, but there was a faint clicking noise and hum coming from the kid's body.

"Are you carrying a bomb?" Jake asked, pulling at the hem of the kid's shirt. Now the kid squirmed to fight, hand down to protect his belly.

Jake loosened up on his mouth. "Quietly. What is this?"

"Artificial heart. Pump." The kid gestured to the bag. "Batteries." He tapped one of the slabs at his side.

Given the way he was huffing and puffing, Jake believed him. "Let's move. Don't say a word." Jake pulled him back down the path, out of earshot from the men at the temple. "Relax, relax, I just want to talk."

Jake let the kid go—it was obvious the kid had no training, Jake could silence him fast enough if he had to. But a frightened civilian would calm down faster, be more coherent, if they were free.

The kid spun away, grabbing at his throat, patting at his belly. He raised his shirt, checked the thick tubing, and then relaxed.

"Who are you?" he asked Jake. His voice seemed loud, too loud. Jake raised a finger to his lips and motioned the kid off the trail and still farther away from Hector's men. "Please, help us. You have to get to the clinic. Before he kills them all."

The sun was up, and Maria was covered in sweat by the time she reached the last screw. Her hands were crisscrossed with small nicks from the chisel, and between the sweat and blood, it was getting harder and harder to hold the tool. Not to mention the way her hands spasmed from the strain. Good practice for digging on an archeological site, she told herself as she gritted her teeth and began to work on the final screw standing between her and escape.

As the night wore on, the other inmates had grown louder and more frenzied. Maria had no idea if this was their usual pattern of behavior, but, as disturbing as the screams and shouts were, she was grateful for the noise that camouflaged her work. It was hard to be quiet when chiseling out rust and pounding at screws to loosen them.

The final screw was more difficult than the others. It was on the bottom corner, and the weight of the panel torqued it so that she had to prop up the panel with one knee while bent over working on the screw with her hands. Within minutes, her back was screaming in pain, but she focused on her task at hand and ignored the pain.

She'd managed to finally get it to turn, although haltingly, when it got stuck. She tried raising and lowering the panel—it was heavy, a solid piece of sheet metal—tried getting under the screw to re-seat the threads, tried pounding it, more for the satisfaction of venting her frustration than any practical reason.

No good. She re-anchored the chisel, repositioned herself to provide the greatest leverage using her entire body weight, and tried one last time.

Crack. The chisel splintered, its edge splitting off and flying against the wall. Left behind was an irregular jagged angle, its point too tiny to be of any good as a screwdriver.

She stared at it, tears flowing without her noticing. Her entire vision filled with the broken tool and the final machine screw. No, no, no, this couldn't be happening. How much longer did she have before they came for her? She had to escape.

Climbing to her feet, she braced herself on the sink's edge. A wave of dizziness swept over her, propelled by fear as much as by the sudden rush of blood to her legs. She wanted to scream but for some reason felt safer if she did what came naturally and remained quiet. Hidden even in the midst of the inmates' cacophony.

She twirled around, hugging herself, the only comfort she had left. Slowly panic eased from her. Beams of sunlight catching dust motes in the empty air surrounding her. The Mayans believed power came from the sun. They often proclaimed their kings as reincarnations of the sun god. If only she could grab hold of one of those sunbeams and fly away.

Stupid waste of time, her father had proclaimed her love of fairy tales and myths. Guess he was right.

She looked down once more at the broken tool in her hand. It might not work as a tool anymore, but the broken edge was sharp. She turned to the door, for the first time realizing the inmates' screams had died away. There was silence outside. She ran to the door, couldn't see anything except the woman across the hall huddling on the floor in the corner of her cell, one hand over her mouth, swallowing her cries.

Then she heard what had alarmed the other women. Footsteps.

They were here. Coming for her. She stepped back from the door and gripped the chisel. No more hiding. If she was going to make it out of here alive, she would have to fight.

CHAPTER THIRTY-FIVE

"Who the hell are you?" Caitlyn and the handcuffed man said simultaneously. What was even more surprising was their shared tone: whispered frustration combined with the voice of command.

"Caitlyn Tierney, FBI," she answered first. She glanced back out into the hall. No one had appeared, alerted by the sound. Good. She rummaged through her pockets. Grabbing the small Baggie with her keys sealed inside, she approached the man. "And you are?"

"Dr. Kevin Cho. Don't suppose you have handcuff keys?"

"Don't leave home without them." In fact, she usually carried several keys on her—a prudent precaution after a killer grabbed her last summer. She found the right key and unlocked him.

He stood, holding on to the sink for balance as he shook blood back into his hand. "We need to get out of here. They'll be back soon."

"Have you seen this girl?" Caitlyn showed him Maria's photo, sealed into a plastic bag.

"Yes. That's Maria. They took her upstairs to the

locked wards." Not waiting for her, he ran to the door, opened it a crack. "Someone's coming."

She motioned him back into his corner, where he pretended to still be chained to the sink while she took up position behind the door, weapon at the ready.

The door opened and a man carrying a tray of instruments covered in a sterile drape entered. "Almost time, Doctor. Hope you're ready."

"Where's Maria?" Cho shouted at the man. "What have you done with her?"

Caitlyn took full advantage of the doctor's well-timed diversion, closing the door behind the man, and settling into a fighting stance, gun aimed. She wished there were more distance between her and her target, but the room was too crowded with surgical equipment.

"Don't move," she ordered.

The man stopped, hands still holding the tray. He glanced over his shoulder. His face had a scar down its right side, and his glare approached lethal intensity.

"He's the one," Cho said, climbing to his feet. "He took Maria. Where is she?"

Before Caitlyn could warn him to back off until she had their prisoner restrained, Cho stepped forward, closer to the man. The man saw his opening at the same time as Caitlyn, flung the tray of instruments into Cho's face, then grabbed the doctor, twisting him to use as a shield, his thick arm pressing against Cho's windpipe, choking the life from him.

"Drop the gun," he told Caitlyn. "Or he's dead." He was taller than Cho and strong enough to leverage the doctor off his feet, ignoring Cho's attempts to claw his way free.

Caitlyn could have just shot the scar-faced man but the noise would have alerted the entire building and she'd lose any intel he had. Besides, he didn't know that her Glock wasn't her only weapon.

She lowered the gun to the floor, sliding it to her side so it was equally out of reach for her and Scarface. "Okay, okay. Now, just let him go."

"Away from the door." The man jerked and Cho's body flailed like a puppet with its strings cut. His face turned an alarming shade of purple.

Caitlyn sidled forward, leaving a clear path to the door. She didn't think the man intended to escape—given Cho's restraints, she bet the man was going to get help. Which would ruin everything.

He surprised her. Instead of opening the door, when he came abreast to her, he launched Cho's body at her, quickly following with his own.

Cho stumbled and fell, knocking Caitlyn off balance. Her impulse to catch Cho gave Scarface time to reach her. He pushed her against the operating table with one hand, raising his other in a fist, ready to punch her.

She didn't give him the chance. He'd made his own mistake, not restraining her hands. She raised her backup Glock and pressed it against his throat, using it to pivot him until their positions were reversed and he was the one pinned against the bed. "Answer the doctor. Where's Maria?"

Cho climbed to his feet and grabbed a key ring from the man's belt. The man glared but said nothing.

"Lie down and relax," Caitlyn commanded. Soon she and Cho had the man gagged and restrained by wide leather straps on the patient table. She retrieved her Glock and took a revolver and a knife from the man, and they left, closing the door. Caitlyn didn't like leaving him at their back. "Hang on a second."

"What? We need to find Maria." The doctor's voice

was a husky whisper, but all he seemed to care about was Maria. She had to admire him for that.

There was no lock on the door. What had Carver said the other night? She fished the change she'd received at the café yesterday from the pocket of her cargo pants, where it'd traveled with her all the way from Santo Tomás. The coins were thin and small enough to fit between the gap in the door and its frame. Smiling— Carver was going to love this—she pushed her weight against the door to enlarge the gap as wide as possible, then jammed the coins into it.

By the time she'd finished, the door was wedged into place and wasn't going to move without someone taking the time to dig the coins out. Not easy, since the frame extended far enough to cover them.

"Okay," she told Cho. "Let's find Maria and get the hell out of here."

Cho declined the offer of one of her pistols but did take the knife she'd confiscated from Scarface. "They took her upstairs. To the locked ward. With the inmates."

There was no one on the stairs, and any noise they made was masked by the inhuman screeches and shouts from the ward above them. Not just shouts, Caitlyn realized—singing. Someone was singing. It was a language Caitlyn had never heard before, not Spanish, at least she didn't think so, and it was beautiful. Haunting.

They reached the third-floor landing. Cho came to a stop in front of a very thick, very solid metal door blocking their passage onto the ward. She handed him Scarface's keys and he worked the lock while she stood lookout. The song had gotten louder, sadder, as more women joined in. It echoed through the stairwell like a hypnotic dirge.

"So Carrera really has been running a psych hospital?" She was still trying to figure out Carrera and what he wanted. Usually if she understood what a subject wanted, she could find a way for things to end peacefully, as she had back in Pennsylvania with the little girl holding the gun on her.

"Maybe once upon a time," Cho said. "But from what I've seen, he's the one driving these women crazy. Stealing their minds as he steals their body parts."

Maria's grip on the chisel was sweaty. Her legs shook as she stood, poised, knees bent, ready to attack. Could she actually kill someone? Maybe all she'd have to do was maim them, distract them enough so she could run.

No. Then they'd be behind her, able to chase after her. If they had guns, they wouldn't need to be very close to shoot her. Okay. She'd run out, lock them inside her cell.

And just where and how would she strike this magical, debilitating blow? A sour taste filled her mouth as her stomach bottomed out. Who was she kidding? She had no idea what she was doing. You couldn't learn how to kill someone or be a hero just by reading a bunch of books.

The footsteps grew closer. She was tempted to run to the door and look outside again. What good would that do? No. She needed to be ready. She might fail. She might die. But it wasn't about her, not anymore. If she could make it out alive, she could save Kevin, find Michael. They could all escape this nightmare.

All she had to do was be strong. Strong enough to be willing to take a life.

Could she do that?

Her father could. He'd been in the army before she was born. What would he do?

Aim for where they're most vulnerable—that's what he always said when he was talking business. But she always had the feeling it was more than a business philosophy with him. Something about the glint in his eyes when he said it. As if he was searching his past, removed from the here and now.

Sometimes she felt that way when she got lost in a good book. She closed her eyes, squeezed them hard, wishing this were just an exciting story or, better yet, a dream . . . opened them again. Same metal door scratched and dented and with that haunting bloody handprint on its edge. Same empty cell. Same Maria.

The footsteps were outside the door. She had her back to the wall the door was in—the better to surprise them when they stepped inside—and couldn't see anyone at the small slit of a window, but she heard a key rattling in the lock. She tried to swallow but couldn't. Her hand cramped and she quickly transferred the chisel to her other hand, rubbed her sweaty palm dry against her jacket, then clenched the chisel once more.

The lock clicked. She focused on the area a few feet inside the cell. Her strike zone.

The door swung open, hitting the other side of the wall. A draft of fresh air entered the cell. She pushed her back against the wall, hiding the chisel down at her side, out of sight of whoever stepped through the doorway.

"Maria?" a man's voice called. "It's okay. It's me. Kevin."

Maria froze. No. It was a trick. It had to be. She wanted to answer, but she didn't dare. Instead she held her position and waited.

A woman stepped into the cell. But she didn't move straight ahead as Maria had planned. She sidestepped, keeping her back to the wall on the other side of the door, pivoting to scour the room, ending with her gun aimed at Maria.

"Stop it. You're scaring her." Kevin rushed into the room and stopped exactly in the space Maria had focused her energies on. She raised her hand for one split second before he spun around to face her. "Maria. It's okay, everything will be okay."

The chisel clattered to the floor as she collapsed into his arms, unable to speak as fear and adrenaline choked any words she had. He held her tight. The woman's voice sounded very far away, saying, "We don't have time. Let's go."

Maria allowed Kevin to escort her from the room. She looked up and met the gaze of the woman imprisoned opposite. They'd started singing again, that strange crooning song that was both comforting and disturbing. "What about them?"

"We'll send help later," the woman with the red hair said, marching ahead and gesturing for them to hurry. They reached the metal door and she looked through it, then held it open as they passed out into the stairwell.

"Michael," Maria whispered to Kevin. She didn't know who this strange woman was, didn't trust her. But she trusted Kevin. "We need to find him."

They stumbled down the stairs, Maria feeling better once they exited into sunlight. Here, behind the hospital building, was a clearing bounded by the jungle and the mountain. Almost there, almost free. Kevin held her hand in his and had a knife in the other. He kept pivoting his gaze to make sure there was no enemy nearby, but he always came back to look at her, making sure she was okay.

"I think they took him to the house," he said. "I didn't see him in there." He jerked a chin to indicate the hospital behind them.

"C'mon," the woman urged. "I'll cover you while you cross the field."

Maria stopped. "No. I'm not going anywhere without Michael."

The woman frowned, stared at Maria for a long moment. "There's no time. Carrera won't hurt him."

"Dr. Carrera is insane," Maria argued. Was that really her talking? She sounded so calm. So confident. "We need to save Michael."

"She's right," Kevin said. "I can't predict what Carrera will do. He's totally irrational."

The woman sighed. "Okay. There's a break in the wall, there." She pointed to the far end of the field. "Beyond it is a trail leading past the waterfall. Wait for me there. I'll try to find Michael."

Maria was both disappointed and glad that the woman had taken charge and didn't expect her and Kevin to brave the man with the scar and the doctor's other guards at the house. "That trail leads to the temple. We could hide there."

The woman shook her head. "No. The temple isn't safe. Wait for me at the waterfall."

Kevin squeezed Maria's hand and they began running into the field. They hadn't gone more than a few steps when a gunshot cracked through the air. A clod of dirt leapt into the air a few yards in front of them.

A man shouted, "Stop right there!"

Maria whirled. Two men were at the corner of the hospital, both aiming machine guns at Kevin. They hadn't seen the redheaded woman who was crouched against the back wall of the hospital, taking aim at them, ready to shoot as soon as they stepped forward.

"Stop!" she shouted to the woman. "Don't shoot! That's my father."

She dropped Kevin's hand and raced through the

field, leaping into the arms of her father. He'd come to save her. She'd prayed for this moment, and her prayers had been answered.

Everything was going to be just fine now. Now that her father was here.

CHAPTER THIRTY-SIX

It was all Jake could do to restrain his laughter. Here he was, alone, taking on a squad of well-armed, well-trained special forces, needing to find their explosives—somewhere in a freaking Mayan temple—disarm them, and save Itzel's people . . . and God sent him a civilian with a bum ticker to protect?

Seriously, there was something drastically wrong with the universe if that's how it worked.

"Tell me everything," he whispered to the kid.

"I'm Michael. They locked me up—my father and Helda—and, well, they didn't expect me to, I broke the window and climbed out and I ran here as fast as I could but being stuck in bed for so long, I guess I'm kinda out of shape—"

Jake shook his head. "No, tell me the important shit. Who are you running from, how are they armed, and why did you come here?"

The kid, Michael, nodded. Then he began again. "My father. He's, I don't know, he's sick, gone mad. Deranged. He kidnapped a surgeon to give me a heart transplant and he was going to take the heart from, from Maria—"

The kid sputtered into silence as if he was just now realizing the truth behind his words. His gaze bounced around, landing on Jake, ricocheting to the jungle, to the sky, back to Jake. Disoriented. Jake knew just how he felt, but there was no time for coddling or any of the crisis-counseling shit the psych guys talked about. Time was running out and he needed intel, fast.

"Got it. Crazy doctor running amok in a crazy bin. Does he have weapons? Is he coming after you?"

"No. I don't think they know I'm gone. But yes, his men have guns. Like yours." He nodded to the AK-47 Jake carried. "I came here because other men showed up, more men with guns, and they blocked the road, so I thought if I made it to the temple and climbed to the top, I could maybe get a signal out?" He pulled a cell phone from his pocket.

"Good thinking, kid," Jake said. Figured a word of encouragement couldn't hurt—the kid looked scared enough, he might be ready to piss his pants. Definitely way out of his league. "Only problem is Hector's men—the same ones who stormed the clinic compound—are also at the temple planting explosives to blow it up."

Michael's eyes somehow went even wider—so wide, the whites showed all around. "But we need to help Maria. And Dr. Cho."

"Hector is Maria's father. He won't hurt her." At least Jake hoped not. Hector hadn't exactly cared too much about blowing up a cavern with two federal agents and dozens of civilians trapped inside. But it did say something that he went after his daughter instead of taking care of the temple first. Of course, that could just be good tactics—as soon as the temple blew, Carrera would know Hector was on the warpath.

Whatever. Jake still had a mission. And time was running out. "How many men did you see?"

Michael thought for a moment. "Two SUVs, maybe five, six men? I'm not sure."

"Two?" Damn, that meant Hector had gotten reinforcements, if he had more men and vehicles. Jake guessed Romero probably had something to do with that. The friendly neighborhood CIA officer would have figured out that backing Hector was his best bet to clean up the mess here—past and present—with the least amount of public attention. Or scrutiny. "Wait here, I've got a job to do."

"Where are you going?"

"Hector's men are planting explosives inside the temple. I need to find them and disarm them." Jake turned to leave, but Michael stopped him.

"I'm coming with you."

"What about your heart?" Jake gestured to the bag.

"No problem as long as we're not running a marathon." Michael stood tall, arms flexed like he was ready to take on the world. Jake had to admire the kid's bravado. "I know my way around the inside of that temple. If you want to find those bombs, I'm your best bet."

"You know anything about defusing bombs?" Jake asked, halfway hoping the answer was yes. He himself knew nothing more than the few classes he'd had at the Federal Law Enforcement Training Center at Glencoe when he'd joined Criminal Investigations. And those were almost a decade ago. Not like IRS agents got a lot of time to practice their bomb-disarming skills.

"No," Michael said. He appeared calmer. And very serious about going with Jake.

Jake looked up at the peak above them that was the top of the temple. No way the kid could make it out of the blast zone in time if the place blew. Might as well let him be of some use.

"Stay on my back, be quiet, and do exactly what I

say." He handed Michael the solar-powered lantern Caitlyn had given him before she left. "Don't turn it on until I tell you it's safe." They started down the trail. "Know how to handle a gun?"

"No, sir."

Jake considered it. He didn't like to have anyone at his back with a weapon if he didn't trust them to know what they were doing. But an extra man carrying a weapon could make all the difference if they were spotted. He pulled out the revolver he'd picked up back at the church and handed it to Michael. "There's no safety, just point and pull the trigger, hard."

Michael hefted the gun, raised it to aim. Jake laid a hand on his arm, pushing it back down. "Don't point it at me and don't shoot until I tell you to, got it?"

Michael nodded and they headed down the path to the temple. Another troop of the damn screaming monkeys flew past overhead. Jake rolled his eyes at the howling primates. He knew exactly how they felt.

Hector and his men corralled Caitlyn and Cho into the courtyard and made them kneel, hands behind their heads. Across the courtyard, Maria spoke earnestly with her father, gesturing to Cho and then the house, obviously filling him in on what had happened. Caitlyn decided the best thing, especially as she was unarmed and Hector had already tried to kill her once today, was to wait and let events play out.

While they waited, Romero brought a middle-aged woman in a nurse's uniform from the house; she was struggling and cursing in German. "Found her in the study," Romero told Hector as he showed Hector a light-weight laptop. "She was using this to track something— think it could lead to Carrera?"

"Where is he?" Hector thundered at the woman. The

nurse held her ground, looked him square in the eye, then spit at him.

One of his men hit her with his rifle butt and she fell to the ground. Cho ran to her, ignoring the weapons trained on him. But she was already sitting up by the time he reached her.

"He's gone to save his son. And you can't stop him." She looked around at all of them, glaring. "None of you can stop him." Then she focused on Maria. "You, you are nothing compared to the man Michael could have been. Silly girl."

Maria blanched. Not because of the woman's words. Because she'd gotten a look at the computer Romero held. She took it from the CIA agent. "Kevin, does the LVAD have a tracking device?"

"What's an LVAD?" Caitlyn asked Cho.

"Left ventricular assist device. Artificial heart, if you will. I implanted one into Carrera's son, Michael, last month."

Michael, that was Maria's twin. Caitlyn wondered if the girl knew.

"Is there anything on there that can track Carrera?" Hector demanded.

Cho got to his feet to take a look. Hector gestured to his men to stand down. "It's got a RFID device to keep track of battery charge, outflow, and the like from a remote computer. I guess you could use it to also monitor location."

Maria pointed to the screen. "This isn't tracking Dr. Carrera. It's tracking Michael. He's on his way to the temple."

"Michael ran away," the nurse said. "All because of you and the ideas you put into his head."

"He must have gone for help," Maria said.

"If so, he doesn't have much time." Cho nodded to

the laptop. "The LVAD only has an hour of battery life left. At most."

Maria's eyes grew wide, but Hector actually smiled at the doctor's grim prognosis. "Come, Maria."

His men yanked Cho away and forced him to his knees again.

"The only place I'm going is to the temple," she told her father. "To save Michael."

"I'll take you to the temple," Hector agreed. Too readily.

Maria had no idea about what else her father had planned. But Caitlyn did. "Tell her, Hector."

He ignored her, taking Maria's arm and steering her away.

Caitlyn stood. Her guard nudged her with his AK-47, but if she was going to die, she'd rather be standing. Maria needed to know the truth about her father.

"He plans to blow up the temple, Maria!" she shouted. Maria spun back to look at her. "If he does, an entire village will die."

"What is she talking about?" Maria asked her father. Then she faced Caitlyn again. "Who are you?"

"Caitlyn Tierney, FBI. I came here to rescue you. Wasn't counting on your father having other ideas."

Hector made a motion and Caitlyn's guard hit her in the back, sending her sprawling.

"No. Stop," Maria cried. "I want to hear what she has to say."

Caitlyn licked blood from her split lip and looked up. "If you don't tell her, Hector, I will."

He remained silent, the first sign of indecision she'd ever seen in him. Maybe he really did love his daughter. Or maybe he was simply deciding how best to protect himself.

Caitlyn didn't wait to see what his decision would

be. "Your father was an army colonel. He ran this prison—that's what it was before it was whitewashed into a hospital. The doctor was his second-in-command. Together they tortured and executed hundreds."

"No," Maria gasped. "That's not true. My father, his company, he saves lives. He would never—"

"Their bodies all disappeared before the UN commission came to investigate," Caitlyn continued. Maria's expression twisted in anguish. "Buried in the temple, so conveniently hidden nearby. Last thing your father wants is for that temple to ever be found again, much less picked apart by archeologists."

Maria pulled away from her father's grasp, whirling to face him. "That can't be right. Tell her she's wrong. Father, say something!"

There was a faint crack in his stony expression. Sorrow—and maybe regret. "Maria, it was a long, long time ago. We were following orders, fighting a war. Nothing to do with us now."

"Not as long as he can finish destroying the evidence," Caitlyn put in as she climbed back to her feet. The guard watched her warily but didn't hit her again. She rubbed her sore back, could feel the bruise forming below her rib cage. "That includes killing Carrera and Michael. Your brother. Not to mention dozens of innocents trapped nearby—including your mother, Maria. Your real mother."

Helluva way to orchestrate a family reunion, but if it helped stop Hector, Caitlyn was willing to try anything.

Maria's mouth opened, then shut again as her face twisted with pain and confusion. "No. Father, no."

"Maria, you must trust me in this. It's the best way to protect you. Carrera has gone mad. To think what he almost did to you. To my precious, beautiful baby?" Hector placed his palm against Maria's cheek.

She slapped his hand aside and took a step back. "No. Don't you touch me. How could you—all those people dead? Because of you?"

"It was my duty. Just as my duty now is to protect you. Come with me. Now." It was clear that Hector's patience with his daughter had run out.

Maria stood her ground. "Unless you want to kill me as well, you will let these people go and help me save Michael."

Hector's face flushed dark with fury. His hand fell to his weapon and for a heartbeat Caitlyn wondered if he was going to shoot his only child.

Caitlyn lunged toward him, although he was much too far away for her to have any hope of stopping him if he drew his weapon. Her guard tackled her, shoving her to the ground.

Cho leapt to place himself between Maria and Hector, ushering her protectively behind him, using himself as a human shield.

Hector looked at Cho in surprise. "Get away from my daughter," he thundered.

"Why? So you can kill her? You'll have to go through me first."

Now all the guards had their weapons trained on Cho. The surgeon looked around, as if he'd surprised himself, but stood his ground. Hector raised an eyebrow and drew his sidearm, aiming it at Cho.

Maria screamed. "No!"

CHAPTER THIRTY-SEVEN

Maria couldn't believe this was happening. In a way it was worse than the nightmare of finding Prescott's mutilated body or being locked away with the insane prisoners on the ward. Those were horrors so beyond comprehension, she could almost pretend they weren't reality.

But this, this was her father. The man who had taught her to swim, who'd urged her to always face her fears and never back down, the man she'd spent her entire life trying so desperately to please.

And now he was a killer? Had executed and tortured people? Wanted to kill Michael and Kevin and destroy a temple that held knowledge that could change history? All to cover his crimes?

The questions came at her from every direction until she was dizzy and not sure what was real and what wasn't.

Then Kevin stepped between her and her father's gun. Just as he'd moved to protect her from Dr. Carrera earlier. She didn't even know him, yet he valued her life more than her own father did.

She looked past Kevin's shoulder at her father. His face had an expression she'd never seen on it before. Gone was the haughty arrogance that made him seem so young and confident, able to handle anything. Instead he looked . . . haggard. Old. Tired.

And in pain.

"No," she repeated. This time she moved to stand between Kevin and her father. She kept walking toward her father until she stood inches away. She laid her palm on his hand holding the gun. "No more killing, Father. Not if you love me." Tears choked her words. "I don't know the man who did all those awful things twenty years ago. I only know my father. The man I've looked up to all my life. The man I used to love more than life itself."

He looked down at her and it felt like they were the only two people in the world. Exactly the way it used to feel when he'd challenge her to climb higher on the diving board or to pedal faster on her bike. The way it felt when she'd taken her First Communion and turned to find him staring not at the priest, but at her, only at her.

"Father—" She swallowed hard. "It's your turn to make me proud."

His gun slid back into its holster and he wrapped his arms around her. "Maria, my angel. I would do anything for you."

She gripped him tightly, then pulled back. "Then help me save my brother. Help me save Michael."

Hector rode with Maria alone in the backseat of one SUV, Caitlyn and Cho crowded in with three of his men in the second one, while the rest secured the clinic. As they raced over the bumpy, twisty road, Cho filled her in on Carrera's plans for Maria.

"Can you believe it?" he finished. "The man actually

thought I'd use a living donor for a heart transplant. Bad enough he kidnapped me—but to lure Maria here just to harvest her organs? He's crazy. Deluded, paranoid, psychotic—take your pick."

The way the surgeon kept talking and talking, Caitlyn guessed that most of his captivity had been spent in isolation. His speech was pressured, as if he was now making up for lost time. Not to mention the adrenaline rush of everything that had happened to him.

"Any idea what's wrong with him?" She'd like to know how volatile Carrera was. Especially as he was heading towards the temple as well.

"I was thinking Huntington's, given the strange muscle spasms and the neurodegeneration. But I'm not a neurologist, just an overpaid plumber."

Caitlyn liked Cho. The way he didn't shrink from a leadership role, the way he'd stepped in to protect Maria when he thought she was in danger.

She struggled to remember the name of the cannibal disease Jake had told her about. "Could it be a form of kuru?" That wasn't the right disease, Jake had said it was something similar, but hopefully Cho knew what she was talking about. "We know of a patient who received tissue Carrera harvested contracting that."

"You mean Creutzfeldt-Jakob? That can be spontaneous, especially if you're genetically prone to it. But—" He stared out the window for a long moment. "—yeah. That could fit. Carrera could have inhaled infected brain tissue or cut himself and been exposed while he was harvesting tissue from an infected patient. Too bad for any patients who got the tissue, but I say it's poetic justice as far as he's concerned. He's been like a cannibal preying on those women—driving some of them mad, I'm certain they all didn't start out that way, and after they came to him for help. Let him die of a cannibal's disease. It's a horrible, awful death."

Cho didn't sound very distressed by the prospect. More like he approved of Carrera's fate.

The man beside the driver held his radio to his ear, then turned around to the guard with Caitlyn and Cho, relaying a message in Spanish. Caitlyn wished she knew what they were saying. Cho leaned close, as if a bump in the road had thrown him off balance and whispered, "They've lost contact with their men at the temple. Is that good or bad?"

Jake. She smiled. Knew she could count on him to take care of business. "It's good news. Very good news."

"Does it mean Maria's out of danger? I don't trust her father."

"I think Maria's safe. Not so sure about us. Just follow my lead."

He frowned but nodded. They spun around a steep curve, splashing through mud, and Caitlyn saw the blackened remains of their helicopter sitting in the middle of a small cleared cornfield. A few more turns and they stopped.

Hector's men climbed out and gestured for Caitlyn and Cho to join them. The road had dead-ended in the middle of the jungle, no obvious landmarks except for a steep hill that loomed over them.

Maria's temple, at long last.

CHAPTER THIRTY-EIGHT

When Jake and Michael reached the temple's entrance, Hector's men were gone. Jake cursed. Were they outside, watching the perimeter? If so, then he and Michael would be totally exposed and vulnerable once they entered the temple.

Were they inside, still placing the charges? Or had they finished, received word to blow the charges, and evacuated to a safe distance?

Any of the three could add up to very bad news.

Nothing to do but complete his mission and try to keep the kid alive. He only hoped Caitlyn was having better luck at the clinic.

Up close, the temple's entrance was imposing. The limestone walls were carved with intricate designs, some that sparked scarlet and gold where the light filtered through the trees to strike them.

"Cinnabar mixed with gold flakes," Michael whispered, tracing one of the hieroglyphs with his finger. "Can you imagine how the temple appeared before the plants covered it? When the sun hit it, it would have been like a blaze of fire in the middle of the jungle."

Jake was more concerned about what awaited them inside. The entrance had an inverted triangular ceiling and the floor was irregular, sloping up into the darkness. As they climbed inside, he realized that the ground was unsteady, like walking through gravel or pebbles. Part of the damage from the earthquake, he guessed. It made for slow and noisy going.

They made it past the first archway, and the tunnel branched to travel around the perimeter of the temple as well as leading deeper inside. There was a surprising amount of light filtered down from openings overhead along the outside wall. Clever. Even with the overgrowth of jungle outside, the air smelled fresh and although it was dark, it wasn't impenetrable. Large vines and tree roots had forced their way down through the openings, creating a vertical carpet of organic flesh.

"Which way?" he whispered to Michael.

"Straight to the cenote."

Sound traveled strangely, the farther inside they ventured. The debris underfoot changed to solid limestone, muffling their footsteps. The call of birds were audible through the air holes and small tunnels that acted like ductwork leading from the temple's interior to the outside world. The engineering was fascinating, as were the glimpses of more murals and carvings, but Jake had to stay focused on locating Hector's men.

They came to a second intersection. This one was guarded by a five-foot-high carving of a bat, its wings spread wide and fangs bared. It was darker and quieter here. Jake realized that not only had they journeyed deeper into the heart of the temple, they'd also traveled down, underground.

"The bat symbolizes the entrance to the underworld," Michael whispered. "The tunnel gets smaller, forces you to bow your head in homage to Chaac."

Jake passed the bat and climbed into the next tunnel. Bow your head was a relative term, he soon discovered. The ancient Mayans must have been a lot shorter than he was. Finally he was reduced to duck-walking through the small passage, trying to ignore the claustrophobic constraints of the tunnel. He thought about having Michael turn on the lantern but was afraid the limestone tunnel would reflect and amplify the light, announcing their position to anyone waiting at the far end.

Finally they emerged onto a ledge leading out to a large cavern. They were at the heart of the temple, the walls soaring up several levels, each lined with openings, until they reached the skylight at the top. Vines and roots hung from the openings, some reaching several stories down, traveling past the ledge he and Michael were on, going down, down, seeking water.

Jake could make out the water line etched into the limestone, maybe thirty feet down from where they stood. But there was no water there now. Instead it had receded down another twenty feet, where it twinkled in the faint light. Not just water reflecting the light, he realized, but glints of gold and the stark white of human bones.

They'd found their mass grave.

At this level, the cenote was about thirty feet in diameter, the ledge they stood on running its circumference. Thanks to the thick tapestry of vines and tree roots, there were plenty of places to hide along the outer wall of the chamber. No one was visible, but the air was eerily quiet. Strange, because he'd expect birds and smaller animals to be living in here, sheltered from the jungle predators.

Jake motioned for Michael to follow him as he edged behind an outcropping. It would make a safe place to ditch the kid while he searched for the explosive charges.

"Stay here and be quiet," he told Michael, who merely nodded.

Jake inched his way to the edge of the cenote and looked down. There were more ledges below. Across from his position was a stone staircase leading down to them. On the next level down, almost immediately below him so Jake hadn't seen him at first, one of Hector's men was kneeling, positioning several bricks of C-4. More than enough to bring down the temple. And Jake was certain it wouldn't be their only charge.

He debated how to best get the jump on the guy. His current position, directly overhead, offered concealment, but he was too far to do anything but shoot the guy—which would alert his partner. He decided to instead circle to the top of the staircase and wait to ambush the guy when he climbed out of the cenote.

Jake sidled around the chamber's outer edge, keeping his back to the large stone gargoyle-like carvings and hiding behind the vegetation when possible. There were four tunnels leading into the chamber, one at each compass point. No way to tell which of them the second man might come through. Jake reached the first one, saw no sign of movement in the irregular shadows inside, and crossed it. He was almost at the top of the stairs when a small, muffled cry came from behind him.

He whirled, AK-47 raised.

Hector's second man stood, a knife held to Michael's throat. He shouted something in Spanish. Jake shrugged, stalling for time. He didn't have a shot, not from this angle. He sidled to the side.

The man shouted again, this time in English. "I'll kill him!"

Jake had to decide. Michael's life or the lives of the villagers trapped below the church. He shifted his weight and aimed to cover the man below him, the one setting the C-4. "Drop it or I'll kill your partner."

The man below was exposed, no cover in sight, so he lunged for his rifle. Jake aimed a salvo that hit the limestone inches from the man's hand.

Suddenly the cavern filled with thousands of whirling, screeching bats, so many that they blocked the light from above as they dived, aiming for Jake. The air thrumped with the vibration of thousands of wings as the bats swarmed past him—some of them so close, their claws brushed his hair. He flung himself onto the ground as the bats turned into a cyclone of black circling around the cavern, desperate for escape.

Just as the air cleared, the bats swarming out through the tunnels, a shot rang out.

Jake leapt to his feet, AK-47 in his hands, searching for the origin of the gunshot. Hector's man down in the cavern had ducked for cover beneath the rock outcropping, so it wasn't him. Jake swung back to where he'd last seen Michael and the other soldier from Hector's squad.

Michael wasn't there. The soldier lay facedown on the ground, head blown open. And an older man stood at the tunnel opening, holding a large semiautomatic pistol.

"Drop the weapon," the man commanded.

Michael stepped from his hiding place behind a curtain of tree roots. "Father. What are you doing here?"

"I came to save you." The older man didn't lower his weapon, keeping Jake in his sights.

"Dr. Carrera?" Jake called, putting two and two together. The man down below began creeping up the steps to the ledge where Jake was. Jake wasn't sure whether to warn Carrera or let Hector's man take Carrera down—except that would leave Jake caught in the crossfire. "I'm Jake Carver with the FBI. I came here to help."

"We don't need your help!" Carrera shouted. "Put the gun down."

Hector's man was almost to the top. Jake crouched to lower his AK-47. As he did, Carrera spotted the man behind him and another shot blasted through the cavern. Hector's man fell from the steps, falling, falling, falling until he landed in the shallow waters below. Jake peered over the edge. The man was dead, not moving as he lay facedown among pieces of skeletons bobbing around him, blood blossoming on the jade green water.

Slowly, Jake straightened. Carrera waved at him to back away from the AK-47. For a second Jake thought Carrera was going to shoot him. He met the doctor's gaze, tried to gauge the man responsible for the deaths of hundreds—what was one more? Jake wondered if he'd be better off taking a chance with a leap into the cenote.

Michael saved him. The kid moved to stand in front of Carrera, stare him down. "I never asked for your help. I don't want it. Not at this price."

To Jake's surprise, Carrera lowered his pistol, face twisted as if he were near tears. "Michael. My son. You never have to ask. No price is too high to save my son. Can't you understand that?"

Michael shook his head. He backed away, hands spread wide, palms up, as if he weighed his father's words. "No, Father. I won't let you do this."

"Michael, stop!" Carrera shouted as the kid approached the edge of the cenote.

"Not until you promise to give yourself up. Get help. Father, you're sick, terribly sick." Michael was so close to the edge that bits of limestone crumbled beneath his heels, tumbling into the chasm behind him.

"Michael, come back. Away from the edge. We can discuss this."

"No. Not until you promise me—" Michael's face contorted with pain. He gasped for air.

Jake watched in horror as Michael's balance wavered. He was closer than Carrera, so he rushed the kid, grabbing him just as he was about to collapse into the pit.

The kid was pale, his lips dusky, breath coming in short, tight gasps.

Carrera ran to join him. "Michael!"

CHAPTER THIRTY-NINE

Maria stared at the temple's entrance. Brilliant blue butterflies hovered in an iridescent cloud, a sight conjured from a fairy tale. As if this wasn't real.

But it was. Her temple was real.

The light glinted off something in the dirt at her feet. She bent down. A piece of jade inlaid with gold, the size of her thumb. Thousands of years old and just waiting here. For her.

She felt giddy. Started to race inside, but her father grabbed her arm. "Stay in the car, Maria."

"No. I have to see—"

A noise like thunder cracked through the air. But it didn't stop. Not thunder, Maria realized as the blue sky clouded black with the crashing of thousands and thousands of beating wings. Thousands, maybe millions of bats poured out from the temple through air holes along the sides; then a stream of them roared through the entrance before her. Their wings were like drums pounding the air as they shrieked past.

The men raised their weapons but quickly realized the futility and instead covered their heads. Maria ducked, arms over her hair—what if one of the bats got tangled in it? The sky grew dark and she couldn't see anything as she ran.

Caitlyn, the FBI agent, caught up with her. "You okay?" she asked, pulling Maria out of the path of the bats and into the shadow of a palm tree.

Maria nodded.

"Stay here." Caitlyn ignored the bats and picked her way through the undergrowth, past Maria's father and his men, heading into the temple. No way was Maria going to miss going inside, not after everything she'd been through. Besides, Michael was in there somewhere with his crazy father.

She followed Caitlyn's footsteps. Crossing into the land of her dreams.

She hadn't gone far when a hand touched her from behind. Maria yelped and jumped. It was Kevin.

"Hurry," he whispered. "Your dad is right behind us."

"What about his men?"

"He said something about a perimeter guard." In the eerie green-hued light of the tunnel, Kevin looked worried. "I don't think he realizes I speak Spanish. He told them not to let anyone out alive. That's when I ran in here after you."

"You misunderstood, I'm sure." She hoped. Wished. Once upon a time her father was the bedrock her world was built on. Suddenly in the past few days, she'd begun to question everything and that foundation was crumbling.

If her entire life was a lie, then what did she have left to stand on? To believe in?

She was glad when Kevin took her hand and led the way through the tunnel. It wasn't as dark as she thought—clever architects had allowed for vents to pull in natural light and fresh air—but it was still very claustrophobic, especially when they reached the final tunnel.

It opened up onto the cenote at the heart of the temple, just as she knew it would. She looked over Kevin's shoulder, her pulse thrumming in anticipation. But instead of finding treasure and the archeological discovery of a lifetime, she saw Michael, lying on the ground, not moving, with a stranger and Caitlyn hovering over him.

Kevin ran to Michael, leaving Maria behind. A man's hand grabbed her arm, hauling her from the tunnel and jabbing a pistol to her head.

Dr. Carrera had found her at last.

"Save my son, Dr. Cho!" Carrera shouted. "Or the girl dies."

Caitlyn stood, putting herself between Carrera and Jake and the civilians. "Dr. Carrera, let her go. We'll do everything we can to help your son. I promise."

As she spoke, she circled the edge of the cliff, gaining ground on Carrera. His eyes were wild, his gaze jerking in all directions, and she had the feeling he didn't hear her, but instead was listening to voices inside his head. The man truly was insane.

Suddenly he turned his pistol from Maria to aim at Caitlyn. Before she could move, he fired. It didn't hit her, but it ricocheted off a boulder near her, a splinter of stone striking her head.

"Down on the ground," he ordered.

Caitlyn obeyed and dropped to the ground. Blood smeared her hand when she touched her head, but it wasn't too much. Stung like hell, though. She turned her face to look at Jake, who was across the chasm, shaking her head at him when he looked ready to spring to her rescue.

He gave her a small nod and sat back, ready to make a move when she gave him the sign.

By now Carrera had marched Maria to the edge of the cliff, the curve of the gaping abyss between him and Caitlyn. Jake could circle around from the opposite side if she could create a diversion, take Carrera's attention away from that side of the pit.

"If Michael dies, so does she," he called, his words echoing through the chamber.

Before Caitlyn could do anything, Hector Alvarado stormed into the cavern. "Let her go!" he shouted, aiming his weapon at Carrera.

Maria squirmed in Carrera's grip, struggling to get free. Carrera pushed her dangerously close to the edge of the chasm. Caitlyn sprang to her feet, ignoring the blood stinging her eyes. If she could grab Maria, use her weight to pull Carrera off balance . . . Jake met her gaze and she knew he was thinking the same thing.

Carrera whirled, his gaze and pistol aiming at Hector then Caitlyn then Hector then Caitlyn and finally Hector again. He pulled the trigger.

A gunshot rang out. Hector fell. Maria called out, "Father!"

Jake made his move, Caitlyn right behind him, coming from two different angles, Carrera and Maria at their intersection.

As she ran over the uneven ground, Caitlyn realized that she wasn't scared. Not for herself, not of dying. It was Jake she was terrified for. What if something happened to him?

Carrera spotted the movement and aimed at Jake. Another shot pierced the air. Jake flung himself to the ground.

Time slowed to a weird, one-step-forward, two-steps-back stuttering slow motion. Caitlyn whipped her head around just long enough to make sure Jake was okay. During that split second, she realized nothing else mattered.

She remembered the terror she'd felt when he plunged into the river and was swept out of sight below the mountain. And realized that everything she'd fought so hard for had been for nothing.

Yes, she had her career. Yes, she had the quiet life she thought she wanted. She'd even deluded herself that all she wanted was to be left alone.

For decades, after surviving the pain of losing her father, she'd barricaded her heart behind razor wire and brick walls. Built the walls higher and higher so she'd never need to face that kind of loss, that kind of pain, again.

Silly her. Jake had tunneled beneath her barricade. A long time ago, she realized now, even as she ran toward a crazy man with a gun and a hostage.

There was no turning back. She couldn't face losing him again. Not when she'd just discovered what was right in front of her all along.

She plowed into Maria, spinning the girl's weight to propel them both away from the cliff's edge. Jake jumped to his feet and leapt for Carrera's gun hand, twisting the pistol away from where it was aimed at Caitlyn.

The momentum threw Carrera off balance. He flailed his hands, trying to stop his fall. And grabbed on to Caitlyn's arm.

Two pairs of hands wrenched her back: Maria and Cho. Caitlyn fell backwards against them, just in time to see Carrera's other hand hook Jake's ankle.

The look of shock on Jake's face filled her vision. He lurched from one side to the other, trying to catch his balance and shake free of Carrera's grip.

Both men fell. Vanished into the abyss.

"Jake!" Caitlyn rolled to the edge of the cliff.

Carrera's body spun through the air. He shrieked in terror as he hit the shallow water, releasing a wave of bones as if his victims had come to life to greet him. Then there was silence. He didn't move.

"Jake," she called again, craning her head over the edge.

Jake was about ten feet lower than the ledge below her, dangling from one of the vines. A vine too short to reach the bottom and too far from any of the ledges for him to jump to safety.

She leapt to her feet as he swung his weight, trying to reach the ledge above him. Running around the perimeter of the pit, she hit the stone steps and sped down them. Above her, she heard Maria run to help her father, Cho calling instructions to her on how to stop the bleeding as he continued to work on Michael.

At the bottom of the pit, Carrera's body splayed across the top of the water, arms spread wide, held in the embrace of several skeletons.

He had died a horrible death, just as Cho had predicted. Caitlyn didn't know the doctor well enough to feel much of anything except anger that he'd cost the lives of so many. There was no way in hell she was going to let Jake be his final victim.

Jake pendulumed back and forth, but his arc wasn't taking him high enough or far enough to reach safety. He twisted his body, and she could see he was planning to make a leap for it.

"No, Jake! Wait!"

She ran out onto the ledge, ready to reach for him. He swung toward her, his eyes met hers, and then . . . a sharp crack as loud as a gunshot echoed through the space between them as the vine he clung to broke.

Pressing her knuckles to her mouth, she swallowed

her scream as he fell through the air. He hit the skeletons at the bottom of the pit, mud and water splashing over him. Then he disappeared from sight beneath the dark ooze.

"Jake!" Caitlyn slid-slipped down the steep pit wall to reach him, using the vines to stabilize her headlong rush. His fall had been half the distance as Carrera's, but even that could have been high enough to kill him if he hit the rock wall or if the water was too shallow or . . . She pushed aside her fears. Skidding to a stop at the edge of the water, she waded past the skeletonized remains of Carrera's victims and made it to Jake's side, hauling his head and torso from the water. He sputtered and coughed.

"You shot me! Why did you shoot me?" He gasped in pain as Caitlyn moved to support his head and slide his body free of the water. She palpated his chest, arms, finally his legs.

A shard of a skeleton's rib protruded through his calf. From the angle he lay at, he couldn't see his leg, although his hands were grabbing his thigh, trying to stabilize the limb.

"Jake, you're not shot," Caitlyn told him. There was a little blood, but given the filth they were lying in, she thought it probably best not to remove the shard of bone until they got someplace where she could clean and dress it properly.

"I'm not? It feels like I am."

"You're not shot. But—" She shifted so he could see past her.

"Oh, shit." His face blanched when he saw what his injury actually was. He turned to face her. "You know I'm really just a CPA, right? Good with numbers and details?"

Had he hit his head on the way down? Of course she knew that. "Yeah, so?"

"So you won't think any less of me if I get a little queasy at the sight of blood? Especially my own?"

Laughter broke past her panic and she hugged him hard. He winced, but then looked her square on and asked, "Hey, did you call me Jake?"

Before she could answer, he took hold of her shoulders to reposition her, then planted his lips against hers. Despite the moldering corpses and the stench of jungle rot and the fact that neither of them had been near a shower or toothbrush in days, it was the sweetest, most satisfying kiss she'd ever had.

A thousand memories crowded through Caitlyn's mind as fast as a hurricane. The joy she felt when she opened the door to the Blue Ball sheriff's office and found him there waiting for her. The way she missed him when they were apart. The funny noises he made when they made love. The tears he didn't try to hide as they climaxed. The fact that he didn't make her feel crowded or smothered or trapped. When he held a door open for her, it wasn't just the act of a gentleman, but the respect of a fellow law enforcement officer who trusted her to lead as she entered a room before him.

The first man in is always right, the tactical instructors drilled new agents at Quantico, teaching them how to clear a room of danger. Jake wasn't her first man, not by any means, but she wanted him to be her last.

"Yes," she said when they parted for air. "I called you Jake."

"I like it. A lot." He kissed her again. "Don't ever stop."

CHAPTER FORTY

Turned out it was more difficult leaving a country after you'd entered it without documentation, helped to uncover evidence of genocide, and been a witness to murder.

Caitlyn didn't really mind the two days' delay. It gave Jake time to get his leg fixed up—more damage to his pride than anything—and her time to see Itzel's people saved from the cavern where they'd been trapped.

When she saw Maria and Itzel together, Caitlyn realized that Itzel would have been only Maria's age when she escaped U4, was rescued by the Lutherans, and then returned to save her home. So young to have rebuilt a community from burnt-out ruins. Sometimes, it took a child to raise a village.

Maria stayed at Michael's side—Caitlyn thought Dr. Cho had a lot to do with that. Apparently after Michael's heart pump failed, his own heart had taken over. Cho said it was slowly gaining strength, and there was a chance Michael might not need the transplant after all.

Jake had rolled his eyes at the irony when Maria told

them that. Caitlyn had given him a look that shut him up before he could say anything stupid. Especially since Michael wasn't out of the woods yet.

Once they made it to Guatemala City, Hector volunteered BioRegen's jet to fly Michael, Maria, Itzel, and Dr. Cho to Miami, where Michael could get the care he needed. Jake and Caitlyn went along for the ride, glad to leave the politicians still squabbling over what to do with evidence of past war crimes, the impact it would have on the civilian population once the news got out, and what to do with the people of Cubiltzul, since the temple and its treasure belonged to them.

Somehow along the way, Hector had turned into the hero of the day rather than a war criminal who'd escaped prosecution. After he was discharged from the hospital, he remained under house arrest in one of the most exclusive hotels in Guatemala City while the Guatemalan authorities decided his fate.

It was tough saying good-bye to Maria in Miami. Caitlyn felt that she knew the girl, even though they'd spent less than a day together. Maria seemed to be handling learning about her father's past fairly well—better than Caitlyn had coped when her own mother's secrets were unearthed.

Of course it helped that Hector had risked everything to save Maria and that he was now cooperating with authorities. Unlike Caitlyn's mom, who was still manipulating the criminal justice system and her own daughter in hopes of walking away from murder charges.

"You'll be okay?" she asked when Maria dropped them off at their gate before heading to the hospital to be with her mother, Michael, and Cho.

"I'm not sure," Maria admitted. "How do you forgive someone for who they once were when you know how good they could be?"

Caitlyn had to look away. It was a damn good question—one she was still working on herself.

"I guess," she said slowly, her thoughts half-formed, "sometimes we have to accept that we can't change someone and we can't always expect them to change for us. All you can do is live your own life the best you can. Honor the memory of the person you thought you knew and loved."

Jake raised an eyebrow at that and she knew he was thinking of her mother. His expression said she needed to take her own advice.

Maria gave her a shy smile, then hugged her fiercely. "Yes. Yes, I will. I can. Thank you, Caitlyn."

Caitlyn had to laugh at that. "Don't thank me. You pretty much saved yourself. We were just along for the ride."

Maria blushed and turned to hug Jake. "And thank you, Jake."

He hugged her back, lifting her off her feet. "Anytime, kid. Promise to let me know how it goes with that Canadian doctor—I have friends with the RCMP, I can have him checked out for you."

Her blush deepened and she giggled, looking like a college kid again. "Could you have him detained here in Miami so we have more time together?"

"Sure thing. Just say the word."

"Seriously," Caitlyn said, resting a hand on Maria's arm. "Are you going to be okay? Staying here, with your mother—Sandra, I mean—and all? There's bound to be a lot of fallout from your father's past, and you might find yourself in the spotlight."

Maria looked down at her feet, hesitated. "I want to make sure Michael is okay. And get to know my mother—my real mother. But then . . ." She raised her head, chin high, meeting Caitlyn's gaze straight on.

"Then, I'm going to transfer. Maybe to Toronto, I'm not sure. Switch my major to forensic anthropology. That way I can help Itzel protect the temple while also bringing my father's victims and their families justice. It's the least I can do."

Caitlyn smiled, proud of Maria's decision. "You need anything, you know where to find us."

They watched as Maria climbed back into the SUV and drove off into the bustle of the airport traffic.

"She's going to be okay," Caitlyn said with a sigh.

Jake hugged her with one arm. "Yes. She is."

There was no one to meet them when they arrived at BWI, but for once coming home didn't feel lonely. Since they had no luggage, they held hands as they strolled through the throngs of people immersed in their own worries, rushing from one gate to the next.

Jake stopped to buy some silly socks at a kiosk, one pair with giraffes wrapping their long necks around the socks and another emblazoned with smiley faces.

"Should I be worried?" Caitlyn joked. Obviously, neither pair was for her.

A sad look crossed his face. "Gift for my niece. And a friend her age."

"The little girl with kuru?"

"Creutzfeldt-Jakob," he correctly automatically. She loved how his mind hung on to trivia that escaped her memory. "Do you think they'll ever trace it back to Carrera's clinic? Might help her folks get some closure."

The epidemiology was beyond her, so all she could do was shrug. "Carrera's autopsy showed he had it, but who knows where he got it from."

"Must have been while dissecting one of his—" He broke off. What to call the women who'd been mutilated by Carrera in the name of greed and science? Surely not patients. "Victims," he finished.

They walked on in silence, no need to rush, no need to fill in the silence with aimless conversation. In their own world, separate from the hustle and bustle of the travelers surrounding them.

"Feels kind of nice," she said.

"Going home?" He squeezed her hand and smiled at her. "Yes. It does."

The spell was broken as both their cell phones rang simultaneously. Caitlyn wished she'd lost the damn thing back at the temple, but no such luck.

Jake dropped her hand to answer his.

"Is it the AUSA?" she asked, worried about what his little excursion might have cost his career.

He shook his head as he listened.

"Yeah? How'd it go? Really?" His voice had a bounce to it. Good news.

She wasn't so sure about her call. It was Assistant Director Yates. "Tierney, you're back."

"Yes sir."

"Wanted to tell you, nice work. Hector Alvarado got the Guatemalans to sign on with the drug interdiction plan State was negotiating."

She brightened. Maybe Hector was serious about living up to Maria's faith in him after all. "That's good news, sir."

"And BioRegen is forging the path to create a governing body that will have oversight over the entire tissue industry to prevent something like this from ever happening again."

Then again, maybe Hector hadn't changed so much after all. Still protecting his own interests. "So they won't be facing criminal charges?"

"For what? As far as we know they haven't broken any U.S. laws, and there's no proof that they're liable for the what-cha-ma-callit disease transmission. Plus, Hector has agreed to be a cooperating witness if or when a war crimes tribunal is convened. But don't worry. The IRS is taking a long, hard look at BioRegen and the Alvarados. You know them. Once they bother to open a case file—"

"They don't stop until they have a conviction," she finished for him, relieved that some justice would be served. Even if it came at the hands of the accountants. Jake would love that.

"Oh, and that kid, the one with the bum heart? Some doctor, Cho, called—said to tell you he's doing fine, is out of the woods. You do know I'm not your damn message service, right?"

"Yes, sir. Thank you, sir." Michael was going to be all right. Somehow it made everything else seem worth it. She glanced at Jake, who was laughing at something the person on the other end of his call was saying. Decided that maybe there was one more good thing that could come from this disaster of a case. "Ah, sir, would it be okay if I dropped by your office tomorrow? I need to pick up some paperwork."

"Paperwork?"

"I need a relationship disclosure form."

Jake stopped walking and talking. He stared at her, then held up two fingers as he bounced on his heels, grinning.

"Make it two relationship disclosure forms, sir," she amended. Jake pumped his fist in the air.

"You and Carver?"

"Yes, sir, that's right."

"It's a shame. I was going to have him assigned to work with you, but that would put him in your chain of command." Yates was giving her a choice: a personal life with Jake or a work life with Jake.

Easiest choice she'd made in days. "That's all right, sir. But you really should think of a long-term assignment for him—"

"Got it covered, Tierney." Yates always had a plan B, C, D, and E waiting in the wings. "There's an opening at the Academy. Tell him he can start full-time on Monday."

"Wait, sir. A full-time position at the Academy, that means—" Now she was the one grinning. You couldn't teach at the FBI Academy full-time unless you were a Supervisory Special Agent.

"Put him on, I'll give him the good news myself."

"Yes, sir." She covered her phone and whispered to Jake, "The Assistant Director wants to speak with you."

He nodded. "Thanks again, Shapiro. I owe you one." He hung up from his call and took her phone. "Yes, sir?" He grew serious for a moment, raised an eyebrow in disbelief, then jerked to attention. "Really? Yes, sir! I'll be there. Thank you, sir."

Then he hung up. She grabbed her phone back and pocketed it. "I have never heard anyone use so many *sir*s in one breath in my life, Special Agent Carver."

"That's Supervisory Special Agent Carver, and don't you forget it." He raised her in a hug that pulled her off her feet. Ignoring the stares of the passengers around them, he twirled her in a circle and kissed her so hard that Caitlyn was dizzy when he finally set her back on solid ground. "I've got a little surprise for you as well."

"You better not have traded in my Subaru for a Harley—I told you I have more common sense than to be racing around at ninety miles a hour with nothing between me and the pavement except freezing cold air and a wish."

"No. Well, not yet. Maybe when the weather gets warmer. I'll make an old lady out of you yet."

"Then what?"

"You don't have to worry about your mom trying to subpoena your medical records or sabotaging your career."

Now it was her turn to stop short. "What? How did you do that?"

"I have a new friend over at the IRS. And I realized that an audit on your mom's accounts would probably turn up enough tax evasion felonies that she'd be facing longer federal time than she would if she took the state's plea bargain for the homicide."

"You had your friend blackmail my mother to save my career?" She was stunned. Amazed.

His expression dampened. "Are you upset?"

Now it was her turn to hug him. "Hell no. I'm kicking myself for not thinking of it first. Jake Carver, you are amazing!"

"That's what all the ladies say."

"Really? And who are all these ladies? Maybe one of them can give you a ride home."

"Nope. There's only one lady I'd trust to drive me anywhere, and she's right here."

"And not going anywhere, so don't you forget it." They passed outside, shivering as the Baltimore March wind cut through their thin clothing. Jake wrapped his arm around her, sharing his warmth. Sharing so much more.

Caitlyn snugged her arm around his waist, giving it right back. Together, their steps in synch, they headed home.

But where did the nightmare begin
for Caitlyn Tierney?

Have you read the first book in the trilogy?

**The huge *New York Times* bestseller:
a thriller to keep you up all night . . .**

Read on for an extract.

Available in paperback and ebook now.

June 6, 2007:

Walls Prison Unit, Huntsville, Texas

CHAPTER ONE

Sarah Durandt flinched as faded blue-checked gingham curtains rattled open to reveal the prisoner strapped to a gurney.

One of the women behind her gasped. Sarah leaned forward, one hand flattened against the glass that separated them from a monster. She breathed through her mouth. It was the only way to choke down the heavy air trapped inside the tiny cement-walled room.

She and the other witnesses were gathered behind glass so thick halos circled the objects in the white-tiled execution chamber on the other side. Bulletproof glass. Who did they think would be doing the shooting? The condemned man already woozy from sedatives or those who came to watch him die?

Sarah curled her hands one into the other and held them still on her lap, shivering as the air-conditioning blew a frosty stream down on her. Eleven others were crowded into the room with her, families representing the other victims. She barely noticed them. They were here for closure. She needed answers.

Her gaze narrowed to a laser-sharp focus aimed at the prisoner beyond the glass. His arms were extended, needles inserted into veins on both sides of his body. Seven leather straps crossed his body and limbs, holding him in a position eerily reminiscent of a crucifixion. But this man was no Messiah.

This man was the devil incarnate.

Damian Wright was medium sized, someone who would not stand out in a crowd with his bland face, blander features.

Sarah knew better. She knew his cunning. Hidden behind his façade of normalcy smoldered a sick desire to torture and maim. Even here, on his deathbed, he persisted in tormenting her. Denying her the slightest measure of comfort or peace.

She wasn't sure why, of all the victims, Damian had focused his sick power plays on her. She wasn't anyone special, just a schoolteacher from upstate New York who lived in a village of less than five hundred souls. Her brown hair was usually pulled back into a ponytail and forgotten about, leaving it free to fall around her shoulders on special occasions like today—the execution of a serial killer.

Damian's sweat-beaded skin glistened as he lay beneath a large, round surgical light. His eyes were squeezed shut against its unflinching illumination. The warden nodded to a black-suited man with a small silver cross on his lapel. The man stretched out his hand, his wedding ring shimmering as it passed through the beam of light, and pulled a black microphone down. Sarah rubbed her own ring finger, tracing the plain band Sam placed there six years ago.

Uncoiling like a cobra, the microphone bobbed hypnotically above Damian's lips. A click, like a muffled gunshot, echoed through the witness room as the warden switched on the intercom. The scratchy sound of Damian's breathing filled the room.

Sarah found herself inhaling in time with Damian, could almost smell the antiseptic and surgical tape and the stench of sweat and nerves emanating from beyond the window. Alan Easton, who sat beside her, gave her hand a comforting squeeze.

"You okay?" he asked, his tone that of a friend rather than her lawyer. She was the only family here to bear witness for Sam and Josh. The only family Sam had left. And Josh, how could she not be here for her son?

She nodded, her attention focused on the events in front of her. The execution chamber held only three men: the warden in his navy suit, bleached white shirt, and narrow tie; the black-suited minister; and Damian Wright, the man who had destroyed her life.

If Sarah were to describe the Death House to her sixth-grade students back home, she would have said the theme of the room, of the entire building set far apart from normal prison housing, was containment.

Nothing was meant to ever escape this tiny building with its cement walls painted an institutional green. The utilitarian execution chamber beyond the viewing window made no efforts to soften or hide its purpose. A flat surgical table, arms splayed wide, bolted to the floor was its only piece of furniture.

"Any last words?" the warden asked the condemned man.

Sarah came to attention. A fly trespassed into the profane proceedings and beat its wings against the cage shielding two flickering fluorescent lightbulbs, its buzzing deafening. Damian Wright, convicted murderer and child rapist, opened his rheumy eyes and stared directly at her. She pulled her hand free from Alan's, fisted it tight.

Tell me. Say something. Give me a clue.

Her prayers went unheard. Damian remained silent, muscles slack, not fighting his restraints. Only his chest moved, rising and falling as he counted down to his last breath. Sarah's lungs squeezed tight, ready to burst from pressure. Damian stared at her, a smile creasing his eyes.

She blinked first, not ashamed to surrender; she'd do anything if it helped her to find Sam and Josh.

Damian's smile widened. But he remained silent.

Fury knotted her gut. Did he torment her, refuse her the closure she so desperately yearned for, because she'd been away at that damn mandatory in-service on the day he took Josh? Or was it because of all the boys he'd killed, only Josh had a father willing to fight, to die for him?

Alan said it was probably because Sam interrupted his ritual with Josh. Forced him to deviate from his sick, twisted fantasy to kill Sam before he could return to Josh.

The minister intoned from his Bible, his eyes never rising from the written word to gaze upon the lost soul he prayed over.

The words of the Psalm, words that twenty-two months ago would have brought Sarah comfort and solace, were now reduced to meaningless noise with less significance than the buzzing of the fly. She pressed her palm flat against the cold glass, more intent on gleaning the answers she needed from Damian than listening to the word of God.

She'd spent her entire life listening. Where was God when she'd needed him most? Where was he when her husband and son needed him?

"I'm sorry we couldn't stay the execution," Alan whispered. "I know how much you hoped—"

She shrugged his words away, her entire universe consisting of the gaze of a killer. The man who had confessed to killing Sam and Josh—but who refused to tell her where they were buried.

For a year and a half she had fought. Fought Damian Wright's silence, his refusal to see her. Fought the new Texas law that allowed executions to be "fast-tracked" with an unprecedented efficiency. Fought her own desire to see Damian die. A desire superseded only by her need to find her husband and son.

The warden strode forward, reading from a document in a monotone that floated just beyond the periphery of Sarah's awareness.

Where are they, you sonofabitch? Sarah tried to broadcast all her loathing and hatred into her glare, hoping to loosen Damian's tongue in these, his last seconds on this Earth. Her fist pounded against the thick glass, creating only the smallest of muffled thuds.

The killer didn't flinch or look away from her. Nor did he speak. Instead his expression turned to one approaching pity. As if she were the one condemned, not him.

The warden finished and removed his glasses, aiming a small nod in the direction of the executioner's booth. Sarah had researched the procedure. Behind the one-way mirrored glass, an unseen man flipped a switch. Medication flowed into Damian's veins. First more sedatives, then a paralytic, finally the potassium chloride to stop his heart.

Time stopped. Sarah didn't blink. Damian didn't blink.

Three minutes later, the minister stood aside as a man clad in a white coat stepped forward and listened with a stethoscope. He straightened, reached a hand out to Damian's face, and closed the killer's eyes.

The blinds snapped shut.

A collective sigh swirled through the room as the other

witnesses shifted in their seats. Through the haze filling Sarah's vision she heard several women and a man sobbing, felt the rustle of their movements as the room emptied. She remained frozen, not blinking, eyes burning.

Alan touched her elbow, pulled her fist away from the glass, and drew her up onto unsteady feet. "We have to go now," he murmured.

She kept her face craned toward the darkened window until the last possible moment. Finally, Alan led her out into bright sunshine, Texas heat and humidity bearing down on her with the intensity of a ten-ton truck.

For a moment she was the one suffocating under the weight of paralyzed lungs. Her chest tightened. For an instant it was her heart that stopped.

She blinked and pain returned. An ice-pick stabbing behind her eyes, her constant companion for twenty-two months, unmitigated by any sedatives or hope of release. Unlike Damian Wright's pain.

And she knew she was alive. At least her body was. Her mind was. Her soul—that was buried in some unmarked grave back home, up on Snakehead Mountain.

Alongside Sam and Josh.

It's over, it's over, it's over . . . The words threaded themselves through Sarah's mind, spinning a cocoon that blocked out all feeling, providing a soft, safe place to hide. A place where there was no need to think, to do, to react. To be. *It's over, it's over, it's over* . . .

Sarah hugged herself tighter and leaned against the car window, her back to Alan as he drove them away from the prison. She'd promised herself no matter what, she wouldn't break down, at least not in front of anyone.

But Alan wasn't anyone. Alan understood—he'd been through it himself. His wife had been killed by a drug addict who stormed their house looking for cash. That was why he'd left his corporate law practice to focus on victims' rights, to help people like Sarah.

How could she have survived the past two years without Alan?

The tires spinning against the highway carried her away from Damian Wright, away from her last chance to find Sam and Josh. *It's over, it's over, it's over . . .*

Her body sagged against the door frame, her right hand automatically reaching for the single ring on her left. She had no engagement ring. Instead, Sam had given her his most valuable possession, a guitar pick used by the legendary Stevie Ray Vaughan, and promised that when he sold his first song he'd replace it with a diamond. Seven years later, the pick still sat in its black velvet jewelry case on her dresser.

Her hand felt cold, but her wedding band radiated warmth, as if she touched Sam. She spun the ring in time with the words weaving their way into her soul, inviting her to surrender. *It's over, it's over, it's over . . .*

No! It can't be. Not like this.

Tears pressed against her closed eyelids, burned as they fought to escape. Sarah's grip on the plain gold band tightened. Her last link to Sam and, through him, Josh. She was tired, so very tired. She should give up. What more could she do?

After all, she had a life to live. Sam would want her to be happy. Someday. A ragged breath tore through her and she felt Alan stir beside her. Alan—could she imagine a future with a man like him? A man who'd devoted almost two years of his life to guiding her through this morass of pain and grief, who'd brought her back into the light, had given her this one last chance.

Last chance, last hope, last rites.

It's over, it's over, it's over.

Sarah straightened, opened her eyes, and blinked against the harsh Texas sun. She uncurled her legs, smoothed out the soft cotton of her navy blue dress. She refused to wear black, not until Josh and Sam were laid to rest. The dark highway stretched hypnotically into the future.

"You all right?" Alan's gaze left the road to stare at her for a long moment.

A sad smile curled Sarah's lips. "Yes. I'm fine."

It's over, it's over, it's over . . . the words sang through her mind, pounding insistently like a toddler throwing a tantrum, banging his head against the floor when he didn't get what he wanted. Josh had thrown a few of those in his day. Until he learned that when he did, he never got what he wanted.

It's over, it's over, it's over!

Sarah gave a small shake of her head—the only warning Josh needed now. She'd shake her head, smile, and he'd leave his whining behind, take her hand, and snuggle against her. *Sorry, Mommy. I forgot.*

But I haven't.

It's over, it's over, it's over . . . *No. It's not.*

It's just begun.

Wednesday, June 20

TWO WEEKS LATER

CHAPTER TWO

Supervisory Special Agent Caitlyn Tierney didn't look up at the tentative knock on her open door. Instead she raised a hand in the universal palm forward gesture of "wait" and kept reading the report on her computer screen. Her latest group of New Agents in Training was in their final week of training before graduating from Quantico. Nerves were frayed as they waited to learn their field assignments, so this hadn't been the first interruption of Caitlyn's morning.

She finished reading her NAT's scores on their critical incident projects and nodded with satisfaction. They'd done as well as she'd hoped. Even Santos, the diffident, intense twenty-six-year-old with a background in particle physics, had managed to integrate himself as part of the team. Caitlyn shut the lid to her laptop and looked up at her visitor, half-expecting to see Santos himself.

Instead, it was one of the lab geeks. Ah, man, she knew his name; he worked in DNA. Not Rogers, no, something close. She smiled, keeping her face blandly genial as she forced her brain along its circuitous route to match the face of the man before her with his name.

Finally, it clicked. But it took at least twice as long as it would have two years ago, before her accident. Something she'd never admit to anyone.

"Hi, Clemens," she said heartily, gesturing the tech to one of the two wooden chairs beside her overflowing bookcase. "What brings you over here to Jefferson? Teaching a class?"

He shook his head. "Thought it would be easier than asking you to make the trip to the lab building." He was right; the forensic analysis center had more security than Fort Knox. Even FBI staff like Caitlyn needed a special invite and authorization for a pass to enter. Clemens glanced at the open door and shifted his weight in his chair.

She might not be as good with names as she used to be, but Caitlyn was still a pro when it came to nonverbal communication. She rose to her feet, folded her reading glasses, and nonchalantly closed the door as she crossed over to sit beside him.

"What's up?" she asked, leaning forward and engaging him in direct eye contact.

He fumbled a file folder from his briefcase. It wasn't marked "top secret" or even "sensitive," so she wondered what all the cloak-and-dagger was about. Then she saw the name on the file. Damian Wright.

Her first assignment two years ago after she'd returned to work. She'd hated everything about that case: the crimes, the travel, the blinding migraines that blurred her thoughts and almost crippled her with their unrelenting pain and nausea, and most of all she'd hated her fatuous asshole of a boss, Assistant Special Agent in Charge Jack Logan. Logan had swooped in and taken over the case without any warnings or explanations, something unheard of. ASACs led from behind their desks via memos and directives; they never ventured into the field.

"You know Damian Wright's dead?" she asked the lab tech. "Executed in Texas." She glanced at the calendar. "Two weeks ago."

"I know." Clemens' voice was mournful. "I'm sorry."

Caitlyn's spine went rigid. Bright flashes of light sparked at the periphery of her vision. "Sorry? You can't be saying you found anything exculpatory?"

Caitlyn agreed with most law enforcement officers that death was too good for a lot of these sickos—but it was the best punishment they had. That didn't mean that she, like other LEOs, didn't also live in fear of putting an innocent man on death row.

Which was why she'd reviewed the Texas evidence against Wright herself, even though by the time Texas took over she was off the case. Their case had been rock solid. Not only had he been caught with the still-warm body of his last victim, butchering the boy, but Wright confessed to everything, refused to allow any appeals on his behalf, and became the first person under Texas' new law to be fast-tracked to execution. Twenty-one months from arrest to death, a new record.

Clemens shook his head. "No, Wright killed those boys in Texas, Vermont, Tennessee, and Oklahoma." He paused. Caitlyn took a deep breath, forcing the flashing lights to fade into the distance. "It's the ones in New York I'm not too sure about."

"Hopewell, New York. Josh Durandt and his father. Right before Katrina hit." Caitlyn remembered. No bodies recovered in that one. The crime scene had been halfway up a mountain; she'd been wearing a skirt after being whisked away from a memorial service for the second

Vermont boy. Logan had laughed, giving her no time to change into more appropriate attire and cutting her no slack when her migraine made her sick during the drive down. After she puked her guts out on the side of the road, he'd joked, asked if she was pregnant, adding that was the problem with "today's FBI." He never had to worry about any of the guys letting him down because they went "hormonal" on him.

"See, I was clearing the backlog and I found these samples in the pile to be disposed of," Clemens said, his tone hesitant as he shifted in his seat, obviously having second thoughts. "You know the new director's protocols. All evidence reviewed prior to disposal, even in closed cases. Turns out the results from Hopewell were never recorded. Not anywhere. Case like that, they should have been top priority. Instead they were almost trashed. If it wasn't for the new rules—"

"What do you have?" she asked, sliding the folder from his hand and spreading it open on her lap. The familiar dark lines of a DNA analysis filled the first page.

"The DNA from the Hopewell crime scene—it wasn't Wright's."

"There were two blood samples found, right? The dad's and one other. We assumed it was Wright's since the field kit said it was his blood type and we had his prints on the memory card found there."

"Yeah, it was his print and the card came from his camera. Wright's reflection can be seen in some of the photos. He definitely took them."

"Who was at the crime scene with him? Are you saying he had an accomplice? There was no evidence of that at any of the other scenes." She ran her hand through her shoulder-length hair, absently rubbing at the puckered skin above her right ear. Her hair hadn't even grown out when she was in Hopewell. Back then it had been so short it barely covered the surgical scar.

Clemens blew his breath out. "That's where it gets a bit weird."

Caitlyn straightened. It never boded well when a lab geek called evidence weird. "How weird?"

"Conspiracy theory, cover-up, Area Fifty-One, political and career suicide kind of weird." He grimaced. "I've gone over everything a dozen times. The data is correct. It's the facts surrounding it that are wrong."

"You mean *my* facts, *my* investigation?"

He looked down at his scuffed Adidas and nodded. "Yeah." He looked up again, pushed his hair back when it fell across his forehead. "Well, yours and Assistant Special Agent in Charge Logan's. He was the agent of record. His name was on all the paperwork. But since he's retired, I thought I better come to you." He gave her a hesitant smile. "Maybe you could tell me what to do with it."

Caitlyn stared past him, through her small window that looked out over the expanse of forest home to the Yellow Brick Road, the academy's famed obstacle course. Sunlight streamed in, reawakening her headache. She'd always suspected Logan of hiding something. He'd hustled her off the Wright case as fast as he could, claiming she was needed to help with the Katrina cleanup efforts. She'd spent weeks working with the National Center for Missing & Exploited Children, identifying over forty-eight hundred kids and reuniting them with their families. An area more suited to a woman's talents, in Logan's words. Since they'd had Wright cold on the other murders, she'd let it go.

She turned to Clemens. "Tell me everything."

Make sure you complete the trilogy.

Book two in the series is Black Sheep.

**A young girl is taken. A father is silenced.
The lies run deep.**

Read on for an extract.

Available in ebook and paperback now.

CHAPTER ONE

"Drop the gun!" Caitlyn Tierney shouted to the FBI agent.

The agent hesitated, chin bobbing as she tried to decide the correct move to make. Tough choice since Caitlyn held the agent's male partner against her chest as a shield. She'd grabbed his weapon and now used his greater height as an advantage. The only portion of Caitlyn's five-six frame visible to the female agent was Caitlyn's hand holding the male agent's own weapon to his head.

The female agent held her weapon steady, aiming at her partner and Caitlyn behind him. Fat lot of good that was going to do her, but it was standard procedure.

Caitlyn braced herself against the larger agent. He smelled minty fresh, as if he'd chewed gum or used mouthwash before following his partner into this squalid dump of an apartment. Sweat trickled down from his hairline, beading at the back of his collar. His hair had been freshly trimmed; his skin still held tiny nicks from the razor.

She glanced around. He was her only cover. The rest of the apartment was bare of furniture except for a sagging tweed couch shoved against the far wall and a coffee table made of cheap two-by-fours. Back to the wall, Caitlyn's only exit was the door to the right of the female agent across from her.

"Let's talk about this." The female agent's voice quavered, but her aim didn't falter. "Let him go and we'll talk."

"Shut up or I shoot him!" Caitlyn responded, effectively removing the agent's best weapon: her command authority. Hard to negotiate or intimidate when you can't speak. "Drop your gun. Now!"

Make a choice, make a choice, Caitlyn thought. The overhead ceiling fan swooshed, barely stirring the air with its listless movements. The place stank of mold and sweat, of windows that didn't open, shag carpet decades out of date, and too many years of too many people making too many bad decisions. The FBI agent was just one more, standing in the weak light of a naked sixty-watt bulb, her mind stuttering through a minefield of options.

Don't make me do it. Choose. Just choose.

The agent didn't choose. Her aim faltered, dropped down, then raised halfway up in indecision.

Caitlyn shot her in the forehead, followed by a double tap to the chest.

Then Caitlyn touched the muzzle of her weapon to the male agent's temple. "Bang. You're dead."

"Tierney!" The scenario leader yelled her name from his observation post. "What the hell you doing?"

Trying to teach them how to stay alive in the real world, Caitlyn thought. She'd been where these New Agents in Training were: forced to choose between following procedure and taking a chance on her instincts.

Six months ago when she'd had a gun to her head and another pointed at her partner, Caitlyn surrendered her weapon. If she hadn't, she'd be dead—and so would five hundred innocent civilians. But she'd done it consciously, knowing her Glock wasn't her only weapon. That it wasn't even her best weapon.

These NATs needed to learn to think like that. It might save their lives someday.

The scenario leader, Mike LaSovage, one of the FBI Hostage Rescue Team members, clomped over to her, aiming his clipboard as if it were a weapon. "Supervisory Special Agent Tierney, a word, please."

Caitlyn removed her helmet and rubbed her right temple, lifting her short red hair, matted by the training gear, away from the itchy scar. She glanced at the female NAT she'd shot. The woman trembled. Her hand touched her face shield, coming away with neon green paint on her fingers—the color of Caitlyn's Simunition.

"She needed to make a decision," Caitlyn muttered, wiping her own sweaty palms against her black cargo pants. Simulation or not, the scenario hit close to home, awakening memories as well as a surge of adrenaline.

"The purpose of this exercise is to allow agents in training a chance to follow proper arrest procedure, not to throw them into a hostage negotiation." LaSovage turned so his back was to the NATs. Didn't want them to see Mommy and Daddy fighting. The Bureau was above that. Follow the bible—a four-inch binder crammed full of rules, regulations, and standard operating procedures—and you'd go home at night, was the catechism the kids were meant to learn from these exercises.

Despite the fact that a few were close to Caitlyn's age, they *were* just kids. No idea what the real world held for them. Decisions made in a heartbeat, bullets fired that could never be unfired, good people lost because of your actions—or inaction.

"You saw the way they entered," Caitlyn argued, feeling older than her thirty-five years as she spied the crushed expressions on the NATs' faces. Nine years carrying a loaded weapon, almost dying twice, killing a man in close-quarters combat, watching a good man sacrifice his life to save hers: Permanent scars crisscrossed her body and her soul. She couldn't remember ever being as young as these new agents. "He was more concerned about following her lead than the threat I posed. Totally opened his weapon side to me. How could I resist? No real suspect would have."

LaSovage looked over his shoulder to where the two dead agents huddled together commiserating and, hopefully, dissecting their mistakes. "It was a sloppy entrance. But this is their first exercise outside of FATS video training. First real-life scenario. You didn't need to push it that far."

"I'll bet they don't make the same mistakes next time."

He grimaced in agreement. "Maybe. But let's play the rest of these by the book, okay?"

Caitlyn had never done "by the book" well. Used to be she could fake her way through it, pretend her actions were guided by rules and regulations, but after returning from an extended medical leave for emergency brain surgery that saved her life, she'd given up the pretense. Which was why the powers-that-be had left her in limbo, on temporary assignment here at Quantico.

"You doing okay?" LaSovage asked, trying not to stare at her hair, still not fully grown back after her operation. "Can't be easy after—"

"I'm fine." How many times a day did she have to tell people that? Or pretend she didn't notice their stares as she walked through the halls at the academy.

Six months ago she'd have embraced the idea of continuing on as a permanent instructor—she enjoyed teaching and loved challenging her students. But to be stranded here as temporary duty, merely so she could remain under the scrutiny of the bosses without becoming a PR risk? Suddenly her office in Jefferson Hall felt as cramped as a prison cell.

Her last case had earned her an unofficial reprimand from the Office of Professional Responsibility and an official, but grudgingly given, commendation for uncovering corruption in the FBI's higher ranks, the U.S. Marshal Service, and even the sacrosanct FBI National Laboratory.

The brass would have preferred if she'd taken their offer of a medical pension and left the Bureau quietly, but no way was she going to let them bully her into quitting. Given that she knew of several embarrassing skeletons hidden in the FBI's closet, they couldn't fire her, not without risking another blot on the Bureau's public image.

Which left Caitlyn and her career in limbo.

"You sure?" LaSovage persisted. "We could grab a beer or something after we're done here. If you want to talk."

His glance dropped to the top part of the scar that ran vertically up her chest, visible above her tactical vest. The rest of the scar formed a letter *K* with the crossbars slashing above and below her left breast. If it weren't for her fair skin the scars would have been less noticeable, but after six months they were still reddish and she'd given up trying to hide beneath turtlenecks. Just like her attitude, they were now part of her, take it or leave it.

His concern seemed more genuine than the morbid curiosity most of her colleagues had exhibited. Interesting since, although LaSovage was a four-year veteran of the Hostage Rescue Team, the FBI's vaunted equivalent to an elite SWAT unit, he'd never actually had to kill anyone.

During the course of their careers it was rare for FBI agents to draw their weapons outside the range. Which made Caitlyn, so young, yet already almost dying a violent death twice and killing a man up close and personal, a distinct anomaly. She heard the whispers: *Was she reckless? Stupid? Or just plain unlucky?*

She wished she had an answer. "Thanks, but I need to be somewhere tonight," she told LaSovage. "Maybe next time."

He nodded, gave her an uncertain smile as if wondering if she was trying to protect him or herself, then turned to usher the next group into position.

They finished out the remaining training for the day, and she returned to her office in Jefferson Hall to grab her laptop and car keys. She was surprised when the female agent in training from the earlier scenario appeared at her doorway, now wearing clean regulation khakis and a blue polo shirt.

"What would you have done?" the NAT blurted out, ignoring the strict protocol that usually guided NATs' interactions with their instructors. Belatedly she added, "Ma'am."

"What's your name?" Caitlyn took the seat behind her desk, but left the NAT standing at attention. This group was new, hadn't taken any of her classes yet, so she didn't know them personally; she'd merely been playing a bad guy in today's scenarios to help with evaluations.

"Garman, ma'am. Mary Agnes Garman."

Mary Agnes? Sounded like a nun's name. She was only a year or two younger than Caitlyn, in good shape but not as fit as the recruits coming from the military or law enforcement, with an hourglass figure that did not fit her name. Although who knew what nuns looked like under those habits?

Caitlyn filled her mind with an image of a mother superior holding a compass—a mnemonic technique she'd cultivated after her brain trauma made remembering things like names a struggle. Not that she'd ever share that secret with anyone.

"What did you see as your options, Garman?"

Mary Agnes hesitated, not in indecision as she had earlier, but in thought. "You didn't give me any."

"Exactly. What's wrong with that statement?"

Her rigid posture sagged. Caitlyn nodded to the chair across from her, and Mary Agnes slumped into it. "I gave you the power. But—" She scowled in thought, her gaze drifting past Caitlyn to the window, already dark with the early-January sunset. "But I still had no options."

"Tunnel vision. The adrenaline makes you focus on what's in front of you, the direct threat. It does that to your mind as well. But there are always possibilities. Don't ever forget that."

"I could have lowered my weapon, but regulations—"

"Do the bad guys play by the rules?"

"No, but—"

"In here"—Caitlyn gestured to the cement-block walls surrounding them—"you have to know the rules, live by them. And that's not a bad thing. Nine times out of ten they'll save your butt."

"And the tenth time?"

"Look for options. You never considered any other

options today. Instead you hesitated, couldn't commit to a course."

"I froze. I got my partner killed." The remorse and fear in Mary Agnes's voice was real. Good. Better she learn the hard lessons now before the gun pointed at her shot something more lethal than a paintball.

"You did. Next time you won't."

"What would you have done?"

"You still controlled the exit."

"It was too far away."

Caitlyn shook her head. "No. It was only three steps to your right. Adrenaline. It distorts everything. Good thing is, the bad guys are affected as well, have the same limitations."

"I could never abandon my partner." Her voice made it sound like sacrilege, reinforcing the mother superior image in Caitlyn's mind. As if what Caitlyn suggested was as bad as betraying a family member. Which, in a sense, it was. Unless you imagined past the knee-jerk blind obedience to ethics and codes of conduct.

"Yes. You could. Three steps and you would have been behind cover, able to observe, negotiate, call for backup, or shoot if the hostage taker took further action."

"Further action. You mean kill my partner."

Caitlyn stood. Stretched her arms wide. "Look at me, Garman. I'm all of five-six, can bench one thirty, maybe one fifty on a good day. What good would a six-foot, two-hundred-pound deadweight do me?"

"You wouldn't have shot him?"

"Not unless he was no longer useful. And that would only happen if—" She arched an eyebrow, waiting for Mary Agnes to put the pieces together.

It took a moment, but the frown faded as the answers

fell into place for the agent in training. "I blocked your escape. If I was out of the picture, dead, you could make a run for it. By standing there, I gave you *more* reason to kill us both."

"Exactly. You were thinking about what you wanted, but you should have been focused on what the hostage taker wanted. Embrace the possibilities, decide how you can control the outcome."

Mary Agnes took a deep breath, chin bobbing in agreement. She stood with renewed energy. "Thank you, Supervisory Special Agent Tierney. You gave me a lot to think about."

Caitlyn smiled, remembered why she enjoyed teaching so much. "No problem, Garman. Have a good night."

Mary Agnes headed back to the dormitory while Caitlyn took the steps down to the lobby, waved to the guard there, and jogged through the cold, her coat flapping open, to her Subaru Impreza WRX parked in front of Jefferson Hall. A thin coating of frost crackled across the Subaru's windshield, but she didn't waste time scraping it clear. She still had thirty-six miles to drive to Paul's place in DC.

She took back roads, avoiding 95 and the constant snarl of traffic on the interstate. Usually she enjoyed the hour-long drive. It provided needed breathing space.

As extroverted as she was introverted, Paul often joked that if it weren't for him, she'd be living the life of a hermit. She never let him know how close to the truth that was. She'd yet to invite him to her place in Manassas for a night, was more than willing to let him think it was because as a neuroradiologist he had to stay close to GW.

In reality, she simply didn't do entertaining. Or strangers in her space. So much easier to make the drive, enjoy Paul's company, and leave when she wanted. She liked the freedom, needed the control—another thing Paul teased her about.

Only lately he wasn't teasing. He was hinting. Emptying a dresser drawer and shelf in the bathroom for her. Talking about how much her drive took away from the time they had together.

He was ready to settle down. With her. For the long term. And it scared the shit out of her. Caitlyn didn't do relationships, never had. She did longer-than-average flings that ended in shouting matches, bruised egos, guys storming away, and her sighing in relief at another bullet dodged.

Paul didn't shout. He wasn't an alpha male, not like her usual guys, and his ego didn't bruise. He cuddled. Comforted. And actually enjoyed it.

Worse, so did she. Being taken care of was a foreign experience to Caitlyn. Paul wrapping his arms around her, sharing his strength, putting her first—it was sweet and sexy and so very addictive. Another thing that scared her. Ever since she was nine and lost her dad, Caitlyn had lived her life and guarded her heart with one rule: Trust no one.

Paul had snuck past that barbed-wire rule and now she was at a loss how to handle things. Part of her wanted to embrace the life he offered: a normal, stable, caring, trusting relationship.

The child in her screamed to run, run, run before she exposed herself too much.

She'd loved every moment of their six months together. Paul had reminded her that there was more to life than just her work. After almost dying, she'd needed that, needed a little of what everyone else seemed to have: someone to come home to, a connection with the world outside the FBI.

Despite the fact that Paul had given her more than any other man she'd ever been with, she knew she didn't have the feelings for him that she should have. It worried her. What was wrong with her that a normal relationship with a terrific guy terrified her more than facing an armed felon? Paul had saved her life six months ago when he diagnosed her brain aneurysm. If she couldn't bring herself to trust him, would she ever be able to trust anyone?

Caitlyn hesitated before pulling into the underground garage at his building. She could call, make an excuse about the training going late, drive back to Manassas and the peaceful solitude of her apartment. He'd never know she was lying—she was pretty good at it. Her chest tightened. Mouth went dry. She didn't want to lie. Not to Paul.

But she was afraid of what she might be facing when she went inside. Afraid of what she'd do when he forced her to make the choice. She didn't want to lose him, wasn't ready to return to her solitary ways.

Not a ring, please not a ring, she thought as she left the Impreza and waited for the elevator. Her cell rang and she grabbed it like a drowning woman lunging for a lifeline.

"Tierney."

"Excuse me, Supervisory Special Agent, this is the operator at the Washington Field Office. I have an urgent call for you from the prison chaplain at Butner Federal Correctional Institution. Will you accept the call?"

The elevator came and she entered, hit the button for Paul's floor. Who the hell did she have behind bars at Butner? Maybe one of the convictions from her time in Boston had turned and they moved him to the facility in North Carolina? After all, Bernie Madoff and Jonathan Pollard were doing time there, as well as a smattering of mobsters turned witnesses for the prosecution.

As always, her curiosity got the better of her. Not to mention an excuse to delay seeing Paul—the thought felt strange, as if she were betraying Paul, but it also gave her a weird sense of relief. Why did relationships have to be so damn confusing? Give her a felon to take down any day of the week. "Sure, put him through."

"Caitlyn Tierney?" The man's voice was unfamiliar. "I'm Pastor Vince Whitford, one of the chaplains at Butner."

She left the elevator and stopped outside Paul's door. No sense knocking if this was something that was going to take her back to work. "Yes. Why are you calling, Pastor?"

He cleared his throat, obviously uncomfortable. "I've been counseling a prisoner here at Butner Medium who tried to kill himself a few days ago. Eli Hale."

Hale, she'd never arrested anyone—oh, hell. She did know that name. Hadn't heard it in twenty-six years. The image of a man, taller and broader than her father, as black as Sean Tierney was pale, his voice low and husky and shaking with laughter as he chased after his daughter and Caitlyn, playing the scary monster to their damsels in distress, a game that always ended with Caitlyn and Vonnie gathered under Eli's massive arms, giggling as he twirled them around until they were dizzy with delight.

"Eli Hale?" It was her turn to clear her throat as childhood memories flooded through her. Vonnie, her best friend in the whole world—until they'd been yanked apart after Caitlyn's dad was forced to arrest his own best friend, Eli Hale. For murder. "Is he okay?"

"He is now. The doctors are releasing him from the medical unit tomorrow, but I convinced him to agree to meet with you. I think you're the only person who can help him."

Anger and confusion twisted through her, tossing her childhood memories aside. Except the one that never left her: the image of her father lying dead, killed with his own gun, by his own hand. Unable to stand the guilt of seeing his best friend convicted of murder.

She swallowed bile. "I think you have the wrong person. There's no reason on earth why I'd want to talk to Eli Hale. Or him to me."

"Please, Agent Tierney. Don't hang up. A girl's life is at stake."

Caitlyn's fingers closed around the cell phone, almost but not quite touching the end-call icon. She wanted to hang up, to end this painful trip down memory lane. But . . . "What girl?"

"Eli's youngest, Lena."

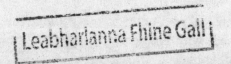